Beautifully Broken

Beautifully Damaged Series Book Two

J.A. Owenby

Trigger Warning

Beautifully Damaged is recommended for readers 17+.

Due to dark and mature content, graphic sex scenes, and sensitive topics, please consider this your ***trigger warning***!

Download Your FREE BOOK

Prologue

The sunlight glinted off River's brown hair as she stood, her hands framing her slender hips. Excitement rippled in the air as our penthouse's first pieces of furniture were unloaded from the delivery truck.

I was ecstatic, not only because our place was finally ready, but because River had agreed to go to New York with me and turn an existing club into another 4 Play. At one time, I'd been thrilled about expanding, but honestly, as long as she was by my side, I'd be happy anywhere. She was my future.

"What do you think?" I slipped my arm around her waist as we eyed the black Italian leather couch that the men had unloaded in front of us on the loading dock. The walnut dining table caught my attention. I was counting the minutes until I could pick her up, place her on the edge, and eat River for dinner.

"It's all beautiful." She grinned at me, and my heart jumped. "You're beautiful."

"This is just the beginning, babe." I leaned down and pressed my mouth against hers. "I can't wait to make love to you in our bed. Then

I'm going to bend you over and fuck you on every possible surface of our new home," I whispered against her ear.

River discreetly grabbed my ass, and I nearly moaned as her tongue darted over her lower lip.

"What if I'm a bad girl?" She peered at me through her eyelashes, and my cock pushed against my jeans, ready to be freed and buried deep inside her. I could almost taste her sweet pussy on my lips and tongue.

"I hope you are. I have a surprise for you later."

A flicker of regret danced across her features, then morphed into relief. "Surprises used to suck, but I love yours." River leaned against me, and I pulled her closer.

She placed her hand on my chest and smiled. "Holden, I need to go to the bathroom. I'll be right back."

"Okay, babe."

She kissed me on the cheek and walked away, my gaze landing on the soft sway of her hips and the curve of her ass. Not only was River physically beautiful, but I loved her heart. Her mind. Her fight. And I was the lucky son of a bitch she slept next to at night.

This moment marked a new chapter for us—a new beginning. River finally had her fresh start. I briefly closed my eyes and imprinted this memory on my brain for eternity, promising myself that I'd never take her for granted.

Chapter One

I clutched the little black velvet box in my hand, nerves tingling up my arm as my heart hammered against my chest. Maybe spending so much time together had bonded us faster, but I knew without a shadow of a doubt that I wanted to ask River to marry me. It was rushing things with River, but I'd had more sex than most men would in their lifetime, drank more booze, used more drugs, owned a successful club, and shared secrets that I'd take to my grave. I'd lived a full life already at the age of twenty-two. River's presence made me a better man, and I wanted to wake up next to her for the rest of my days.

With a smile on my face and love bubbling inside of me, I sat on the edge of our brand-new bed. The sheets, blankets, and light blue and white comforter were still in bags, resting on top of our dresser. *Our* dresser. It was funny how furniture could make me feel so connected to River.

I gazed out of the bedroom windows, overlooking the city of Spokane. River had fallen in love with the gorgeous view of the rushing water of the river. Maybe we could get married on a boat, or at least honeymoon on one. The mental image of River in a skimpy bikini made my dick instantly hard. I couldn't wait to fuck her on every surface of our new home.

A pop of lightning split the sky as stormy, blue-grey clouds rolled in and plump raindrops splattered against the glass. I was grateful the weather had held off until we'd moved the furniture.

Flipping the lid of the box open, I stared at the two-carat diamond surrounded by emeralds on the engagement ring. It was one of a kind. I'd had it designed with Brynn's help. While River and Brynn shopped, Brynn would peruse the jewelry stores, collecting information for me on River's tastes. And tonight, surrounded by our friends, I planned on dropping to one knee and popping the question. I sighed with contentment. Even though I wanted River to have the wedding of her dreams, I wasn't opposed to marrying her tomorrow. The moment I'd found her sleeping in my recycling bin, I realized there was something different about her. Something fierce and beautiful. My life had drastically changed over the last five months. She'd taught me to live again, to love again. My heart had opened up, and instead of running from it, I ran to her.

I gently closed the box as my mind reeled. Pierce had informed me that my father, Tim, was back in Spokane, and shivers of disgust tiptoed up and down my spine. Once I'd learned more about who he really was, I referred to him as Tim. In my mind, he was no longer my dad. The sorry son of a bitch had tried to rape River, but she'd put him in his place. If he were smart, he'd stay the hell away from us.

My hand balled into a tight fist. While he was in town, I'd make sure that River had security with her twenty-four seven. I couldn't take any chances. If Tim was tangled up in illegal weapons, then the men he associated with were as dangerous as he was, if not more. The hairs on the back of my neck bristled at the mere idea that Tim might hire someone to come after River. It was my responsibility to keep her safe. Guilt twisted my gut into knots as memories of Hannah's smile haunted me. I hadn't kept her from harm, but I wouldn't fail this time.

Hopping up, I busied myself with opening the package of the

Frette Bold sheet set. I couldn't wait to bring River home that night. This was our bed, not one that I'd had other women in, including Becky. I was still in shock about Becky's behavior toward River. I'd known Becky for several years, and if anyone had mentioned to me that she would hold a knife to someone's throat, I would have told them they were fucking crazy. Man, had I missed that one.

I quickly fluffed our pillows and tucked the blankets into neat corners under the mattress. I was ready to give Tim, Logan, and Becky a swift kick in the ass and file them and their shitty behavior in the past. Since Dan had died owing Logan a ton of money, Logan was willing to take River for payment, and that shit didn't fly with me. From what River had mentioned, Logan was a meth dealer and bad news. I didn't want him anywhere near her. Besides, River and I were off to New York soon. We had a new and exciting future in front of us, and that's what I wanted to focus on.

My cell buzzed in my back pocket, and I removed it. Zayne's number illuminated the screen.

"This is Holden."

"Is River with you?" Zayne asked, his voice thick with tension.

Goosebumps pebbled my arms. "No. Isn't she with you?"

Silence filled the line for the length of a heartbeat.

"She ditched me." There was no way that I could ignore the seriousness in Zayne's tone.

Anxiety punched me in the stomach. "Where are you?" My palms grew sweaty, and I wiped one against my jeaned thighs.

"At the loading dock," Zayne responded.

I didn't even bother telling him I was on my way. I just hung up and dialed River's number. No answer. I tried again, but it went straight to voicemail.

Opening the new nightstand drawer, I placed the ring in the back where River wouldn't find it. Then I bolted out of the penthouse, my mind clamoring with possibilities of where she might be. The first stop was our office.

I called River three more times as I searched for her everywhere on the third floor, including the conference room. Nothing. Absolutely no sign that she'd even been there.

I swore under my breath as I paced in front of the elevator, willing it to hurry the hell up. My brain told me there was a logical explanation for why she would ditch Zayne, but a storm was brewing in my heart. Had Logan found her? Had Tim done something to her? Fear wrapped its cold fingers around my chest, and I rubbed my sternum. Surely, she was okay, and this was all a misunderstanding.

The doors whooshed open, and I hurried inside, selecting the main floor. As soon as I reached my destination, I darted out and ran to the loading area. Vaughn had joined Zayne, concern flashing in his mismatched gaze.

"What the hell is going on?" I asked, placing my hands on my hips, remaining beneath the overhang with Vaughn and Zayne.

Zayne turned slowly, and my stomach plummeted to my toes when I realized he was holding River's purse. Time stood still. The sound of my heart drowned out the rolling thunder and sheets of rain slamming against the side of the building.

"This was left here on the loading dock." Zayne's voice was low, his expression grim. "They'll take prints, so if you want to look through it before the police, then I'd grab some gloves."

Nearly stumbling backward from what Zayne was implying, I whirled around and headed inside for the bar. Someone had taken River. Frantically, I rummaged beneath the sink until I found what I needed. I shook out a white pair of latex gloves, then returned to Zayne. He handed me her purse, and I cringed. I'd never gone through her belongings unless she'd given me permission, but this was different. I swallowed, my throat thick with fear.

Without pause, I opened her bag. "Fuck. Her phone is here." I glanced at the men, then pocketed her cell. If the cops found out, I'd get in trouble for withholding evidence, but I didn't give a shit. If she was really missing, I needed to know what the hell was going on. I offered a silent prayer to the universe as I unzipped the middle compartment. I could hardly breathe when my attention landed on a clear, zip-top baggie. Its only content was a little white stick—a white stick with two blue lines and the word "positive."

My heart rate exploded into a frenzied gallop. I couldn't catch a breath. Sheer terror coiled in my chest.

Reality seeped into my soul as I slowly dropped to my knees. River was pregnant ... with my baby. I was going to be a father. Shock clouded my mind briefly, then I rose to my feet.

Tears blurred my vision. "River is pregnant. We have to find her. Now!" Anger churned beneath the surface as it dawned on me that Zayne hadn't kept up with her. I replaced the test into her purse, then set her bag down. My hands clenched and unclenched, itching to slam my fist into his face. "How the hell did you lose her? This is why I fucking hired you! You're supposed to be keeping her safe!"

Zayne straightened and met my furious gaze, which made me crazy. He was going to be a man and own his fuck-up.

"She ran out of her office and down the hall. The elevator must have been on our floor already because she was on it before I reached her. I ran back to the opposite end to take the stairs, but the door was locked from the other side." Zayne's green eyes narrowed. "River didn't want me to follow her, Holden. I don't know why, but something had her spooked pretty badly. It took almost five minutes before the elevator returned. I could see that it had stopped on every floor. By the time I got here ... all I saw was her purse. I called her, searched this area, and had Vaughn search the other floors." Zayne swallowed visibly. "Maybe she's with Brynn?"

"I don't understand why the door to the stairwell was locked. It never is. I use the stairs every day. Did you let River out of your sight long enough for her to lock the stairwell?"

"No. We went straight to the third floor. She went into her office for a few minutes, then flew past me to the elevator. Unless you have access from one of the offices directly to the stairs, it's not possible. The only other person she was with this morning was you, then me," Zayne said.

I scrambled for his explanation to make sense, but Zayne was right. River had eyes on her all morning. Something wasn't settling right inside my gut. "Zayne, call Chance. Vaughn, if you'll reach out to Jace, I'll contact Brynn."

I grabbed River's purse, entered the club, and sat at the bar. I tapped the green icon on my iPhone and pulled up Brynn's number in my favorites.

"Hey," she answered.

"Is River with you?" I asked, cutting out the pleasantries.

"No, I haven't seen her today."

My pulse skyrocketed. Sweat broke out over my skin as fresh anger coursed through my body.

"Holden?"

How had I let this happen?

"Holden, what's wrong?" Brynn pleaded, concern bleeding into her normally perky tone.

"Have you talked to her? Texted or anything?" I mentally begged River to come home ... to be safe.

"No. We were all meeting at your penthouse this evening, but I haven't talked to her yet." Brynn paused. "What's going on, Holden?"

I hung my head and ran my fingers through my dark hair as foreboding iced my skin. "River's missing, Brynn. She was able to ditch Zayne, and now we can't find her. Her purse was on the loading dock, along with her phone and ..." Did I tell Brynn that River was pregnant? I chose to wait in case River waltzed through the door at any second.

"Fuck. Holden, that's not good." Panic seized Brynn's voice. "I'm on my way to the club. Have you called the guys to see if they've talked to her?"

I could hear Brynn moving in the background, and I imagined she was running through her kitchen and to her garage.

I glanced up, eyeing Vaughn and Zayne, who were now inside standing next to me. "I had the bodyguards reach out, but by the sound of it, no one has seen her." My stomach lurched, and bile swam up to my throat. "I think someone took her, Brynn." I nearly choked on my words.

"No. She has to be all right. We have to stay positive. I'm in my car, so I'll see you in a few minutes. But please let me know the second you find her." Brynn disconnected the call, and I placed my phone on the bar top.

"Holden," Zayne said. "You need to file a police report, but I'd like to reach out to my bosses. Pierce and Sutton can help before the cops can. We can keep it quiet and move faster."

My nostrils flared. If Zayne had kept up with River, then she wouldn't be missing in the first goddamned place. I turned slowly, and my fingers clenched. In one quick movement, I hopped off the barstool and closed the gap between us. "This is your fault," I spat.

Regret coasted over his face, followed by a shadow of conflict. "I know," Zayne said, not denying my accusation. I backed away, wrapping my fury into a neat little package, and shoving it down like I always did.

Vaughn stepped in front of Zayne and blocked me. "I understand that you're upset, but handle it later, man. We need to find River and we're wasting valuable time."

My anger simmered down long enough for me to realize that he had a valid point. I'd deal with Zayne later.

Over the next half hour, I called the cops and reported River as a missing person. It helped that I had a few connections with the police, but there wasn't much they could do yet. Zayne was right. I needed Pierce and Sutton's help.

"I'm here!" Brynn said, running toward me. "Have you found her?" She halted in front of me, her hands trembling. Brynn's long, red hair was piled into a messy bun. She must have been in a hurry because her face was free of makeup and her white shirt was untucked.

My heart galloped. I shook my head and pulled her into a hug. "We think someone took her." I grabbed Brynn's hand and led her away from the bodyguards. We'd stay where they could see us, but I needed Brynn's help and didn't want Zayne and Vaughn to know.

I removed River's phone from my back pocket and the pregnancy test from her purse. "I don't want the cops to have these." I turned Brynn's palm up and placed the life-altering contents in her hand, the plastic crinkling beneath my fingers.

"Holy shit." She paled, then glanced up at me. "This is why she has been so sick." Tears moistened her eyes.

"I need you to hide those. I'd rather have Sutton help with River's cell than turn it over to the authorities." I hesitated. "If we get caught tampering with evidence ..."

Our conversation was interrupted by a few officers arriving. Brynn discreetly shoved the items into her handbag. "I've got your back, Holden. You're not alone." She squeezed my shoulder and remained next to me as the cops approached.

Jace and Chance arrived at 4 Play half an hour later and practically ran to me. Chance's expression was grim as he approached. "What can we do to help?" He shoved his fingers through his blonde hair and blew out a breath. Chance was clearly frazzled but remained calm. He'd slipped on black dress shoes with his designer jeans and a white rumpled shirt.

"I don't understand," Jace said, placing his hands on his hips, worry flickering to life in his blue-grey eyes. "How did this happen?" Jace rubbed his chin, most likely analyzing the situation in order to find a missing piece. He kicked the toe of his tennis shoe against the wood floor and bowed his head. "What can I do?" He shoved his hands into his jean pockets, his bulging triceps peeking out beneath his basic black T-shirt.

"I'm not sure yet. Let me talk to the authorities and I'll know more here in a few." I patted them each on the back, grateful that my best friends were with me.

For the next several hours, the police searched the club and delivery area for any signs of a struggle, then reviewed the security footage. I swore a blue streak when I realized there was a blind spot at the loading dock. The camera hadn't picked up shit.

They asked all of us questions concerning the furniture company, names, descriptions of the employees, and who else was on site. Since I'd been in the penthouse, I wasn't sure if anyone had shown up after the men had unloaded our belongings.

The longer we searched, and the longer River didn't show up, hope began to fade away. I'd denied the nudge of my instincts, but I couldn't anymore. The harsh reality had been shoved down my throat until I fucking choked on it.

River was gone.

Chapter Two

After the police cleared out, Zayne drove Jace, Chance, and me to Pierce's house. I'd asked Brynn to remain at the club along with Vaughn and a plainclothes officer. Apparently, Pierce had connections in the community, and I had money, which allowed us extra help even though River hadn't been gone twenty-four hours yet. Although, Pierce and I had spoken on the phone often, this would be the first time I'd meet him and his wife face-to-face.

As the minutes ticked by, the chill in my bones solidified to sharp, stabbing ice crystals. The not knowing and lack of confirmation were the worst kinds of torture imaginable. I felt as if I might shatter into a million tiny pieces from the stress.

I paced Pierce and Sutton's large living room, my brain running a hundred miles a minute as I took in the details of their log home. It was spacious but comfortable. The light, shiny wood floors extended into the dining area and up the stairs. The grey stone fireplace stretched toward the vaulted ceiling, and fans circulated the air. The windows offered a stunning view of rolling hills and snow-capped mountains. River would never want to leave this place.

A tall, muscular guy rounded the corner, his brown eyes landing on me. Power rolled off him in waves. His posture and grim expression signaled that he was ex-military. A gorgeous blue-eyed, blonde woman held onto one of his impressive biceps.

"Hey, Holden. I'm Pierce." He extended his hand, and I shook it.

The woman released Pierce's arm and stepped forward. "I'm Sutton." We shook as well. "I'm sorry we're meeting under these circumstances." She gently patted my shoulder.

"Me too. Thanks for opening your home to us." I sat at the end of the brown leather couch next to Jace and Chance. Everyone introduced themselves, then we got down to business.

"I've already talked to Zayne, but I'd like to hear it from you, as well." Pierce remained standing, but Sutton sank into a matching recliner and tucked a foot beneath her leg.

I relayed the information that I had while Jace and Chance listened intently. "And um ..." I shot up from my seat and laced my fingers behind my head. Tension snaked down my neck and between my shoulder blades. "River is pregnant."

"Shit," Jace and Chance said in unison.

"I found the test in her purse. My guess is that she took it this morning, then tried to ditch Zayne so she could have some privacy and hopefully tell me." I had no clue if I was correct or not, but I was fishing for a reasonable explanation of why she ran from her bodyguard. *Unless she'd been threatened.* I wanted to search her phone before I turned it over to Sutton. Maybe she'd received a call or text that would help me piece together what the hell had happened.

"If River had just found out, she'd definitely need some time to process it all if it were unexpected," Sutton added. "This information adds a layer of urgency. We're protecting two people now."

A sharp pang stabbed me in the chest. "I just want her back unharmed."

"We all do. What suspects do we have?" Pierce asked, stroking his lightly stubbled chin.

I glanced at Jace and Chance. "You guys don't know what's going on. Brynn knows a little bit about it because she and River are close, but ... I didn't want to bring anyone else into the situation. I'm sorry." I scrubbed my face with my hands, realizing this was a full-blown catastrophe.

Chance scooted to the edge of the couch, his brows drawn together, shadowing his blue eyes. "Spill, man. We've got your back. Don't even question it."

"Talk to us. We all care about River," Jace added.

These guys were my best friends, and I trusted them with my life. We'd grown up together. We were in a sex club together. Neither of them had ever judged me, even when I'd made some stupid decisions.

Forcing myself to do what was necessary, I began to share. Pierce and Sutton were aware of some of the details from our phone calls, but I hadn't told the others in the room. "Tim tried to rape River."

Jace's mouth gaped. "That's so fucked up."

Chance's eyes narrowed, but he remained silent. I continued to explain that not only was Tim a sorry son of a bitch for attempting to hurt River, but also what I'd learned concerning his extracurricular activities.

I hadn't asked Brynn's permission to share, so I kept her name out of it. I didn't want her tangled up in this mess any more than necessary.

"Where's Tim now?" Pierce frowned and folded his arms across his chest, his biceps bulging beneath the sleeves of his white button-down shirt.

"The last I knew, here in Spokane, but he might have left again. After he attacked River, I saw him at Mom's once. But that's it. I haven't had anything to do with him," I said.

"What about the guy River was running from when she arrived here?" Jace asked. "His asshole friend grabbed Becky instead."

"His name is Logan," I explained to Pierce and Sutton. "From what I understand, River's guardian, Dan, owed Logan a lot of money. Since Dan is dead, they were looking for River to pay up ... she overheard exactly how they wanted their payment, and she ran. It's how she ended up at my house. River also mentioned that Logan is a meth dealer. I'm not sure what else he's involved in, but years ago he knew Tim."

Everyone stared at me, waiting for me to continue. "River found a picture I had of my family. Logan was standing next to Tim. It was a long time ago, so the details are spotty, but Tim had introduced him as a business partner."

While I'd been talking, Sutton had been taking notes. She was furiously scribbling as I spilled River's and my secrets.

Pierce stepped forward. "I have a guy at the FBI. I want to reach out to him and see if Logan and Tim are on their radar. Holden, go back to 4 Play and I'll be in touch. You guys try not to talk to anyone else about this. If you need an ear, call Sutton or me, or chat between yourselves. Vaughn and Zayne will continue to watch the club. Holden, don't go anywhere alone. Take one of my men with you at all times. I'd like to have someone posted outside the penthouse while you're home, too."

"I understand. But I have to ask ... has Zayne lost a client before?" I shot an angry look in Zayne's direction. He'd been quiet the entire time, stoic and unreadable.

Compassion flickered in Sutton's gaze. "Although we're all trained, Holden, sometimes a situation is unavoidable. The fact that the elevator was already on the floor gave River a head start. I know you're angry, but Zayne is one of the best men we have, and I guarantee you he's not taking this lightly." Her attention zeroed in on Zayne, then back on me.

"What bothers me is that the stairwell was locked," Pierce added. "If it hadn't been, Zayne would have gotten to her in seconds. I've personally seen him jump the handrail and drop a flight to tackle a guy. In this instance, he was literally stuck. It makes me think whoever we're dealing with knew where Zayne was and had this planned."

I groaned in disbelief and frustration. "Those doors are never locked. First, it's against the fire code. Second, Chance is a manager at 4 Play, and both of us use the stairs all the time."

"Someone knew the layout of the club," Pierce said.

"The only people that I wasn't familiar with were the men moving the furniture into the penthouse. There were four of them, and I don't even have their names."

"I do." Zayne stepped forward. "They all had patches on their uniforms. Mitch, John, Alex, and James. I realize those are common, but the company should have a record of who worked that day."

"I can call them and find out," Sutton said, taking more notes. "I'll pretend that I'm a new customer. That will allow me to see if they run background checks on their employees and gather some information. I'll explain that they did a wonderful job for you, Holden."

I appreciated their expertise, and the more we talked, the more the anger at Zayne slipped away. Pierce was right. If the stairwell door had been unlocked, Zayne would have been able to reach River by the time the elevator arrived on the main floor.

A sinking feeling knotted my stomach. "If Tim has her ..." My molars ground together as hate pebbled my skin. "I'll fucking end him."

The room grew quiet as I realized I'd threatened to kill someone in front of five witnesses.

"We've been in your shoes before," Sutton said softly. "My sister was kidnapped, and I plotted a few murders myself. You're in good company with people who understand. Also, every word spoken between us is confidential. Pierce or I will talk to Brian at the FBI, but we won't repeat anything said here, like what you mentioned about Tim."

"Even if your father turned up dead tomorrow, no one would ever know what you said." Understanding flickered in Pierce's brown eyes.

"Thanks. I'm pretty fucked up. I just want my girlfriend back and safe."

"We'll find her," Chance said, his words full of conviction.

I hoped like hell he was right.

Pierce sat down in the brown leather wingback chair. "I'll reach out to the FBI and see what I can learn about Logan and Tim. Sutton will deep dive into Logan, as well. I'll call as soon as we know something. Until then, feel free to check in. I understand everyone's nerves are on end."

My cell vibrated with a text, and I removed it from my pocket. Brynn's name flashed across the screen.

Any news? I'm out of my fucking head with worry right now.

"It's Brynn," I announced as I replied to her.

Not yet. I'll be there soon. We can all go to the penthouse and talk.

Tiny black dots flickered while Brynn typed out her response.

Okay. See you when you get here.

I thanked Pierce and Sutton for their help, then told them goodbye.

Zayne led Jace, Chance, and me to the company Mercedes parked in front of Pierce's garage. Zayne had insisted on driving us. It had been a smart move. I was so upset, I had no business being behind the wheel of a car.

Once we were headed down the driveway and to the main road, Jace broke the silence from the backseat. "I can't believe River's pregnant," he said softly. Compassion laced his words. "Is the test recent?"

I pressed my lips together. "I think it was from this morning. She's been sick the last few days. I have a feeling Brynn might know more."

"That's fucked up, man." Chance massaged the back of his neck. "This whole situation is fucked up. I'll do anything I can to help."

I glanced over my shoulder at him, his blue eyes flashing with a myriad of emotions—support, fear, and anger.

"The stairs being locked is bothering the shit out of me, dude," Jace chimed in. He cracked his knuckles, his tell-tale nervous sign.

"You and me both," Zayne said from the driver's seat. "I'm fast. I would have made it to her in time." His hand tightened on the steering wheel, his fingers turning white from gripping it so hard.

My anger had dissipated the more I realized that Zayne had been purposefully backed into a corner. I swallowed my pride. "Sorry I lost my shit and yelled at you."

Zayne rubbed his jaw. "I would have done the same. Let's forget it and move on."

I nodded. Maybe Zayne was a better man than I'd given him credit for. "From what you said, it sounds like River punched all of the elevator buttons to stall you. I wish I knew why. I can speculate, but I'm not positive. I want to check her phone and see if there are any texts or calls from an odd number. River didn't have many people in her life, so if it wasn't one of us, then it's suspicious."

"Good to know," Zayne said, flipping on the turn signal and turning right onto Division Street.

"So, you think she got spooked?" Chance asked from the backseat.

"Something happened from the time she arrived at the club this morning to when she ditched Zayne." I ran my fingers through my hair, attempting not to fall apart again. I needed to be alone to process what the fuck was happening. I could lose my shit later, but not in front of everyone.

"I know for a fact no one else was on the floor with us. I searched it as soon as she disappeared into her office," Zayne explained.

"She didn't touch anything that I could see," I added, recalling that her desk was clean and so was mine.

Nervous silence stretched between us as Zayne pulled into the parking lot of 4 Play. Without a second thought, I jumped out of the car and ran inside the club. The overhead lights above the bar illuminated a woman, but I couldn't tell who it was. I hurried toward her, my heart dying a little with each step as I realized it was Brynn and not River.

"Hey." I bent down and kissed her on the cheek.

She gripped my arms, her face pale. "I haven't heard from her. Have you?" She peered at me, trust in her gaze.

"No. Let's go to the penthouse and see if we can find anything." I took her hand in mine as Jace, Chance, and Zayne joined us. Brynn's fingers were ice cold, and I rubbed them hoping I'd warm her up. "Please know that I love you when I say this ... you don't look too good."

"I don't feel too good." She gulped, then leaned against the wall as we waited for the elevator.

The doors whooshed open, and we all filed in, then headed to the penthouse. This would be the first time everyone saw it complete and furnished. It wasn't right. River should have seen it before anyone else. We should have made love in our bed—in our new room. I'd planned on cooking for her that night before our friends joined us for drinks and ... My heart nosedived, and a sharp, stabbing pain spread through my chest. I should be proposing to the love of my life tonight. Instead, she was missing, and I was scrambling to try and find her. Her and our baby.

The elevator arrived on the top floor, breaking my thoughts. I strolled to the door and allowed the retinal scanner to scan my eye. I waited for the click of the lock to release, but nothing happened.

Frowning, I jiggled the handle, but it was still locked. I returned to the scanner, but it failed to work a second time.

Before I could verbalize my concerns, Zayne pulled his gun out of his side holster. On high alert, he faced the elevator and watched as the light indicated it was coming our way. The soft ping sounded in the hallway, and Zayne remained steady, waiting.

Chapter Three

Brynn tightly squeezed my hand as Jace and Chance stood still. I'd never experienced a glitch with the retina security, and the timing was too bizarre with River's disappearance.

I released a soft sigh of relief as I stared at a pair of black Louboutin heels, then a large bouquet of pink and yellow roses. Mom lowered the flowers enough to see as she stepped out. Zayne quickly holstered his gun, and we all pretended that my mother didn't almost stare into the end of a barrel.

"Oh, you're all here!" Mom peeked around the arrangement. Her red blouse was tucked into black slacks and every strand of her brown hair was in place. "I'm so glad I haven't missed you."

I moved forward, freeing the vase from her grip.

"I didn't realize you were back in town, or I would have called." I kissed Mom on the cheek.

"I flew in late last night and am flying out again in a few hours. It's an unexpected trip, but that's business for you." She gave me a warm smile.

I shifted my weight from one foot to the other, realizing that I would have to tell Mom about River. "The scanner isn't working, so I have to call the company and find out what happened."

"That's unacceptable. Has River tried it yet?" Mom's eyes swept the group. I assumed she was attempting to assess everyone's mood. "Where is she anyway?"

"Let's go downstairs and I'll update you." Mom was going to flip her shit. She and River had grown close over the last few months.

Quietly, we filed back into the elevator, then down a floor and to the conference room. I placed the flowers on the cabinet and ran my fingertip along one of the velvety petals. River would have loved the bright colors. They were gorgeous, and the sweet fragrance filled the area.

Zayne remained in the hall as everyone sat down.

"Holden, what in the world is happening? You're all acting as though someone died."

I cringed and placed my knuckles on the smooth wood surface of the table, bowing my head. "I hope not."

"Holden, you're scaring me. Please tell me what in the hell is going on." She gripped the arms of the chair, the color draining from her cheeks.

"River is missing."

"What do you mean missing?" Mom's hand fluttered over her chest.

"We found her purse on the loading dock. No one has seen her since the furniture was delivered."

"Good God." Mom shook her head. "I don't understand. She has a bodyguard. Where was he?" Her pitch rose as she spoke.

"He tried to reach her, but someone jammed the elevator buttons. It's a long story, but all you need to know is that Zayne did everything he could." I paused, giving her a minute for my words to sink in. "Mom, is Tim in town?"

"I have no idea where that man is or what he does with his time these days." Mom sank into her seat again, her attention bouncing around the room. "You suspect that your father took her?"

"It's crossed my mind."

Her forehead creased with obvious confusion. "Jesus, do you really think it was Tim? I know he was furious at being made a fool when he ... when River accused ... when he tried to hurt River, and he's irate about me filing for divorce. Maybe he blames her for all of that. But kidnapping?" Her brows furrowed. "I don't think so, Holden. I just ..."

Jace, Chance, and Brynn remained quiet and allowed me to provide the information I was comfortable with sharing. I appreciated them more than they would ever know.

I sat on the edge of the table and took Mom's hand in mine. "I love you, Mom. We've come a long way in the past few years."

"Of course we have, you're my son. I'd move heaven and earth for you."

But not for Hannah. I mentally slammed the door on my anger and continued. River deserved my full attention right now.

"Mom, you can't repeat any of this conversation. I've been advised not to talk about it, but you need to know." I ran my fingers through my hair and willed my racing heart to calm itself. "Tim ... I've recently learned that he isn't who he says he is." Dejected, I continued. "There's suspicion that he's tangled up with some very dangerous men and dealing illegal weapons."

A harsh laugh escaped my mother. "Tim? I don't think so, honey. He's too stupid to be able to pull off something like that without landing his sorry ass in prison." Her smile faltered as she realized I wasn't playing around. "Are you sure?" she whispered.

"Yes," Brynn added.

My head whipped in Brynn's direction, my eyes pleading with her to not share any more. If Tim took River and learned that Brynn had dirt on him, he'd come for her next.

"I don't understand, Brynn," Mom said.

Jace and Chance each took one of Brynn's hands in theirs. We were all in this together, but it helped to see the support.

"I don't have a lot of information, but he met with an arms dealer a few months ago. He's in deep, and he's played you, Catherine. He's dangerous. Please, please hire security and stay safe." Brynn's eyes welled up. "I'm planning on doing the same if I'm not with one of these guys."

I glanced at Brynn. "One of us will be with you at all times, but if you want a bodyguard, I'll take care of it."

My attention zeroed in on Mom again. "I'll talk to Pierce and have a bodyguard waiting for you when you return from your trip."

"Thank you, honey. I'm not sure when I'll be home. These trips can take a while, but I'll give you plenty of notice." A sob escaped and tears rolled down Mom's cheeks. "Does River know all of this?"

"Yeah." I realized Mom would have more questions, but for now, I needed her help. "Mom, I need you to be one hundred percent honest with me. Is Tim in town?" I asked, pinning her with an intense gaze.

She gave me a tearful nod. Chance rose from his seat, located a box of tissues, and placed them on the table in front of her.

"Thank you, hon." Mom grabbed one and dabbed her eyes. "Your father and I had to meet at the attorney's office. Divorce stuff." She sniffled and folded her hands in her lap. "What do you need me to do? You know how much I love River. She's already a part of the family."

"We all love her," Brynn added.

"The police have been here and taken our statements. Now it's a matter of waiting."

"Alastair's don't wait, Holden. They fix shit." She stood abruptly.

"Mom. What are you going to do?" Dammit. She had to stay out of it. "You can't confront Tim. He'll know we're onto him. Please. Give me your word that you won't say anything. If you do, you'll put River's life in even more danger. We're not doing *nothing*. I have some men on it. That's all I can share with you."

Mom shifted from side to side, fear flickering across her features. She glanced around the room, her jaw tightening as tears reappeared.

"You're right. I just want to smack him senseless until he tells me where she is."

My eyes narrowed while I mentally revisited beating Tim to a bloody pulp after he tried to rape River. "I wish it were that easy," I whispered, hugging her. "I think it would be best if you left town and stayed off his radar."

"That's why I stopped by to congratulate you and River. I needed to tell you goodbye as well. I'm leaving tonight. I'm off to London."

"Thanks, Mom." My throat clogged with love and appreciation.

"You keep me posted. Do you understand? I'll stay out of it, but the minute you find her ..."

I gathered her in my arms. "Please be safe." I kissed the top of her head, then watched as she left. I stepped out into the hallway. "Zayne, can you escort her to the car? I'll keep the door locked until you're back."

"Yes." Zayne fell in behind Mom as she strolled to the elevator, her shoulders rigid with tension.

I secured the room, then collapsed into my seat. "Thank you, guys, for following my lead. It's bad enough that Mom is going through a divorce, and now River." I rubbed my face with my hands, suddenly remembering why we were sitting around the table instead of in the penthouse. Pulling my phone out of my back pocket, I called the security company.

Fortunately, they were able to analyze the problem remotely. In less than an hour, I was at the entrance of my new home, testing the scanner. The lock clicked, and I pushed the door open.

"Thank you. Let's not have that happen again," I said to Hal, the technical support guy. "I'll be contacting the owner of the company, Jason, tomorrow. You've been very helpful, and I'll let him know." Although I was polite, I had to express that I was displeased with the hiccup. If they didn't have the information, they wouldn't push to make a better product.

Zayne entered and raised his hand to halt us from following. "I'm going to search the place first. The timing of the scanner not working bothers me."

We waited in the hall while he searched the premises. When he returned, he uncurled his fingers, revealing a small device in his right palm. "I checked for bugs, but the place is clean."

The thought hadn't even occurred to me. Zayne was quickly earning my respect again.

I held the door while Jace, Chance, and Brynn filed in. Zayne nodded at me from the hallway.

"He's a good guy, Holden." Brynn said, slipping her arm through mine. "I realize that River ditched him, but I think I understand why. She needed a few minutes alone to process. My guess is that she ran to the loading dock for some fresh air, and to find you."

Jace made a beeline for the kitchen and tugged on the handle of the stainless-steel fridge. He removed four beers and handed one to each of us. "I know the situation isn't what it was supposed to be but ..." He popped off the cap and held his beer up. "To friends. To family. And to River's safe and speedy return. However this plays out, I'm thankful as fuck I have you guys."

"Cheers," we said half-heartedly and in unison.

Jace was right. The timing sucked ... sort of. Knowing that my family was standing in front of me, and that we had each other's backs no matter what soothed my frazzled nerves a little, though.

"I have her phone," Brynn reminded me as we strolled into the living area. Brynn sat carefully on the new black leather couch. Jace and Chance settled into matching chairs, and I stood at the window, overlooking the city below us. River and I had decided on a contemporary theme—clean lines along with comfort. I'm pretty sure our décor would qualify for a magazine. It was stunning. The pieces of art River had chosen hung on the back wall, the color a gorgeous contrast to the black furniture and white marble floors. My chest ached, and an angry fuse ignited inside me. Once River was safe in my arms again, my mission would be not only to end, but slowly torture the mother fucker that stole her and my baby.

"I placed it in a plastic baggy when you all were at the Westbrooks', just in case there was some incriminating evidence. I mean, I realize we touched it." Brynn crossed her legs, her foot kicking. She was stressed and still didn't seem like she was feeling well.

"Wait. You kept River's phone?" Jace's dark eyebrows shot up to his hairline.

I strolled over to Brynn and took it from her. "Yeah. I have to check if there are any leads. Once I look, I'm handing it over to Sutton. She can track more than I can. But I have to fucking try." I sank onto the couch next to Brynn. "I have to do something. Mom's right, Alastairs don't wait. We make it happen." I nervously ran my free hand along my leg. Brynn gently rubbed my back as I stared at the cell. "I need some gloves."

"Here." Brynn rummaged through her purse and handed me a pair of latex ones she'd hijacked from the bar. "I thought about it while you were gone." She gave me a sheepish smile.

I slipped them on, then removed the phone from its protective baggie. Sucking in a breath, I touched the screen and woke it up.

The battery was nearly full. River hadn't ever really owned a cell before, so she wasn't glued to it every minute of the day like most people. A text message notification dropped down from the top, and I tapped it.

"What the hell?"

Chapter Four

I looked at the message, dumbfounded. When I had the clarity of mind, I checked the time it had been received. It'd been sent a little after two this afternoon. River had already been missing. Suspicion seeped into my veins.

"What is it?" Chance leaned forward on the edge of his seat as he waited for an explanation.

"It's a text from Shirley. She and Ed were the ones that helped River leave Montana, but the phone she gave River had a tracker in it."

"Yeah, we were all there," Jace motioned for me to hurry up and read the text.

"It says: *River, it's Shirley. I've been worried sick and got your new number from Addison. Please call me.*"

"Call her, Holden. It's time to get some answers." Chance stood and cracked his neck. We were all high strung and clamoring for any piece of information that would lead us to River.

"What am I going to say? Did you know that your cell had a tracker in it, and you put my girlfriend in danger?"

I stared at the phone as though it were a bomb ready to detonate.

What if Shirley and Ed were behind River's disappearance, and I fucked things up even worse?

"You won't find out until you call her," Jace said, his expression skeptical and not matching the confidence in his tone.

An intense wave of protectiveness jolted through me. If there were any chance that this woman might know something that could lead us to River, I had to do it. Before I talked myself out of it, I called her.

I placed the call on speaker and leaned forward, elbows resting on my knees.

"Hello?" A woman with a throaty voice answered.

"Is this Shirley?" I asked as I hoped like hell that I hadn't made a mistake.

"Yeah, who's calling?"

"I'm a friend of River's."

"I thought this was her new number. I've been trying to contact her. Do you know if she's okay? I've been worried sick." Shirley's east coast accent was undeniable.

I toyed with the right words to start our conversation. At this point I didn't trust her, and I had to be careful not to provide too much information. "I'm not sure how to tell you this, but River is missing." I rubbed the back of my neck with my free hand. "I was hoping you might be able to help me."

"What? And before I help anyone, who the hell are you?" Her words were sharp.

"Sorry. I'm Holden, her boyfriend. We were moving into our new home today when she disappeared."

"Jesus," Shirley whispered. "I adore that girl. I'll do anything you need me to. What can I do?"

I glanced at everyone in the room. "I need to know something first."

"All right."

"Logan sent a man after River when she first arrived."

I could hear Shirley suck in air. "That dirty bastard."

"You know him?"

"I do. He's a piece of shit. What I don't understand is how he tracked her to Idaho."

Her words knocked the air out of my lungs. Shirley didn't know that River was in Spokane, which meant she was either playing me, or she hadn't led Logan to her.

"There was a tracker in the phone you gave her," I explained.

Shirley's cell clattered and static crackled in my ear, then she swore a blue streak. If she really hadn't put River in harm's way, then she seemed like someone I could quickly appreciate.

"Sorry. Hopefully that didn't break your eardrum." I heard the flicker of a lighter, then Shirley inhaled deeply from what I suspected was a cigarette. "Now I understand why she never reached out to me. She thought I helped Logan find her. I didn't. I swear it. I'd never do that to her. Neither would Ed."

I could picture Shirley pacing. "It had to be the little girl I sent to buy the phone and a few other things for River before I put her on the bus. Her name is Josie. She works at the diner with us. When she brought the items to me, the plastic case on the cell had been opened. She said it was cheaper since it was an open item. I didn't think twice about it. Hell, I've bought some of those marked-down products myself. But the next day, she missed her shift. Josie never came back. I'm gonna make a wild guess it's because she did a favor for Logan with that damn tracker."

I massaged my temple with my free hand, debating to believe her or not. My head ached as if, at any second, my skull would splinter. "So, you think she planted the device?"

"Hell, she had to have. It wasn't Ed. He didn't even touch the phone. I was the only person to handle it other than Josie, and I swear to you on my mother's grave that it wasn't me."

I squeezed my eyes closed, attempting to clear the haze of emotions. I wanted to trust Shirley. What she said made sense, but I still wasn't sure.

"Logan sent one of his buddies to my house. Instead of snatching

River, he grabbed an innocent ..." Brynn scoffed loudly, and I shot her a dirty look. Although we understood that Becky was far from harmless, I didn't have time to explain it to Shirley. "He took someone else and held her at gunpoint. I was able to help River stay out of sight. That's when we learned about Logan and that he was looking for her."

"Good God. Logan is pure evil. Thank you for keeping her safe."

I couldn't ignore the sincerity in her voice.

"Can I ask how the two of you met?" Shirley asked softly.

A slight grin pulled at the corner of my mouth. "I found her sleeping in my recycling bin."

"Wait. What? She was supposed to be at the women's shelter," Shirley said, obviously alarmed.

"She missed her stop in Idaho and ended up in Spokane. When I saw her, I invited her into my parent's place and made her some food. She got spooked and ran out of the house. I tried to catch her but ... she hauled ass into the street and was hit by a car."

"Oh my God! Please tell me that she's okay. How bad was the damage?" Shirley paused, inhaling again. By this time, I wanted to join her. The stress was eating me alive.

"She broke her leg. I rushed her to the hospital, and she stayed with me until she healed." A sharp pain spread through me. River had to be alive. "I fell in love with her," I admitted. "Hard."

"It would be difficult not to fall in love with her. She's strong, beautiful, and smart as a whip. Wherever she is, I have to believe that she's going to be all right." Shirley continued. "Dan, River's guardian, was found a few days later. His death has been the biggest gossip all over town ever since she moved. They're still investigating it. Some animal got hold of the body, so there wasn't much of him left."

I couldn't stop my smile. I was glad the bastard had died painfully. "From what River said, Dan owed Logan a lot of money and they were planning to take River for payment."

"I'm going to kill that son of a bitch myself," she blurted, then grew silent.

"Have you seen Logan lately? Does he come into the diner?" I asked, my heart hammering against my ribcage.

"He's been around, but he mentioned leaving town a few days ago for a while. Do you ... Do you think he took River?" Her voice trembled.

"That's what we're trying to find out. Anything that you learn could save her life," I added.

"I'll talk to Ed tonight. He's at the diner now, but he should be back by seven. We both hear a lot of rumors, so maybe one of them will end up helpful. In the meantime, I'll see if I can locate Josie."

"Okay. We're working on things from this end as well. Can you call me directly with any information? I'll have to give River's phone to the police."

"Of course. Let me grab a pen and paper to write on."

Brynn rifled through her purse and handed me what I needed. Shirley and I exchanged cell numbers, along with the ones for the diner and her landline at her and Ed's place.

"I'll be in touch." I stared at my shoes, my mind scrambling for any clue of who took River.

"I'll let you know as soon as I learn anything," Shirley promised.

"Keep your doors locked, Shirley. Make sure you've got a weapon on you, too. These men are dangerous, and if they learn that you're sniffing around their business it could land you in hot water."

"Don't you worry. I carry. Got one in my purse and another in my car. Not to mention a few around my home. I have a nifty leg holster, too. I'm covered."

I couldn't help it. I liked her. "Excellent. I'll talk to you soon."

I ended the call and blew out a breath. Right now, I wanted to believe the best in Shirley, but the longer that River was gone, the more I questioned my instincts. "Was it only me or do you all believe that Shirley and Ed didn't have anything to do with the tracker?"

"I believe her," Brynn said, then glanced at Jace and Chance.

"She's either an amazing liar, or she really cares about River and wouldn't hurt her." Jace laced his fingers behind his head, his gaze narrowing in thought. "I could be wrong, but I believe her as well."

"Me too, but you need to tell Pierce and Sutton everything. They probably have connections and can find out who Shirley and Ed are, and if they're hiding the truth." Chance folded his arms across his muscular chest.

"Agreed," Brynn added.

I opened the record of calls and texts, but other than Shirley, there were only calls or messages from Addison, Brynn, myself, or our group chat. I'd lucked out with Shirley's timing. At least I was pretty sure whose side she and Ed were on.

Looking one last time, I conceded. There were no hints of who could have taken her. No threats, no ... nothing. "I'll call Pierce now and tell him everything I learned." I hoped like hell it was enough to find my girlfriend.

After talking to Pierce and Sutton, I made an excuse that I was exhausted. I was, but I realized I wouldn't be able to sleep. I just needed to be alone.

I watched as Brynn, Jace, and Chance left the penthouse and entered the elevator. Zayne remained posted by the entrance.

"Can you give this to Sutton so she can see if there are any clues I couldn't find?" I handed Zayne River's phone in the baggie.

He tucked it into his pocket. "Vaughn will be here later to give me a break, so I'll take off for a while and give it to Sutton."

"Thanks, man." Waving goodnight, I returned to my apartment and sagged against the now locked door. I'd been holding my shit together all day. I'd put on a brave face and thought of every detail over and over.

If River returned tonight, she'd use the retina scanner and be able to enter.

My Adidas tennis shoes slapped against the white marble floor as I made my way to the kitchen. I grabbed another beer and set it on the countertop. River had been so excited about this space. She'd even promised to make her lasagna for me the first weekend we were here.

Anger swelled within me and roared to life—anger at myself and at River for ditching Zayne. I was furious that the stairwell door had been locked, trapping Zayne on the penthouse floor. I muffled a cry, my chest burning from burying the pain. Before I realized it, I swooped the beer off the counter, sending it crashing to the floor. Glass and amber liquid sprayed in every direction as I stared at it stupidly.

"Goddammit, River," I whispered to an empty house. "Where are you?"

My body quaked, and nausea bubbled in my stomach. Exhaustion and grief brought me to my knees. I placed my palms against the floor, allowing the cold marble to soothe them. I couldn't lose River. She had to be all right. Quiet sobs tore from me, and my shoulders shook uncontrollably. How could this have happened? We knew that Tim and Logan were dangerous.

I threw my head back and screamed. I screamed at the universe. I screamed at the injustice of losing Hannah and now River. And I screamed at the pain roaring to life inside me. Hannah nearly pulled me under, but if I lost River, it would devastate me. I would cease to exist without her.

Leaning against the kitchen island, I allowed myself to break. All of the dark thoughts and fears I'd kept in check all day came rushing out with so much velocity, my gut rebelled. I jumped off the floor and hurled in our brand-new sink. Cold sweat dotted my upper lip, and I wiped it off, then sucked in a sharp breath and swallowed repeatedly.

I turned on the cool water, washed my face, then rinsed my mouth, and the sink. The brain fog began to clear as I gathered myself together and cleaned up my mess.

Once I'd swept and mopped, I hurried to the bedroom and flung open the closet door. I quickly selected black jeans and a dark shirt to change into. It had been six hours since River had disappeared.

Anxiety sparked through me. It was time to take matters into my own hands.

I grabbed my phone, wallet, and keys before I headed out. Hopefully, Pierce and Sutton were true to their word, and what I did or said remained confidential, because I was about to put Zayne to the test.

Chapter Five

Even as a kid, I was hot-tempered. I wasn't sure why, but I had a simmering anger inside of me, and at any given moment, I'd plummet off the end of that cliff and lose my shit. There was always something at the edge of my subconscious, lurking in the corner and taunting me. As I grew older and participated in sports, I could contain my temper and redirect my energy. It probably saved me from a destructive path. But no matter what, I hadn't ever been able to shake the shadows from my mind—until River.

As soon as I left the penthouse, Zayne fell into step behind me. We rode the elevator without speaking, then strolled through the busy club as though we were on a mission. I was. Zayne just didn't know it yet.

Once we entered the parking garage, I approached a sweet, dark green Mercedes EQS. It was sporty and luxurious and brand spanking new. The only miles were from the drive from the dealership to its parking space at 4 Play. It was River's, and I hadn't even had a chance to give it to her yet.

Ensuring I had the key fob in my pocket, I waved my hand in

front of the car door handle, and the locks popped open. Zayne slid into the passenger's seat next to me.

"Sweet ride," he said, running his fingertips over the light gray leather seat. River would fall in love with the new dashboard, with its multiple screens and controls that spanned the length of the interior.

I pushed the start button, and the vehicle purred to life. The engine was so quiet I had to strain to hear it. "It's River's. She hasn't seen it yet."

Shifting into reverse, I eased out of the parking space next to my BMW i8. The Mercedes handled like a fucking dream. Once I'd realized how excited River was to drive my car, I wanted her to have her own. She deserved it. She'd earned it, but more than that, I bought it because I love her.

My chest tightened, and I struggled to breathe against the pressure. We had to find River soon. I understood how critical the first forty-eight hours were, and it had been six already. When I needed time to slow down, it gave me the middle finger and sped by.

A soft buzzing in my head started as I pulled out onto Division Street. Zayne remained quiet, but I realized he was observing me, looking for any telltale signs of what I was up to. My pulse kicked up a notch as I drove toward my mom's house. Tim had returned to Spokane, and I had a sneaking suspicion that he would visit her and see if she was still in town. Regardless, I was on a mission to find the piece of shit and beat him black and blue until he told me where River was. Even if he hadn't taken her, I suspected Logan had, and somehow Tim was involved.

Twenty minutes later, I slowed and eyed the home I'd grown up in. Oddly, the lights were on, and although the curtains were closed, I could see a silhouette moving in the living room. My eyes narrowed. Mom wasn't supposed to be there. She either canceled her flight, or someone was in her place uninvited.

"Why are we here?" Zayne finally asked.

I responded with silence.

The garage door opened, and Tim's car eased out. I sucked in a breath. What the hell was he doing here? If Mom was there, was she okay?

I was torn. Did I call to see if Mom's trip had been delayed and she was at the house, or find out what that piece of shit was up to? I faced Zayne. "Can you check on mom? I'll be back in a bit."

Zayne full-on frowned. "I'm not leaving you, so wherever you go, I go."

"Goddammit." I made a snap decision to follow Tim. He wouldn't recognize the car, and since I'd parked up the street, he didn't have a good view of us.

If I were honest with myself, he was the only lead I had on River. I had to talk to him.

Tim swung onto our road, then his taillights blinked in the darkness as he slowed at the stop sign. Although he hadn't signaled, he turned left. He was most likely heading back to Division Street. I had to pace myself perfectly. I couldn't spook or lose him.

"Let me guess. You want answers from Tim?" Zayne asked.

"Yup."

"Then let me help."

I squinted at Zayne in disbelief. "Aren't you supposed to keep me out of trouble?"

Zayne smirked. "Depends on the circumstances. I know Pierce and Sutton are digging into who this man really is, but if we get information first ..." Zayne gave me a half-shrug. "We call it streamlining the process." Zayne arched a brow, and a dark chuckle rumbled through him.

If the situation hadn't been so intense, I would have laughed.

A heavy blanket of silence fell over us. I gripped the steering wheel so tightly my fingers turned white. I hoped like hell I wouldn't strangle Tim before I got the information I needed from him.

Hang on, River. I'm coming for you.

. . .

I continued to follow my sorry excuse of a father until he rolled up and parked near an abandoned building in downtown Spokane. He climbed out of his car, and I released my seatbelt.

Zayne's hand landed on my shoulder. "Wait."

"What? Why? This might be my only chance to grab him."

Zayne pulled away. "I understand, but something about this feels off."

I silently grumbled that Zayne had blocked me. Staring into the darkness, I surveyed my surroundings. We were in a shitty part of town. Boarded up buildings lined the streets, and homeless people curled up in the doorways of closed businesses. If I walked down the street, I'd probably spot at least half a dozen used drug needles on the sidewalks.

He disappeared into the building, and I stared at the door. "I think he should be kidnapped the way River was and flung into a trunk." I wasn't sure if River had been thrown into the back of a vehicle or not, but I suspected she'd been tossed into the delivery truck. Anger simmered beneath my calm exterior, threatening to break free at any moment.

Ten agonizing minutes ticked by, then the same door opened that Tim had used to enter the building. I leaned forward, attempting to get a better look through the darkness.

"What the fuck?" I blinked rapidly and tried to clear my vision.

"Do you know who's with him?" Zayne asked.

"I'm not a hundred percent sure, but I think it's Logan from River's old neighborhood." My hands fisted. "I've only seen him in an old photo. Honestly, I don't remember that evening at all, but River found it on my desk, so it obviously happened. My mind is one big-ass blank from the ages of three to five."

Zayne glanced at me as his eyebrow rose. "Nothing?" He asked as he returned his attention to Tim and the man he was talking to.

"Not a fucking thing."

"Do you want to? Remember that is." Zayne rubbed his jawline, his green eyes flashing with curiosity.

"I'm not sure." I shifted on the smooth leather seat. "I need to get closer so I can see if it's really Logan."

I grabbed the door handle and climbed out of the car.

"Holden, what the fuck are you doing?" Zayne fiercely whispered as he followed me.

"Just roll with it." I shoved my hands in the front pockets of my jeans in an attempt not to appear as though I wanted to beat Tim. I didn't want to put him on the defensive. My plan was risky, but I was willing to take that chance if it got me closer to finding River.

Loose gravel crunched beneath my tennis shoes, alerting the men that we were approaching.

"Hey, Dad."

Confused, Tim stared at me. "Holden? What are you doing here?" He squared his shoulders, eyeing me suspiciously.

"I saw you leave Mom's and I needed to catch you before you left town again. I know that our last conversation was heated, but I need your help." I slumped in defeat. "My girlfriend is missing." My voice cracked with tension.

Tim's mouth hung open. "Son, are you sure she didn't run off with another guy?"

My nostrils flared, and I gritted my teeth. "I'm positive."

Tim sauntered over to me, empathy flickering to life in his expression. Then he shocked the shit out of me with a hug. "What do you need, Holden? How can I help?"

I ran a hand through my hair and eyed the man who had remained quiet so far. It was definitely the same guy in the picture. He was older and thinner, but there was no mistaking it was him. From what River had said, he lived in the same shitty and dilapidated trailer park she had, but he was dressed well. Money oozed from his pores. He placed his hands on his hips, and his Rolex reflected the streetlight. He wasn't as poor as he pretended to be. But pretending to be broke was a smart cover when you were running illegal weapons.

"I didn't mean to interrupt your meeting. You seem to be traveling more and I couldn't afford to miss you." My gaze landed on the ground, then slowly drifted to Tim.

Tim patted me on the back, and I willed myself not to shiver with disgust.

"It's all right. You probably don't remember Logan. He was over a lot when you were younger. He's a friend and business partner."

Logan tipped his chin up, then held his hand out. "You're not a scrawny little kid anymore." Logan chuckled. I shook, making sure I gave him a firm handshake, imagining it was my fingers wrapped around his throat.

"Sorry, I don't remember you. Thanks for letting me borrow my dad for a few minutes."

Logan focused his attention on Zayne. "Who is he?" I didn't miss the edge to his tone.

"My bodyguard. He's cool."

To my surprise, Tim bristled. He threw his arm around me and stepped closer to Logan. "We might be able to help, son. Tell me what happened."

Tears stung my eyes. I was totally pretending with Dad, but the gut-wrenching agony that welled up inside of me was as real as the oxygen we were sharing. "We moved into the penthouse today. When I came downstairs her purse was on the loading dock. She was gone. I called the cops and they're looking for her but so far ..." I self-consciously rubbed at my tear-filled eye.

Dad glanced at Logan. "Let me check around and see if I can learn anything helpful. I know some folks that might have some information. I'm not making any promises, though. Until then, keep your chin up. I'm sure she's fine." He patted me on the chest. Either my dad was as good at acting as I was, or he didn't have River. The fastest way to find out was to buddy up to him again. Then, I wouldn't only take the motherfucker down, but I'd burn his body and toss it in the ocean. Fuck with me, fine. Fuck with the people I love and you're going down one way or the other.

"When are you leaving again?" I asked Tim.

"Tomorrow morning at ten-thirty, but that doesn't mean I can't reach out to see if anyone has seen her. Do you have a picture on your phone I can share?"

My gut twisted into knots. If Logan didn't realize we were referring to River, he was about to. I removed my cell from my back pocket and scrolled through all of the images of River. "Yeah." I sent one to him, then looked him dead in the eye. "If you ever touch her ..." *Shut up, Holden.* I held my hand up to him. "I've already been extremely clear with you. I want to move past it. You're my father. We can make things right between us."

"I'm sorry, son. I was horribly out of line. It won't happen again. I found the divorce papers and lost my shit." Tim folded his arms over his chest and tilted his chin up at me. "You're more important than a young piece of ass."

A chuckle pulled my attention away from Tim. "You can have young pussy anytime you want, man." Logan punched Tim in the shoulder. "You can't have your son's girl, though, you know that. No one wants sloppy seconds."

Tim smirked. "Wait until you see her. Leftovers don't mean shit. She's gorgeous."

My entire body stiffened with rage, and I stepped closer to him. "Enough," I seethed. "She's off limits to both of you." I glared at Tim, then Logan.

"No worries, boy. I'm giving your dad shit. We go way back and coming onto your girlfriend isn't cool. I'll keep him in check." Logan sucked on his teeth and arched a dark brow at me. "You have my word."

His word didn't mean crap to me, but at least the conversation was moving in a better direction.

Gravel crunched behind me, and I peeked over my shoulder. Zayne had moved to the right of the small group, his expression and body language unreadable.

"How about we meet for breakfast before you leave tomorrow?" I asked Tim. *Maybe I could learn some more about his business—and River— if Logan wasn't around.*

"Sounds good, son." He placed a hand on my arm. "How about the diner near the airport at eight?"

"I'll be there." I kicked at the rocks on the pavement, then braced myself. "Thanks for your help." I threw my arms around him as though he were the best father in the world. *Little did he know that I was about to hurl all over him.*

"Love you, Holden. See you tomorrow."

"Sounds good. Nice to meet you, Logan." I gave them a wave before I left them standing in the parking lot.

Once Zayne and I were in the car and driving away, I sank into the seat. "That was fucked. I hate that son of a bitch. I thought I was going to blow chunks all over him." I flipped the turn signal on and carefully circled the block. I killed the lights once we neared the building where Tim and Logan were still talking.

"You should be an actor. That performance came off real." Zayne leaned forward in his seat. "Or an undercover cop."

"I want to know where he's staying. I'm not certain that he isn't lying to me about leaving town. At the same time, I think everything that comes out of his mouth is a fucking lie."

"He's definitely hiding shit."

I frowned at Zayne. "How do you know?"

"He made very little eye contact with you, and he shifted his weight from one foot to the other. He's certainly uncomfortable around you. I just don't understand why. It could be that Logan is buying weapons from Tim right now."

Tim hopped into his car as Logan walked back into the building. "Interesting. I wonder what's inside?"

"Duck," Zayne ordered before Tim stared straight at River's Mercedes, then eased onto the road.

I counted to ten and peeked over the dashboard. Tim had reached a stop sign and took a right. I shifted the car into drive and followed him.

"You're taking a huge risk," Zayne said.

"I know. I'm not even sure if it will work, but if it gets me closer to River, then it's worth it."

"I understand." The tone of his voice made me wonder if he'd lived through something similar.

Ten minutes later, Tim parked in front of a white Victorian house. I lagged behind so he wouldn't spot us as he climbed out and retrieved a laptop bag. He strolled up the steps to the porch, and the door opened. A gorgeous, younger blonde smiled as a little girl ran to him, smiling as though he were the best thing in the world. Tim scooped the child into his arms and kissed the blonde's cheek.

"Son of a fucking bitch," I said quietly. "Does Tim have another family? That kid looks about five years old."

"You can't jump to conclusions no matter what it looks like. She might be his new girlfriend and she's got a child."

"You're right. That makes more sense." I grabbed my phone and messaged Pierce and Sutton the address. At least this way, I'd know the truth.

Unease and foreboding clutched my chest. I'd thought I knew who my father really was, but apparently, I had no fucking clue.

Chapter Six

As Zayne and I headed back to 4 Play, I realized I'd gone in search of answers but had only ended up with more questions. Who the hell was my father, and who were the people with him? Was the little girl my sister? My thoughts were scattered all over the place.

Before it got any later, I texted Mom to see if she was all right. Honestly, I wasn't even sure where she was, or if she'd receive my message. She could be in London or still on the plane, but I had to try to reach out since Tim had been lurking around in her home.

Once I was safely inside the penthouse, my stomach growled loudly. I hadn't eaten since breakfast, and it was after nine at night. Pacing to the window, I glanced out at the dark-shrouded city. Was River down there somewhere? Was she close by or across the world? I swallowed hard while my heart splintered into pieces. The minutes ticked by with no leads. Fuck it. I needed to check in with Pierce.

I typed out a quick text, the unbearable silence suffocating me.

My phone buzzed with a new message from Pierce.

First, Sutton didn't find anything on River's phone. Second, we're checking into a lead now. I will tell you more as soon as I know.

My pulse skyrocketed, and I leaned my forehead against the window. I hoped like hell it was a strong tip they were following.

For the moment, I needed some noise before I went insane. Spotting the remote, I pushed the power button and turned the television on. I didn't give a rat's ass what was playing. I just wanted to stay in control of my emotions. Breaking down wouldn't solve anything. I had to figure shit out.

Finally, I realized that in order to think straight, I had to fuel my mind and body. I whipped up a quick veggie omelet with some sausage and toast. My stomach clenched. River and I should have already made love on the counter. I should be eating her for dinner.

My dick hardened immediately at the thought of one of her legs over each of my shoulders and my tongue buried deep inside her. I loved how she arched her back, her nipples hard and begging to be played with. Suddenly, it dawned on me that we wouldn't have to worry about birth control for nine months. My cock deflated as the harsh reality crashed over me again, nearly knocking me off balance. *If River is in danger, so is our baby.*

I picked up my plate and sat at the dining room table. River had talked me into dark wood pieces for the penthouse. Honestly, I didn't care what we chose, but she thought the contrast would complement the white marble. She was right. Everything we'd chosen, from rugs to the artwork, blended beautifully. She had a good eye.

Clenching my fist, I forced myself to pick up my fork and shove the food into my mouth. I nearly gagged on the eggs. The stress was making me sick, but I had to eat. I massaged my forehead, willing the pounding headache to leave. Over the next several minutes, I ate slowly and began to feel better physically.

Exhaustion seeped deep into my bones. Regardless of if I could sleep or not, I had to rest. I wouldn't be worth shit if I were too tired to piece together a complete sentence. It was funny how I realized I needed to take care of myself in order to benefit River. The notion had never crossed my mind before, but I'd never been in love either. I thought I was once, but I think it was all of the sex with Brynn. She was beautiful, and I was pretty sure my dick had been ruling my emotions. Eventually, I saw her again as one of my best friends instead of romantically.

The sex club had brought us all closer in a way I hadn't imagined. We weren't only connected physically. We were tied to each other for the rest of our lives. Images of the group flashed through my mind: Sariah, Brynn, Payton, Jace, Chance, and I were sweaty and tangled up. We passed the ladies around and licked and fucked them until their cries of pleasure burst through the playroom. Sometimes the girls would play together, and the guys would watch. Eventually, we'd get in there as well. Brynn had a mouth on her, and as much as she loved getting fucked by Sariah, she sucked my dick like ...

"Stop." I slammed my fist down on the table, my fork jumping into the air and clattering to the floor.

I bowed my head. The group was my safe place, and the only reason I was thinking about them was to get my mind off reality. And ... to prepare myself if River didn't return. My jaw clenched. I refused to believe that she wouldn't. I should be planning for our future together and welcoming our baby into this world. Although I'd never planned to have kids, River had changed my mind. I couldn't think of anything I wanted more than to marry her and have a family.

My dinner churned in my stomach as horrible questions haunted me. What if she lost the baby? What if she was raped or beaten? I shot out of my chair, sending it flying backward and clattering to the floor.

I rubbed my eyes with the heels of my hands as images of a battered and bloodied River bombarded me. "No," I cried out to no one, shaking my head furiously.

A knock on the door pulled my attention away from my dark thoughts. I wasn't expecting anyone, and although Zayne was in the hall, I peered through the peephole. *Chance.*

I swung the door open, my gaze landing on his. Chance had always been quieter than the rest of the group, but his emotions were evident in his stormy blue eyes. Right now, they flashed with a combination of worry and concern.

"Hey, is everything okay downstairs?" I asked while I stepped back and let him in.

Chance ran his fingers through his blonde hair. He ditched the suit jacket and rolled up the sleeves of his light gray dress shirt.

"It's fine. A typical night. I just wanted to see how you were holding up." Chance shoved a hand into the pocket of his slacks and closed the door behind him. His attention dialed in on the chair that still laid on its side. Without a word or any questions, he strolled across the room and picked it up. He nodded to my plate. "Looks like you ate something."

I nodded as I headed to the wall of windows that overlooked downtown Spokane. "I'm trying." My voice was thick with fear and sounded strange.

"Talk to me, man. We've known each other since we were kids. There's no fucking way you're dealing with this. I don't want you spinning out if at all possible." Chance joined me and stared at the city below us.

"I feel like I'm in a fucking dream. It's hazy and uncertain, then the monsters come out and chase me." I placed my palms against the cool pane of glass.

If River were here, she'd get onto me for leaving handprints. It was one of her quirks, and she'd cleaned the slider at Mom's every time I turned around. She hated fingerprints on computer screens, phones, and refrigerators. I'd offered to buy her a sexy maid's uniform. All it got me was an empty soda bottle flung at my chest. She'd laughed and shucked her jeans and sweater, then returned to cleaning in her red and black lace G-string and bra.

I nearly moaned with the mental image of her ass in the air as she bent over to pick something off the floor. I'd hurried across the room, dropped to my knees, and peeled off her G-string. My tongue had landed on her sweet pussy, and she'd slapped her hands against the sliding glass door for balance as I made her scream my name ... in front of a window where anyone could have seen us. My cock began to throb, and my mouth watered at the memory of her taste. I inhaled slowly. I'd give my soul to have her next to me again, safe, and celebrating our first night in our new home.

"I want to help. Need to help. But I don't have a clue about what to do," Chance admitted, his shoulders sagging. "I can call in some favors to deal with Tim, but what if he's got her? How would ending his pathetic existence solve our problem?"

It was extremely rare to hear Chance offer a violent solution. He usually steered clear of it with his background and family, but he was willing to go down that path if the situation was warranted.

"I know. I've thought about it, too." My throat grew raw with unreleased emotion, and I swallowed. "I talked to him tonight."

A tight line creased his forehead as he observed me. "What happened?"

I folded my arms across my chest. "I wanted to see if he might have kidnapped River. What I hadn't expected was that Logan was with him, the guy that sent someone looking for River when Becky was held at gunpoint."

Shock flickered across his face. "With your dad?"

"Yeah. Since the picture of Logan and Tim was taken years ago, I wasn't sure if they were still speaking. Apparently, they are." I stepped away from the window. A memory I couldn't quite grasp danced at the edge of my mind. *What am I missing?* "I figured if I played it well, I might be able to spend time with Tim and figure out if he's responsible for River's disappearance." I massaged the knotted muscles in the back of my neck.

"That's dangerous, Holden. You're dancing with the devil. This could backfire if you poke your nose too far into his business. You'll be missing right along with your girlfriend." Chance's gaze narrowed. "We have to find another way." He spun on his heel and walked to the couch, then sat on the edge. Chance steepled his fingers together, which told me he was deep in thought.

"I'm having breakfast with Tim in the morning. Zayne will

be with me. I want to try to trip him up and see if he's a solid lead or not. While the cops and Pierce are tracking down other options, this was the only thing I could think of that I could do."

"Not keeping busy is hard. Your mind spins out and makes it even worse." Chance leaned back on the couch and stretched his long legs in front of him.

I joined him. I yawned, exhausted but wide awake. "I was too late for Hannah. I can't be too late for River and our baby." The words caught in my throat.

"If she were here now, do you think she'd keep the baby? You guys are young. She's literally just getting on her feet. She's nineteen and you're twenty-two. You've got your entire lives ahead of you to have a family. Are you sure you're ready to be a daddy?" Chance asked, his gaze full of support.

I tugged on the hem of my shirt. "I don't know. She's had a lot of loss in her life that might affect her decision to keep a baby right now." I drummed my fingers against my jeaned thigh. "I'll respect her choice either way, but we're financially secure, and she's the one I'd want to have kids with. If she says she wants to keep it, then I'm a thousand percent on board and committed. On the other hand, you're right. We're young. We have time. Besides, I'm not sure she'd be too thrilled if she were pregnant in her wedding gown." I winced at my slip.

"What?" Chance grinned. "Did you propose to her and not tell me? If you did, I should beat your ass."

I met his smile with my own. "No. I had it all planned for tonight." My face fell. "I was looking over the ring when Zayne called me and told me that she was missing."

"That's fucked up." Chance shook his head in disbelief. "We're going to get her back, man. I'll make some calls of my own. If we tackle this with all the resources we have, then we'll bring her home faster." Chance stood, his expression grim. "I'd tell you to work off some stress and join us in the playroom later, but River would skin you alive. Honestly, it's not about the sex right now, it's about the distraction."

"I'll have to find another way to stay sane." I rubbed my stubbled jawline. "Will Brynn be there?"

"She says she will, but she didn't look too good earlier today. I suspect it will be Sariah, Jace, and me. You can always watch if you need to take your mind off things for a few minutes."

It was funny how much had changed in such a short time. Before I met River, I wouldn't have thought twice about participating or viewing, but not anymore. She was all I wanted. "I'll pass, but I appreciate you looking after me."

"If you get too wound up, text me and you can help me close the club tonight. Might be best if we try to keep you busy." Chance cracked his knuckles before he grabbed his suit jacket and slipped it back on.

"You're probably right."

We said our goodbyes, and the click of the door closing behind Chance was loud, reminding me that I was once again alone when River should be with me.

I scrubbed my face with my hands, then stretched out on the couch. It was time to try and sleep.

Cries, screaming, and faceless people shuffled by. Terror thickened the air that swirled around me as I ran, then fell. I glanced over my shoulder and struggled to get to my feet. Holden! Holden! Don't let them ...

I jerked myself awake, panting and shaking. Gripping the arm of the sofa, I searched the living room for anything familiar to help me calm down. I'd fallen asleep, and as soon as my eyes had closed, I'd been plagued with nightmares. What the fuck had just happened? Wiping beads of sweat from my forehead with the back of my hand, I attempted to slow my racing heart.

I struggled to piece together the dream, but it was already fading. I stood and hurried to the master bathroom. Nausea rolled in my stomach, and I was afraid I was about to lose my dinner. Entering the spacious room, I waved my fingers in front of the light. Once my sight adjusted to the brightness, I quickly turned on the cold water and splashed my face.

When I straightened, I stared at myself in the mirror. My dark hair was tousled, and shadows rested beneath my brown eyes. My skin was pale, and my expression appeared vacant, as though nothing was left inside of me.

Removing my phone from my back pocket, I looked at the time and swore a blue streak. I'd only slept for half an hour. I dried off with the brand-new black hand towel and hung my head. It felt wrong to be here without her. A low cry escaped me, and I balled my hands into fists. I had to keep my shit together. Otherwise, I wouldn't be able to get information from Tim. I'd miss body language and signs like I had earlier.

On second thought, staying at the penthouse probably wasn't the best idea I'd had. With no one else around, I'd allowed myself to fall apart, but I needed my friends.

I tapped out a text on my cell to our group chat.

Need company. Let's meet at the bar?

My phone pinged, but it wasn't from who I expected. I ran my fingers through my hair as I read the message from Pierce.

Chapter Seven

I've *been able to confirm that Tim and Logan are on the FBI's* *radar. Play it cool when you see him tomorrow.*

I typed out a quick reply.

Thanks for the heads up. Glad someone is aware of his activities.

I wasn't used to Zayne reporting to Pierce, but more than that, the facts were now in front of my face. There wasn't any more doubt about who Tim was. Chills darted down my back. Even though Pierce hadn't said why they were on the FBI's shit list, I assumed Brynn's information, along with mine, was accurate.

My phone pinged with more messages. Jace and Brynn were on their way to the club. Chance was already downstairs.

Most nights, I showed up at 4 Play dressed in an expensive suit and shirt. At the moment, I didn't give a fuck what I looked like, so jeans and tennis shoes were the outfit for the evening.

I grabbed my keys and wallet and shoved them into the appropriate pockets. Minutes later, Zayne and I were on the elevator heading to the main floor. Once everyone got here and ordered food and drinks, we'd move to the conference room. The playroom couches would be more comfortable, but the room had just been thoroughly cleaned. Hiring someone to remove ass prints and jizz off the furniture was bad enough. I wasn't going to mess it up with food crumbs that night. The guys were pretty messy eaters.

Zayne remained quiet as I made my way to the bar. "Take My Breath" by The Weeknd pumped through the speakers. The club was packed, which was a good sign since it was a Thursday evening.

My mind raced with memories of the first night I'd brought River here. I was terrified she'd walk away from me. Us. Owning a sex club along with her past weren't the best ingredients to a lasting relationship, but she'd shocked the crap out of me. Over the months, I'd had the most amazing sex of my life with her. It wasn't about me. It was about making River feel safe, loved, and valued. Her life had been hell, and I wanted to give her so much more. I wanted to show her sexuality could be a loving, positive, and fun experience.

Dread seeped into my veins. Where had I gone wrong in protecting her? A tidal wave of fear and grief slammed into me, and I sank onto the barstool while I waited for my friends.

I ordered a Dr Pepper and my focus bounced over the crowd. I'd always loved to watch people. They were fascinating most of the time.

"Hey, man," Jace said, joining me.

"Hey. Thanks for hanging out. Once everyone is here, I figured we'd get some food and drinks and hang in the conference room where we can talk privately."

"I'm starving, so that sounds good. Did Chance work tonight?" Jace ran a hand down his burgundy button-down shirt. He'd tucked it into his dark wash jeans and paired it with black dress shoes. Jace always looked put-together. The dude could roll out of bed and head straight out the fucking door, and no one would ever know. I was pretty sure that's exactly what he did the first two years of college, too. We all had partied hard and fucked harder, but by then, we'd established the club, so sex was available any time we wanted it. Jace and Chance even lost interest in chasing other women.

"You should figure out how to blow off some steam." Jace propped his elbows up on the bar while he remained standing.

"Got any ideas other than using Tim's face?" I took a drink of my soda, the tiny bubbles tickling my nose and moistening my upper lip. I wiped my mouth as my mind wandered back to River. Was she hurt? Was the baby okay? I squelched the stormy thoughts. I had to remain positive and hang onto hope. River was strong. Feisty. She wouldn't go down without a fight. If she did, she'd come up swinging with a plan.

Jace arched a dark brow at me. "Are you still pissed at him for leading a double life, or did you get some news?" Jace signaled to the bartender, then ordered a Jack and Coke.

"Not much, but some. It's more confirmation than anything. I'll update you upstairs. You never know when someone is listening." I glanced at the row of people to my right. No one looked like they gave a fuck what I said, but I couldn't risk it. The minute I yelled over the music, it would stop, and everyone would hear me.

A gentle touch came from my left. "How are you holding up?" Brynn asked, kissing my cheek.

"Shitty. You?" I stood and hugged her. She didn't look well at all. Her skin was still pale, and her hands shook slightly. I'd never seen Brynn this stressed, but we'd never had someone we loved kidnapped either. "Are you coming down with the flu?"

She gave me a sweet smile that didn't reach her green eyes. "I'm fine. Don't worry about me. You have way bigger things to deal with. We all do."

Before I could answer, she'd turned her back to me and kissed Jace on the cheek as well. Although I sensed there was something off with Brynn, I wasn't sure if it was concerning River's disappearance or something else. I'd talk to Jace and Chance to help me find out what was going on.

One thing was clear. We were all worried about River. Brynn had even joined us in boyfriend jeans and a faded Jeffrey James concert T-shirt instead of her usual classy blouse and black boots.

None of us gave a shit about what we looked like. We just wanted River home.

Everyone ordered food and drinks, then we made our way to the conference room. Zayne remained in the hallway, staring at the elevator. His job had to be boring as hell some days.

We settled in at the table and waited for our food to be brought up. Finally, I gathered my thoughts, then spoke. "Pierce messaged me right after I texted you all tonight. He confirmed that the FBI has Tim and Logan on their list. I don't know why, but they're watching them."

Brynn rubbed her makeup-free face. "This is confirmation of what Dad shared with me." She took a drink of her rum and Coke. Everyone was hitting the alcohol already, but I wanted to stay sober in case Pierce and Sutton located River. Even if Pierce called and said that they'd found her, Brynn, Chance, and Jace wouldn't be allowed to go, so they might as well try to relax.

"Sounds like it." I fidgeted in my chair and finally propped my feet up on the seat opposite me. "I'm having breakfast with Tim in the morning."

The silence between us continued to thicken until the entire room throbbed with tension.

Brynn leaned forward, her gaze narrowing on me. "Holden, no. You're playing with fire. Please, don't go." Tears welled in her eyes. "I can't lose you, too." She slumped, her hand covering her mouth.

I'd only seen Brynn cry a handful of times in the ten years I'd known her. She was tough, and it took a lot to rattle her.

"Brynn," I whispered.

"Come here." Chance pushed his chair backward and pulled Brynn into his lap. She curled into him and hid her face against his neck.

Jace reached over and gently rubbed her back. This is what close, deep friendship looked like. We would do anything for each other, even cover up a murder. I chewed the inside of my cheek, willing the fear and frustration to calm down so I could focus.

"Brynn," I started again. "Zayne will be with me. I'll be safe. I swear." I glanced at Jace for a bit of help.

"I realize everyone is on edge, but we've got to give Holden a chance to figure out if Tim had anything to do with River. Brynn, what if Tim slips up tomorrow and River is home in a few more hours?"

Chance kissed Brynn's forehead. "Zayne's a fucking badass. He'll take care of Holden. If you need us, we'll stay with you until Holden's back."

Brynn fidgeted in Chance's lap. "I want this all to go away. I love River. I love Holden. I love you all. It's tearing me the fuck up and I don't know how to help. I just keep falling apart."

"You're allowed to fall apart, Princess," Jace said. "Every one of us are allowed to not have a goddamned clue of how to handle all of this." Jace nodded at me. He was right. We weren't supposed to know how to cope with River missing. My heart had splintered into a million pieces the second Zayne had handed me River's purse. Reality had bitch-slapped me in the face. I'd failed Hannah, and now I'd failed River.

I cleared my throat in an attempt to rein in the overwhelming guilt. The one difference between Hannah and River? River was still alive. I hadn't reached Hannah in time. I promised myself that I wouldn't make the same mistake twice.

I placed my feet on the floor and propped my elbows on the table. "There's more about Tim. I think he has another family."

Jace groaned and stared at the ceiling. "Dude, I know he's your father, but he's such a fucking asshole."

"He's not my father. I refuse to acknowledge him as Dad any longer. Mom deserves so much better than that piece of shit."

Chance shook his head in disbelief. "The older we get the less I'm surprised. It's like we've belonged to a dark, secret society of evil, but we didn't know it."

Jace smacked Chance in the arm. "Well said. But I think Tim might be taking first place in the evil department." His attention cut over to Chance, then to me. "At least we're exempt from the evil shit. I won't ever allow myself to become a monster."

We all nodded in agreement.

Brynn raised her head, her eyes rimmed in red as she looked at me. "This shouldn't surprise me, but somehow it does." She wiped her tears away and sat up.

Chance continued to hold her. At times I'd wondered if they had feelings for each other, but Jace treated her the same way. Brynn, Sariah, and Payton were the only girls in the sex club, which meant they were doted on a lot. But Brynn had all three of us willing to move heaven and earth for her. None of the guys were that close with Sariah and Payton.

Even though I knew Brynn was happy for River and me, I suspected she missed the closeness we shared like she had with Chance and Jace. I'd still do anything for her, but River was the only woman I'd die for.

I dragged my fingers across my stubbled jaw. "I'm not sure if it will work or not, but I'm hoping Tim will share enough with me to give us something to go on. But there's more."

Three sets of eyes landed on me, and I readied myself for a speech. "I also met Logan tonight."

Brynn jumped out of Chance's lap and marched over to me. If shit wasn't hanging in the balance, I would have laughed.

"Now, you listen to me Holden Alastair. You stay away from them. They're dangerous and are connected to even more dangerous men. For all you know, Tim had something to do with Hannah's death." My face fell with her words. "I'm sorry, but I won't lie. I've always wondered if he was a part of it. Maybe she stumbled on information or someone that put her in danger." She leaned against the conference table and folded her arms. "Please. I'm begging you. Stay away from them."

Shadows gathered in my mind, swirling with memories of River. Her smile, her frown, the way her lips tasted, the feel of her soft skin beneath my fingertips. I'd do anything to bring her home. Not even my best friends could stop me.

"I understand that this is scary, Brynn. Dad won't mess with me in public. We're just having breakfast." I did my best to soothe her nerves, but I doubted that it would do much.

"Brynn," Jace stood and approached her. "Come here." Jace wrapped his arms around her and rested his chin on the top of her head. "What would you do if one of us were missing?"

"I'd wait until Tim and Logan were with some of their men, then come out and fucking eliminate them. I'd look good in thigh highs and machine guns." She attempted a grin. "I realize I'm really emotional and terrified. I'm scared to death that this whole shitshow is going to blow up in Holden's face."

Jace slid his fingers down her arms. "We're all in this together. Chance and I have Holden's back. He also has Zayne, Vaughn, Pierce, and Sutton. We're not going into this blind." Jace cupped her cheeks in his large hands. "We have to find River. We'd do the same for you."

Tears slipped down her cheeks, and she nodded. "I know. I had to try."

Jace released her and leaned against the wall. "This whole thing is fucked up." He cracked his knuckles.

"I don't think we've had this much fucked-up excitement since that night in high school. It was only a week later that I brought up the idea of the club with Sariah and Payton," I said quietly. I hesitated to bring up details. We were all aware of what had happened that earth-shattering evening.

"No one had been kidnapped, though," Chance added. "Don't get me wrong. The reason behind it was messed up. But at least everyone was safe after Holden figured out the logistics ... except for Emerson."

Brynn nodded silently. "We will carry that secret to our grave," she whispered.

I wiped my clammy palm on my thigh. It had been a while since those events had haunted me. At first, it had been a stupid date, then it all went to hell. We'd all been friends with Emerson since Brynn had moved to our school, but that night ... Her life had changed forever. *Our* lives had changed forever, and it had also inspired our group sex club.

We stared at each other. Words were no longer appropriate.

"I saw Emerson a few days ago," Chance said. His blue eyes clouded with regret.

"Is there any change?" I asked. I almost hated to know. It had been four years since Emerson had walked, talked ... or screamed for help.

"No, but I keep hoping."

"Me, too." Brynn rubbed her arms.

The memories of the life-altering event hung over me. Hung over all of us.

"Does River know the real reason behind the club?" Brynn glanced at me, her body tight with tension.

"No. I was hoping to leave it in the past, but we'll see how it plays out when she's home." I leaned over and hung my head. *If she makes it back.*

After we ate, we all headed to the game room. Maybe shooting zombies would help my stress level. Unfortunately, the moment I strolled into the area, I saw River everywhere I looked. I guess that happens when someone owns your heart.

I peeked at the clock on the wall. Only seven more hours before I sat across a table from Tim and hoped like hell he slipped up. I had no way of knowing how that day would forever change the course of my life.

Chapter Eight

I squared my shoulders as I entered and searched the busy diner. For such a simple, bland-looking restaurant, they were known for their incredible breakfast. Dark green booths, and cream-colored tables packed the large space. The only pictures were of famous people who had dined here, including Bill Clinton, Maya Angelou, and Colin Powell. This place had a fascinating history.

Sweat beaded on my spine, and my veins burned with adrenaline. Not only was I exhausted, but I was also begging the universe for a break. I needed River in my arms again, safe and sound. There were times that my hunches were wrong, but deep down in my bones, I felt that somehow, Tim was connected to River's disappearance. I hoped like hell it really was my instincts and not some paranoia driven by my desperation to find her.

If I'd been hungry, my mouth would have watered the second I stepped foot inside. The aroma of freshly brewed coffee, crispy bacon, pancakes, sausage, and eggs reminded me that I hadn't eaten yet. My stomach growled in agreement as I spotted Tim in a corner booth, reading the newspaper and sipping a hot beverage.

"Hey, Holden," a cute waitress said. She appeared in her thirties.

The buttons of her white top gaped from the strain across her ample breasts.

I peeked at her nametag. *How did she know my name?* "Hey, Joanie. I'm looking for my father. Dark hair, in his late forties, a few inches shorter than me."

"Right there in the corner. I'll be over to get your order in a few minutes." She winked at me, then her hazel eyes traveled down my chest, stomach, and long legs. "You look like dessert to me."

I stifled a groan. Not only was I not interested in a quick fuck behind the restaurant, but I also needed to focus on Tim.

Apparently, parts of my past would never stop following me, though. I figured since I'd hooked up with one of the waitresses seven years ago, it would have died down by now. I was fifteen, and Tabitha was twenty-two, so I assumed she would have kept her mouth shut if she wanted more. She hadn't. At all. In fact, our sexcapade stories were passed down to each new waitress that was hired. I guess the other women needed someone to fuck them in places they might get caught as well. In the women's bathroom, next to the back door, at night on the hood of their car. If she didn't have time for a break, I'd slide my hand up the inside of her thigh, move her panties out of my way, and finger fuck her in the employee hallway. She loved it, and so did I. Until I didn't. The fun wore off, but Tabitha wanted a relationship. And that sure as shit wasn't going to happen. First of all, I was a minor. Second, she wasn't my type. No one was. I was in it for the thrill, and that was it.

"Since we're in public and I don't think anyone will cause too much trouble, I'll be right back." Zayne disappeared in the crowd of people waiting in line near the front door.

I frowned but shoved my hands into the pockets of my jeans and strolled over to Tim's table.

"Morning," I said, sitting on the hard leather booth seat. I moved to the middle while Tim folded the New York Times and set it next to him. He smoothed his navy shirt. Although he was dressed for business, he hadn't worn a tie, which led me to believe I was his first meeting of the day.

"Morning, son. I'm guessing you didn't get any sleep?" His expression twisted with satisfaction. He was obviously up to something.

"No." I held my cup out for Joanie, who stared at me as she poured the black coffee. I'd need a lot more than one refill.

Tim placed his elbows on the table and leaned closer to me. "Is there any word of her at all?"

I pursed my lips and shook my head. I blew on my steaming drink, then took a sip and winced, allowing the hot, bitter liquid to seep into every nook and cranny of my being.

Zayne caught my attention as he slipped in and planted himself in the corner nearest our booth. He hadn't been gone long. Maybe he'd had to go to the restroom. He folded his arms over his chest, his biceps bulging against the sleeves of his black Westbrook Security polo shirt.

Joanie returned with a tall glass of water and placed it on the table in front of me. "What can I get you, gentlemen?"

I nearly scoffed. Tim was no gentleman, but I had to keep my shit together. I could lose it after he left Spokane again.

Realizing it would be best if I ate, I ordered scrambled eggs with cheese, bacon, hash browns, and a biscuit with a side of gravy. If I couldn't stomach it all, I'd take some home. It wouldn't last two seconds around Chance and Jace.

The second the waitress left, Tim began talking. "I've been asking around, son, but so far I've hit a wall. What else can you tell me about River's disappearance?"

Was he fishing for information to see how close I was to finding her so that he could redirect me?

"Palmer's furniture delivered and moved everything to the penthouse for us. I was waiting for River to come up, but Zayne called me and told me to meet him at the loading dock. When I arrived, Zayne had her purse. Her phone was in it." I studied him, searching for any clue that he was behind it, but apparently Tim had years of practice because he simply returned my intense gaze as though I was the one under scrutiny.

"I assume the police have spoken with everyone who worked that shift."

I nodded. "They said they were going to, but I haven't heard anything from them." I had no intention of disclosing that I'd hired Pierce and Sutton. They'd be able to find out more information than the cops simply because they had an inside connection to the FBI.

"The fact that her purse and phone were left behind indicates she didn't willingly leave you, Holden." Sincerity flashed in his eyes.

"I never thought that was the case." I leaned back into the booth. "We weren't having problems and there was absolutely no indication that she wanted to move out of the area or end our relationship."

Tim cleared his throat, a faraway look occupying his expression. "People aren't ever what they seem, Holden. You're old enough to start learning that. Trust no one. Always be aware. You're an Alastair and wealthy at the age of twenty-two. Someone will always be after what you love."

What? This conversation was taking a strange turn. "What are you trying to tell me?" I clenched my teeth together, willing myself not to flat out ask him if he took River. It would get me absolutely nowhere.

"I've made choices that put my life on a different path. If I'd realized how it would have affected me today, I wouldn't have ever ... agreed." He gave me a sad smile. "I know I can't repair things with your mother, and honestly I don't want to. But you and Mallory are important to me."

Who was this guy? Was he such a narcissist to think him attacking River was forgivable?

"If I were in your shoes, sitting across from my father, I'd have a few questions." He drained his coffee cup and set it on the edge of the table for a refill.

"Like what?" I toyed with the corner of the paper napkin that was wrapped around my silverware.

"I'd want to know if he had anything to do with River's disappearance." His forehead creased as he analyzed my reaction.

I gave him none. "Did you?" My heart hammered against my chest as I waited for his response.

"No. I swear to you that I wasn't involved in any way."

Fuck. Not involved in any way meant he wasn't behind hiring someone either.

"Again, if I were in your shoes, I'd want some kind of proof that I wasn't lying."

His eyes bored into mine. A flicker of doubt crossed his features. Tim straightened his leg beneath the table, slid his hand into his pocket, then produced a thumb drive and moved it toward me. "This will prove that I'm not lying to you."

I stared at it as though it might burst into flame. "What is it?"

"Security footage of me at the time she was taken as well as my phone records for this month."

Snatching it up, I tightly gripped the small device. "It doesn't prove anything. You could have scheduled everything three months beforehand."

Tim nodded. "I understand that you don't believe me, but when did the furniture company schedule the time and date to deliver?"

I swallowed hard. "Palmer's contacted me three days before the drop off date, but they didn't give me a time. They mentioned a six-hour window. However, they didn't call until they were on their way."

"Holden, I was in the air and on my way to Spokane that entire day. I hadn't spoken to you or your mother. I had no idea what company you were working with, what day, or time you were moving into the penthouse."

My heart sank to my toes. "Where were you flying in from? It would be easy to have cell and internet access."

"Monte Carlo."

Tim might as well have slammed my head face-first into the table. He just didn't know it. The bastard had confirmed the information Brynn had shared with River and me. I turned away from him and stared out of the window, watching the traffic whiz by.

My attention landed on him again. "What's in Monte Carlo?"

"My business. I work with men all over the world." Tim picked up the silver cream holder and added more to his coffee.

I gripped the water glass and dragged my thumb up and down the condensation. Moisture pooled onto the table, creating a ring on the tabletop.

"Do I want to know what you really do?" I quirked a brow at him while my pulse hammered against my wrist.

"That depends."

"On what?" Tension slithered down my neck and shoulder blades. Was he about to confess about the weapons?

"If you want to join me. I came back to recruit you, Holden. To show you a life that you could only dream of." The caring father façade he'd cloaked himself in shed like a snake's skin, revealing his true intentions.

Jesus. What the fuck was happening?

A beat of silence permeated the space between us. Crossing my arms over my chest, I glared at him. "What's the offer?" I suddenly wished I'd placed my cell phone in my lap so I could secretly record the conversation, but the restaurant noise would have most likely blocked out Tim's voice regardless.

"Come with me and I'll show you. I'll introduce you to some of the most powerful men in the world. Leave your life and that girl behind. She's not worth it, son. She's nothing but trailer trash," he said in a matter-of-fact tone, a smirk tugging at his features.

I shot up, reached across the table, and jerked him by the collar of his shirt. "Careful what you say, old man," I ground out past clenched teeth.

Arrogance and fear flickered in Tim's eyes, and I inwardly smiled. He remembered the last time I beat the shit out of him. Realizing the majority of people in the diner were staring at me, I released him and slowly sat back down.

"I understand your reaction, Holden. But after you left, Logan admitted that he knows River. The man who raised her owed Logan a large amount of money. Before you get it into your head, Logan didn't have anything to do with River's disappearance either."

Joanie interrupted our conversation and placed plates of steaming food in front of us.

I unrolled my napkin, the fork, knife, and spoon tumbling free and clattering against the table. I grabbed a utensil in an attempt to busy my hand and not to lose my shit. Unable to calm myself down, I shoveled a fork full of scrambled eggs into my mouth.

"I know this is a lot to consider, but it will be worth your time, Holden. Leave the childish dream of your clubs and friends behind. You deserve so much more." Tim nonchalantly cut into his pancakes, then took a bite as though we were discussing the weather.

For the first time in my twenty-two years, I really saw Tim Alastair. The reality of who he truly was broke through every false idea that I had of him. He was a selfish, sick man. All he cared about was money. Not me, not his other kids, and not his soon-to-be ex-wife. Just money.

I shook my head in disappointment. Setting my fork on the edge of my plate, I wiped my lips with the napkin and tossed it on the table. My eyes connected with his. "Is it true then?"

"You have to be more specific, Holden." Tim took a healthy bite of his bacon, never breaking his gaze from mine.

"Do you sell illegal weapons?"

Chapter Nine

The color drained from Tim's face. *Checkmate, motherfucker.*

Before Zayne and I had arrived, we'd agreed on a few signals in case I found myself in trouble. Rub my chin if I suspected Tim had River or run my fingers through my hair if Tim divulged information about her. What I hadn't anticipated was Tim trying to recruit me, then me shoving my foot into my mouth.

Tim recovered quickly, and with a wicked grin and glint in his eye, he said, "You've been snooping." He took a sip of water, then chuckled. "Well, it makes my job easier. I suspected you'd seen the papers on my desk after your mother kicked me out of the house. I wasn't positive, though."

I nodded. He was giving me an easy out.

"If you work with me, you'll be a multimillionaire before you're thirty. You'll have more money and power than you could possibly imagine," Tim explained.

I was already worth more than what Tim was offering, but he didn't know that. More importantly, if he had River, would he really try to recruit me? But why in fuck's name would I believe anything that he said? He'd lied and hid who he was my entire life.

"Weapons aren't my thing, but thanks for the offer." I looked at my food, my stomach churning.

"Think about it. I'll reach out again in a few weeks." Tim glanced at his watch and smirked. "I have a plane to catch." He grabbed the black briefcase in the seat next to him and stood. Opening his brown leather wallet, he tossed a hundred on the table like it was supposed to impress me. I had my own money. I didn't need his. "I'll be in touch." Tim stalked off before I could tell him not to waste his time. I wouldn't change my mind.

I leaned my head against the back of the booth and cringed. Zayne slipped into Tim's seat, and I peered at him. "You might as well order some food while we're here. He didn't have any information to help us with River's location." Defeated, I scrubbed my face with my hands. "I'm not sure he or Logan had anything to do with River's disappearance."

Zayne lifted his finger to signal the waitstaff, and Joanie nearly tripped over herself when she spotted him. She arched her back, pushing out her chest making her giant tits even more prominent. I was pretty sure Zayne could take her behind the building and do anything he wished with her. She'd probably already creamed her panties. Her attention bounced from Zayne to me, then to Zayne again. I threw my head back and barked out a laugh. I'd seen that look way too many times. Joanie would definitely be down with a threesome at this point. Before River came into my life, I'd have been down with it for sure. Now? I was immediately turned off by the desperation that rolled off Joanie in waves. The only pussy I wanted to play with was River's. My cock strained against my jeans at the thought of her, then my heart cracked open.

Zayne placed his order, and Joanie removed Tim's plates and cup. I was pretty sure that not even a minute had gone by when she'd returned with Zayne's orange juice and coffee. He was getting the fastest service I'd ever witnessed here.

"I bet you're used to that kind of reaction from the ladies." I couldn't help but grin. Under normal circumstances, I would have been laughing my ass off.

Zayne brushed a dark curl off his forehead, and his green eyes followed Joanie as she walked away. "I've been with a lot of women. Seen a lot of life. Not much bothers me these days." He cleared his throat and took a sip of his coffee. "Except evil shit like selling people or molesting kids."

For the first time since I'd hired Zayne, I had a tiny peek into who he was as a man. I was intrigued. "You served in the military, right?"

"Army. I was a ranger." He scanned the diner, then returned his attention to me. "I saw and did a lot of crap."

"I can't imagine." I'd never even considered the armed forces. I was all about sports and the club. As far as I was concerned, my future had been all planned out.

"So, you lost your temper with Tim." Zayne assessed me.

I moved my eggs around on my plate, unsure if I could eat anymore. "He said he was here to recruit me to work for him."

"Interesting," Zayne said without even blinking. "And what about River?"

"That's when I lost my shit." My nostrils flared as I recalled his words. "He told me to forget about her, that she was trash. He admitted Logan knew her, too. Tim mentioned Dan owed Logan a lot of money. But before I could dig much deeper, he insisted that neither he nor Logan had anything to do with River's kidnapping. I find it odd that he offered the information before I asked the question. Makes me wonder what he's lying about." I fished out the thumb drive I'd deposited into my jeans pocket. "He gave me this to prove where he was while River ..." I nervously tugged on the collar of my shirt, struggling to say the word kidnapped as I placed the small item on the table for Zayne.

Zayne took the black and silver drive and looked at it for a moment before tucking it into his pants pocket. "Have you considered the idea that Tim took River to be able to control you, then recruit you? He could have planned every step of the kidnapping and your conversation today."

"As in maybe he paid someone at the furniture company to tell him when they'd be at the penthouse and to grab her?" I hadn't even considered the possibility until Zayne brought it up.

Zayne narrowed his eyes and peered out of the window briefly. "We sure as hell can't rule it out."

I tapped my finger on the side of my coffee cup and tried to sort out what motives Tim would have. "Maybe Sutton can verify if the footage was altered."

"She can. That girl can do anything computer related." He grinned for the first time since I'd met him. "Except fix one."

"How long have you known Pierce and Sutton?" I could only deal with the conversation about Tim and River a little at a time. I should have been out scouring the earth for her, but I had no idea where to start now that I leaned toward believing Tim. Maybe. The back and forth was wearing thin. I needed a straight answer, but it wouldn't come from him. Hopefully, Sutton would know something soon.

"We all attended high school together and trained in karate. Vaughn, too. He's a year behind us."

"Those friendships are invaluable. The trust that they'll always have your back and be there for you ... It's hard to find. I have that with Brynn, Jace, and Chance."

"I can tell. It's good that you have support around you right now. When someone you love is in danger, it drains the life out of you for sure."

I wanted to ask Zayne how he knew, but Joanie injected herself into our conversation with Zayne's breakfast.

Once she was gone, I tried to eat a little bit of my biscuit. I slapped some butter and grape jelly on it, then took a bite.

Zayne nodded at my plate. "Try to finish your food, man. You'll require your strength for when we bring River home. She's going to need you, and you'll slip into caretaker mode and forget to take care of yourself."

I chewed on a piece of bacon, pondering what he'd said. "How do you know all of this? You obviously have some experience."

He stared at the entrance to the diner, watching people as they left and entered. "Sutton's sister, Vaughn's fiancée, was kidnapped a while ago. Sutton and Pierce had a history and had split up right after high school. Years later, Sutton showed up on his doorstep and begged him to help find Claire."

"I didn't realize Sutton had lived through that experience. Going through this fucking sucks." I crushed my napkin between my fingers, wishing it was Tim's face.

"Yeah, but Claire was recovered, and she and Vaughn are getting married soon. She's had a lot of therapy and she's doing really well. It helps that she has a career she loves. She's the choreographer for the band August Clover."

"No shit? They're amazing. I'd love to see them in concert. I bet River would, too."

"Gemma and Hendrix are good friends of mine. I can get you and River tickets when they tour again. They're taking some time off since they just got married."

I drained the coffee from my cup, then set it down. "I saw that in People Magazine and every other gossip rag. They don't have a lot of privacy these days."

"They miss it." Zayne polished off his pancakes and wiped his mouth with his napkin. "Do you believe Tim? That he and Logan didn't have anything to do with River?"

I hesitated, wracking my brain and heart for my first response. It was often the one I really believed, but this time … "I can't. If he's being honest with me, it means we don't have any fucking leads and …" I looked out the window, willing myself to think clearly. It was one thing if I lost my shit in the privacy of my own home and another in public.

"I get it. I'll have Sutton look at the video today and see if we have any other leads. I think we should swing by and talk to her and Pierce face-to-face. Sometimes you get more of a sense for what's going on behind the scenes. Just because you might not have any other ideas, doesn't mean they don't."

Zayne stood and removed his wallet from his back pocket. I raised my hand. "Don't. Tim dropped a hundred." The money had wedged itself under my extra dish with the gravy. I picked it up for him to see. "Breakfast is on him."

"At least the motherfucker is good for something." He slipped his Ray-Bans on. "We should go. I'll call Pierce and let him know we're on the way."

I rose from my seat and brushed off the biscuit crumbs that had collected in my lap. Zayne and I walked to the door, then it dawned on me to ask him a question.

"When we first arrived, you excused yourself. Where did you go?" I stepped outside and winced. My eyes cowered from the burning light of the morning sun, and I wished I'd grabbed my sunglasses out of the Mercedes.

"I'll tell you when we're out of earshot."

I tried to read Zayne for a hint, but there was none.

Once we were settled into his Mercedes and he eased out of the parking lot, he grinned. "I planted a tracker on Tim's car."

That was the best news I'd heard in a while. "That's fucking awesome." Gratitude for nifty gadgets washed over me.

"As long as he's in his vehicle we can also record his conversations." Zayne smirked. "Sutton's work."

"Oh, God, this is exactly what I needed to hear. Maybe we can find out if he has River or not." I nearly choked on my words, my emotions spinning out of control. One thing I'd learned was that hope could be a dangerous thing, but I had to hold onto something.

"Sutton is already on it. I texted her as soon as I had everything in place. It was pretty easy to break into and he'd parked behind the building, so it was a quick job." Zayne flipped his turn signal on and headed east toward Pierce's house. He tapped the button on the steering wheel and messaged Pierce that we were on our way. Maybe the meeting with Tim had been successful after all.

My phone vibrated. I leaned forward and pulled it out of my back pocket. I gawked at the message from Chance, dumbfounded.

"Holy fucking shit." I looked at Zayne. "Pierce and Sutton will have to wait. We have to turn around. Now."

Chapter Ten

I hadn't meant to sound like a demanding asshole, but Zayne did as I asked without question. He glanced at me. "I need to know where we're going."

"4 Play," I choked out. I could barely breathe, much less get the words out. "Chance just texted. The club is on fire."

Zayne swore as I'd never heard him before. "Hang on."

I grabbed the oh-shit bar as Zayne began zigzagging in and out of traffic. I would have complimented him on his mad driving skills, but I was too fucking terrified that I'd lost everything.

"What did Chance say?" Zayne asked, his attention on the cars in front of us.

"That he was trying to handle it and would tell me more when I got there." My knee began to bounce as my anxiety climbed through the goddamned roof.

"Fuck!" I slammed my fist into my leg. "The engagement ring is in my nightstand drawer." I squeezed my eyes closed, willing this nightmare to stop.

"You were going to propose, or already had and needed to get the ring sized?" Zayne sped past several cars, and I wondered how many speeding tickets he'd received and managed to get out of.

"I was supposed to ask her to marry me last night."

"Sorry, man. That fucking sucks." Zayne flipped on the turn signal, then moved into the right lane, passing a car in the left.

I peeked at the speedometer. He was pushing ninety. There was no way we would be able to move this fast on Division Street. There were too many stoplights and too much congestion.

Glancing through the front windshield, I spotted a plume of black smoke. "Goddammit." I pointed at the fire that was visible from Interstate 90.

A police siren wailed too close for comfort, and I glanced behind us. "Fuck, we're getting pulled over. This shit's just getting better and better."

Zayne slowed down enough to pull off onto the shoulder of the highway. Blue and red lights flashed behind us. I sank into the seat, my eyes glued to the billowing smoke that was now blotting out the sun from my view.

"Put your hands on the dash," Zayne ordered.

I did as he asked. I'd never had any problem with the cops here, but I wasn't interested in having any issues either. Zayne lowered his window and placed his palms on the wheel where the officer could see them.

"Sir, are you aware that you were going twenty-five miles over the speed limit?"

"Yes, sir. My name is Zayne Wilson. I'm the bodyguard for Holden Alastair. Right now, his home and business are on fire. You can see it behind you. If you'd be kind enough to give us an escort, I'd appreciate it."

The cop talked into his radio and confirmed Zayne's information. "Let me verify who you both are, then I'll be happy to help. Mr. Alastair, can I have your driver's license?"

I slowly moved my left hand and removed my wallet from my

jeans pocket. "Open it up. My license is on the left side." I handed it to Zayne, who gave it to the officer.

Once the cop verified that I was Holden Alastair, he hurried back to his vehicle, turned on the sirens, and pulled out into the traffic. Zayne stayed right behind him.

"This actually worked out better," Zayne said as he rolled up the window and pushed the button for the air recycler, then switched it on full blast. "The air flow will keep the smell of the fire out."

"Thanks. I'm sure I'll inhale more than my fair share once we're there."

The next ten minutes were painstakingly slow as I continued to stare at the black, thick cloud of smoke. Zayne drove into the parking lot across the street from the club. Before he rolled to a complete stop, I bolted out of the car and to the other side of the road. Fire trucks and ambulances were fucking everywhere.

I grabbed my phone and called Chance, hoping like hell he wasn't inside.

"Yeah?" Chance's breath came out ragged and uneven as though he were running.

"I'm here. Where are you?" I frantically searched around the crowd of people.

"I'm helping the employees, man," he said, coughing as he attempted to talk.

I stopped abruptly, my hand rubbing the back of my neck. "Where? I'll help. This is my club. Get your ass out here and I'll go in."

A loud clatter echoed through the line, and I suspected Chance had dropped his phone.

"Chance? Chance!" I darted over to one of the firefighters. "My best friend is in the building. Chance is also the manager so he's trying to save the people that are still in the club. How bad is the fire? Can someone look for him?" Panic seized me. This wasn't good.

Zayne coughed from behind me, and I was grateful he was there.

"I'll make a call and let the men know," the firefighter stated.

"Thank you. You have no idea how much I appreciate everyone." I pulled my shirt over my nose and took a deep breath before I released it. "I'm Holden, this is my residence and business. Do you have any clue about how the fire started?"

"Not sure, but the penthouse is *where* it started from what we can tell at this point. The lower floors will be all right if we're able to contain it fast enough."

The second the words left his mouth, an explosion erupted on our side of the building.

Zayne threw me to the ground and covered my body with his. I struggled to breathe from the impact.

"Chance! Chance!" I yelled. "Zayne, we've gotta fucking find Chance."

"Stay down, Holden," Zayne ordered.

Another ball of fire ripped through the air, and people screamed and ran as I lay on the asphalt, overwhelmed with fear and worry.

Embers from the fire landed all around us, sending men and women fleeing in the opposite direction as fast as they could move. *What the fuck is happening? First River and now 4 Play.*

Zayne hopped off me and pulled me to my feet. "Go!" He pointed to the parking lot where he'd parked the Mercedes. We hauled ass across the street.

"Chance is in the fucking club, Zayne!" My throat was dry and raw from the smoke and screaming for my best friend.

Zayne's face fell as my words registered with him. "Holden." He nodded, and I slowly turned to see what he was pointing at.

My pulse galloped, and goosebumps broke over my arms as my attention flew around the space. The fire raged to life, consuming this side of the building. I rubbed at my chest, where my heart continued to hurl itself against my ribs. The palpitations were full of fear, adrenaline, and shock. There was no way that Chance would be able to walk away from the destruction in front of me. Fuck the penthouse and club. I had insurance, but I'd never be able to replace my best friend. My brother.

I sank to my knees, unable to rip my eyes from the flames as an anguished cry tore through me. The mere idea of Chance not surviving fucking gutted me and ripped my insides apart.

It was more than I could take. Between losing the love of my life and now Chance, I was done. Whoever had decided my fate had won. I placed my hands against the asphalt, pebbles digging into my palms, but I didn't give a fuck.

My phone rang, and I answered it without glancing at the number.

"How's that offer looking to you now, son?"

White-hot rage coursed through me, and I rose to my feet, my jaw clenching so tight it shot pain through my head. Everything I'd worked so goddamned hard for had been destroyed the minute I'd told that son of a bitch no.

"You did this?" My voice cracked, and I ground my teeth together. "Did you set fire to my club to force me to work with you?" My attention cut over to Zayne.

"*I* personally didn't. I have plenty of people to take care of those annoying jobs for me. And a piece of advice, don't look at it as if I'm forcing anything, Holden. Simply consider it a nudge in the right direction. Since you'll be tied up for a while, I'll check in soon. Until then, think about my offer."

Tim disconnected the line, and my hand lowered to my side. I looked at Zayne, dazed. "Tim just admitted he set fire to the club to persuade me to work for him. I hope like hell that motherfucker was driving his car when he confessed to it." Whether Tim realized it or not, he'd put a target on his back because, at that moment, I swore that I'd hunt the piece of shit down, torture him, and if I was in a good mood, end his miserable life. However, I wasn't opposed to the idea of making him suffer for years.

Zayne placed his hand on my shoulder. "Holden." He pointed to a body bag.

Fear squeezed my heart and crushed my lungs. Without even thinking, I ran toward the stretcher and prayed like a desperate man that Chance wasn't in it.

Chapter Eleven

"Excuse me. Excuse me!" I weaved through the crowd that had gathered after the explosions. Why people gravitated toward the building, I wasn't sure. At least the officers had a barricade now, but I needed to find out what the hell was going on, even if I had to be sneaky about it.

"Holden, I know the officer," Zayne said from beside me. I'd been so focused on the body bag I hadn't realized he was still next to me.

"Can he give us some information?" My eyes gravitated to the building, to the flames licking through the shattered windows. The thick smoke made it difficult to see, and I used my shirt to cover my nose in order to breathe.

"Officer Walters," Zayne said, approaching the cop.

The officer grinned and shook Zayne's hand. "Never expected you to be here, Wilson. How the hell are you?"

Zayne motioned for me to join them. "I've been better. I need a favor if possible. This is Holden Alastair. He owns the building, and his friend was inside when the explosions went off."

The cop's face fell. "I'm sorry, it's not safe for anyone to get any closer. Is there another way I can help?"

My hands trembled at my sides, and I balled them into fists. "Are you able to tell me who is in the body bag? Or at least if it's Chance Anderson? He's my best friend and the manager of 4 Play. He was working when the fire started." Little beads of sweat formed on the nape of my neck, and my pulse throbbed wildly.

"Let me see what I can find out." The officer nodded at us, then walked over to the stretcher with the black bag. He blocked our view as the EMT lowered the zipper. Officer Walters nodded, then hurried back to us.

"Holden, it's a female." Before I had time to feel relieved, panic seized me again. What if River had returned to the club?

"What color hair does she have?" Zayne asked before I even opened my mouth.

"Blonde. It looks like she was in her early forties."

I bent over and propped my hands on my knees, attempting to calm my galloping pulse.

"Holden? Excuse me. Excuse me, coming through."

I straightened to see the top of a redhead moving through the crowd. "Yes, I understand but I need through please."

"Bitch, stop being so damned pushy. We're all trying to see here!" A female voice scolded Brynn.

"Fuck. You. I'm not trying to see anything. I am a partial owner of the club that's on fire. Now get the hell out of my way." Brynn had always been crafty when she needed to be. Of course, people would let her through if they thought she owned 4 Play.

I began moving in Brynn's direction, so I could grab her and pull her through the crowd. If I didn't, she'd beat that woman's ass, and I couldn't deal with any more chaos.

"Holden." I looked at Zayne, and he tossed me a few masks he'd been able to obtain from a firefighter. His was already in place. At least it would help filter the smoke some.

I slipped mine on, then made my way to Brynn.

"Brynn! Take my hand."

Brynn's expression overflowed with relief as she reached for me.

"Excuse me, I'm the club owner and I need everyone to please let her through," I said in a commanding tone.

The crowd parted, and Brynn finally reached me. She gripped my hand so hard I thought my fingers would lose circulation.

"You're okay!" She hiccupped. I pulled her to me in a tight hug and she buried her face in my chest.

"I'm fine. I wasn't at the club." We stepped apart, and I gently slid the mask over her nose and mouth. "This should help you breathe better."

Brynn nodded and adjusted the straps behind her ears. "What happened?"

I draped my arm around her and spotted Zayne a few feet away from us. "Let's join Zayne, then I'll tell you what we know so far."

She nodded, her features full of fear. Her skin was still pale, and she shivered against me even though the blaze of the fire heated the air, making it toasty.

"Brynn," Zayne nodded at her as we stood beside him.

"Hey, Zayne." She eased her arm around my waist and looked up at me. "Fill me in."

I pursed my lips, not wanting to stress her out even more. "We're waiting for Chance."

"What? He was inside?" Panic flashed in her green eyes.

"Yeah. I thought ..." I pointed to the body bag. "I thought he was in there, but it's not him. It might be a salesperson from one of the liquor companies. We have a standing appointment every week."

Brynn gasped, her attention zeroing in on the body.

"When I got here, Chance answered his phone, then he dropped it. There were two explosions, and I haven't been able to reach him."

"Oh, God." She shook her head, shock evident in her gaze. "He has to be all right. Holden ..." Her body shook violently, and I wrapped my arms around her. We clung to each other as we waited, the seconds stretching on forever.

"Holden!" I peeked over my shoulder and identified a familiar hand waving at me over the crowd.

"Jace!" I motioned for him to come on over. I grabbed another mask from Zayne and handed it to him when he joined the rest of us.

Jace engulfed us in a huge hug. "Man, am I glad to see you guys. I sped like a bat out of hell when I heard the club was on fire."

I watched as Jace glanced around, then worry twisted his expression. "Chance?" His focus bounced from me to Brynn, then back to me.

"We don't know yet." I laced my fingers behind my neck, the stress of the situation eating me from the inside out.

"Fuck!" Jace rubbed his forehead as he continued to search through the multitude of cops, firefighters, and EMTs. "Fuck!"

Brynn stood in the middle of us and slipped an arm around Jace and me. We stood silently with heavy hearts as we waited for our friend. We silently witnessed the fire as it continued to rage through the building. I'd decided to wait to tell everyone that Tim was behind it. At the moment, I didn't care. I just needed River and Chance safe and sound and next to us where they belonged.

"Holden, we've got great news," Officer Walters said to me. "We found Chance."

"You said great news. Chance is alive?" I held my breath while I waited for his answer.

"Yeah. He's good." Even with his mask in place, I could see the officer's smile touch his warm brown eyes. "He's behind the building getting checked out by an EMT. He'll join you shortly."

Brynn burst into tears, and I fought mine as well. We all hugged each other.

"I knew that son of a bitch wasn't dead," Jace laughed.

"I didn't, but I was on the phone with him right before the explosions."

Brynn pointed ahead of us, and we stared at a dirty and exhausted Chance walking toward us. Brynn scooted beneath the yellow tape and sprinted to him. I laughed as he braced himself, and she jumped up and wrapped her legs around his waist, looping her arms around his neck. I quietly watched them as Brynn planted a kiss on his lips. I was relieved that he was all right, but witnessing Brynn and Chance together reminded me that River was still missing.

It was nearly midnight by the time they'd contained the fire. Once we thought the blaze was over, the embers would start smaller flames again. It was a constant touch-and-go waiting game.

When Chance had rejoined us, we all headed to his place so he could shower and change clothes. I wasn't able to do anything at the scene anyway. Brynn stayed glued to Chance's side after he got cleaned up. I think we all wanted to stay close to each other, but Brynn was the one that could get away with hovering, and it not be weird.

Brynn ordered a few pizzas, and we huddled in Chance's living room. I gave Zayne a plate piled high with several slices, then he resumed his post near the front door of Chance's house. I sat on the floor with my back against the black leather couch and stretched my legs out in front of me.

Chance had remodeled lately, and the light wood floors gleamed. He hadn't known the first thing about interior design, so he'd hired someone. A mocha-colored loveseat and couch occupied the living room, and a black rug covered the floor between them. A white-washed brick fireplace was the focal point on the far wall. A large Samsung flatscreen was mounted to the left. Tan, full-length blackout curtains hung over the windows. The home was comfortable and sophisticated but not stuffy.

Brynn and Chance sat next to each other on the love seat while Jace and I took the sofa.

Surprisingly, I was starving. Maybe the adrenaline of almost losing Chance today kicked my appetite into high gear. I scarfed down four pieces of cheese and pepperoni along with a Heineken.

"How did you find out about the fire?" Brynn asked, nibbling on the crust of a piece of Meat Lovers.

"I texted him," Chance said and took a drink of his beer. "The alarms went off and I used the cameras to figure out what the hell was going on. I finally realized it was the penthouse."

I rested my plate in my lap. "When we were waiting to see if you were alive ..." I gripped the neck of the bottle, anger rolling to a boil beneath my calm exterior. "Tim called me. He admitted to starting the fire."

"What?" Jace nearly shot off the sofa.

"Why?" Chance leaned forward. His expression grew intense as Brynn pursed her lips.

I took a drink, then set the beer on the floor next to me. "He tried to recruit me to work with him. I said no, and the next thing I realized, the club was up in flames."

Brynn's mouth gaped, then she slapped a hand over it, her eyes wide with shock and realization of how fucked up my father really was.

"Fuuuckkk," Jace swore, scooting to the edge of his seat. "That's twisted."

"Oh shit. I'd totally forgotten that you met him for breakfast," Brynn said. "Is that when he asked you to join the dark side?" She flashed me a sheepish grin at her lame attempt at humor.

I massaged the corded muscles in my neck. "Yeah. And he swore up and down that neither he nor Logan had anything to do with River's disappearance."

"Do you believe him?" Chance asked, disbelief lacing his words.

"After he burned my club down? Fuck no. But Zayne was able to put a tracker on his car, as well as a recording device. If he was driving when he admitted to coordinating the fire, then we have evidence against him."

"Oh my God. I hope so." Brynn folded her legs beneath her. Color returned to her cheeks after she'd eaten a little. "Honestly, I'm still stunned that he asked you to work with him. And did he happen to tell you what kind of job he was referring to?" Brynn tilted her head slightly, an indication she was chewing on the new information.

"I asked if he was involved with illegal firearms. He didn't lie to me. He said yes."

"Man, he's even dumber than I thought if he thinks you're not going to take that information to the cops. I mean you haven't, but you're talking to Pierce and Sutton who are connected to the FBI." Chance shook his head.

My phone rang, interrupting our conversation. I leaned on my hip and raised my ass off the floor in order to remove it from my back pocket. I glanced at the screen. It was nearly one in the morning, and Mom was calling, which meant she'd heard about the fire.

I tapped the screen and answered. "Hey, Mom."

"Honey, are you all right? I called as soon as I heard the news. Is everyone safe? Oh my God, I can't believe this," Mom nervously rambled.

"Everyone is fine. The club isn't, but I have insurance so it will be taken care of. Chance was inside the building when the fire started. He gave us a good scare." I peeked at him while I spoke, but he seemed content with Brynn next to his side.

"I don't know what I'd do if I lost another child." Mom hiccupped, and I imagined she was dabbing away her tears with a tissue.

"You don't have to. I promise I'm okay. Pissed, but I'm all right." I had to be careful not to let slip that Tim had something to do with the fire. I didn't want Mom involved.

"Please tell Chance I'm glad he's okay." Mom sniffled.

"I will. We're all at his place tonight."

"You move back in with me, Holden. Someone needs to live there. Your father won't be back. He moved the rest of his belongings out of the home. We're officially done with the whole property issue."

That's why he was at her place the other night. At least she was aware that he was skulking around.

"Mom?" I glanced at my friends. "Please stay away from Dad. He's not who he says he is."

I could imagine her puzzled expression. "I don't understand. Why would you say something like that?"

"Because he admitted to me that he set my club on fire." And there it was. My heart winning over my logic once again. The desire to protect her was stronger than the need to keep her in the dark. She'd be in more danger if she walked around blind to the situation.

A pause lingered over the line. "Are you sure? I mean, maybe you misunderstood what he said?"

"I'm a hundred percent sure. He's dangerous, Mom. Now that the divorce is almost finished, stay away from him. Promise me," I insisted.

"Holden, this doesn't make any sense. Why would he do something like that?" Shock permeated her voice.

"He asked me to work with him and I declined. He said the fire was to nudge me in the right direction. He's pushing pretty hard for me to join him."

"Shit. Goddamn him. You *cannot* work with him. Not under any circumstances, do you hear me? Swear to me, son."

Shocked shitless, my cell slipped from my ear, and I caught it before it hit the floor. *She knew.*

"Mom? What in the hell is going on?"

Chapter Twelve

"We can't discuss this over the phone, honey. It's not … safe."

I cringed and leaned my head against the couch. "You know he's dangerous?" I wanted to ask if she knew about the weapons, but she was right. We'd have to wait to dive into the conversation until she was in town again.

"I didn't until recently. When Brynn mentioned it before my trip, I dug into what she said," she admitted, her voice soft. "I'll be back soon, and we can talk about everything then. In the meantime, move back into the house. And is River back yet?" Her tone filled with worry.

"No. I'll let you know as soon as she is." I glanced at the pizza crumbs that dotted my white paper plate. "Where are you?"

"London. It's gray and dreary and I can't wait to return to our sunshine. It will be nice to have you home while you're figuring things out as well. I realize we have a new security system, but it needs to be reset now that your father won't need back in. Ugh, that man makes me sick."

"That makes two of us." I crossed my legs at the ankles, exhaustion settling over me. Depression clung to the edges of my mind as I realized I'd live at Mom's place without River. I wasn't sure I could do it. It might be mentally better for me if I stayed with Jace or Chance. At least there wouldn't be the constant reminders of her presence. She hadn't been to either of their places.

"I'll see about moving in again. With all of the memories of River, I'm not sure it will be the best option. I'll let you know. I'm happy to reset the system and check on everything, though."

"I'd appreciate the help with the security codes. As for River, I hadn't considered that. You do what you need to, son. Keep me posted."

"I will."

"I need to go. I have a meeting in a few minutes. I'm so relieved you're safe. I love you, Holden."

"Love you too, Mom." I ended the call and bowed my head. The shit was getting thicker and thicker.

"Are you going to move in with Catherine?" Brynn asked softly. "It will be hard to be there without River." Tears welled in her eyes, and she sniffled.

"You're welcome to stay here, man," Chance offered. "Hell, I'd rather help you with whatever you need concerning the club. Maybe you can rebuild or design it from the ground up. It will give me something to do. I don't have to work, so I'll simply take time off and help you."

"Thanks. I'm not sure what I'm going to do about 4 Play yet. It depends on how much damage there is. And, at least for tonight, I'll take you up on crashing here." I took a long drink of my beer. "I need another one of these, too." I rose from the floor and stretched.

"The guest room is ready. Hell, no one has even slept in it yet." Chance batted his eyelashes at me. "You'll be my first."

Jace chuckled, then his expression grew serious. "Damn, I wonder if the playroom is destroyed."

"Regardless, it's too dangerous to be in the building. It will take a while before we'll even be allowed in and that's only if it's safe. For all I know, I'll have to knock it down and start over." I grimaced at the idea. "Right now, all I want is River beside me." I kicked at the rug with the toe of my tennis shoe. "I hadn't told you guys, but when everyone came up to see the penthouse for the first time, I was going to ask River to marry me. I was looking at the ring in our new bedroom when Zayne called me, and I learned that she'd been taken." Fire squeezed my lungs and burned up the back of my throat. I couldn't breathe as panic ripped through me. She had to be okay.

"Dude, that's harsh the way it worked out. You'll have another opportunity so hang on to that." Jace fisted his hand over his heart.

"I guarantee you one thing," Chance began, "River is bound and determined to make it back to you. She loves you like mad."

"Thanks. I obviously feel the same way."

"Holden," Brynn said, standing and approaching me. "She'll be back. You'll still get to propose." She slipped her arms around my waist and hugged me. I rested my chin on the top of her head and eased my free arm around her.

"I hope like hell you're right. I'm not sure I'll make it if I lose her and the baby."

Brynn peered up at me. "Did you suspect about the pregnancy when you bought her engagement ring?"

"No. I had no fucking clue. I swear I thought she just had the stomach flu. It seemed like she was too sick to be pregnant."

"Honestly, I think it was a bug on top of morning sickness." Brynn stepped away from me, then returned to her seat next to Chance.

"I'm with Brynn. River will make it. Shit, that girl survived Dan, then Logan, and a car accident. She's smart and strong. She'll make it back to you, dude." Conviction danced across Jace's face.

"I agree with Jace," Chance added. "She's had a lot of life experience and she's street smart. This shit isn't over yet."

"When I find out who took her ..." My hand clenched and unclenched.

"We'll all take care of the problem. We love River, and no one can fuck with our family," Jace added, a threatening tone in his voice.

My heart warmed with the support of my friends. God only knew where I'd be without them.

We all crashed at Chance's place. It was a two-thousand square foot, one-level home with three bedrooms which meant that Brynn would share a bed with either Jace or Chance. Neither of them minded. If I hadn't been with River, I'd have brought her to mine. And even though we wouldn't have crossed a line, it didn't feel right to have her next to me when all I wanted was River.

Thank God Chance and I were almost the same size. He loaned me a clean basic T-shirt and black basketball shorts. We tossed my clothes into the washing machine. I wasn't sure if the smell of smoke would ever come out, but it was worth a shot since I had nothing else to wear.

I stared at the ceiling, the red numbers on the clock were an ever-changing beacon in the dark. Although the queen-sized mattress was comfortable, it was firmer than mine and Rivers. The décor from the living room flowed into the bedroom as well: a black dresser and bed frame, flatscreen TV on the wall, and a small but adequate en suite bathroom. Chance's designer had done a spectacular job with the house.

It was after three in the morning. I was mentally and physically drained, but my mind was racing with the events of the day. Thank God no one else had died in the fire. I hoped Tim would be caught and charged with arson and murder.

I muddled through my meeting with him at breakfast. He swore he didn't have anything to do with River, but how could I trust a man that possibly had another family? More than that, Tim had hidden his true nature from me. He'd obviously perfected lying through his teeth.

Lacing my fingers behind my head, I closed my eyes. They were burning from the smoke and lack of sleep. My mind began to wander back to River. Was she hurt? Was the baby okay? My eyes snapped open, and my heart hammered against my chest. I took a slow, steady breath, willing my overactive pulse to calm down.

I threw my legs over the side of the queen-sized bed and placed my feet on the plush, tan rug. Dragging my fingers through my hair, I stifled the scream threatening to tear through me. I'd never been good at waiting, and I was afraid I was going to lose my sanity.

A soft knock at the door pulled my attention away from my dark thoughts.

"Yeah?" I asked softly.

Brynn joined me in the room. She had a glass in her hand. "I know your mind is probably running a million miles an hour. Mine is." She placed the water on the nightstand, then a tiny white tablet. "It will help you sleep. Take it."

Brynn sat on the bed, assessing me. She'd swapped out her blouse for one of Chance's tees and still wore her jeans. "You're exhausted. It's not a heavy-duty sleeping pill, just enough to relax you. So, if Pierce or the police call, you'll hear the phone and wake up easily."

"You're sure?"

"I promise. Holden, you're burning the candle at both ends. Tim, River, your club. You're going to get sick if you don't get some rest." She tucked a piece of hair behind her ear and stared a hole through me.

"I know. I'm afraid I'll miss something important, though. Like what if she calls and I'm passed out and I don't hear my phone?"

"I'll stay with you. I'll wake you if your cell rings or a text comes in. I swear."

I looked at the floor, debating if I should try the pill or not. "I thought you were with Chance tonight."

Adoration overflowed from her. "I was, but you need me more. I might not be able to do much to find River, but I can take care of you." She rubbed my back, and my shoulders sagged.

Conceding, I nodded. "Thanks, Brynn. I really don't know if I'd make it through this without you and the guys." I popped the tablet and downed the water.

I laid back again while Brynn walked around the bed and climbed in on the other side. We rolled over and looked at each other.

"It's been a long time since we've slept together." I gave her a sheepish grin. "We have a lot of history."

"More than most friends that's for sure." She studied me for a second. "Do you ever regret starting our sex club?"

I looked at her quizzically. "No. Not for a second. I regret why I felt the need to start it."

"We all do," she whispered, still haunted by our past. "But it was to protect Emerson—to protect all of us."

Shoving those nasty memories back behind the door where they belonged, I tried to focus on the present moment.

Brynn's tongue darted across her lower lip, then she looked at me. "She'll say yes."

My brows knitted together. "I'm not tracking with you."

"River will say yes to your proposal." She offered me an exhausted smile. "I can't wait to go with her to try on wedding gowns. Maybe I'll take her to Seattle where there's a better selection. We can have a girl's weekend if I can pry the two of you apart." Brynn's gaze narrowed. "I have an idea. I overheard Zayne talking to Pierce the other day. I think they know Gemma and Hendrix, the lead singers of August Clover. Maybe we can have Zayne ask Gemma for the name of the designer that she used. I bet she'd create River the perfect dress. Did you see Gemma and Hendrix on the cover of People Magazine? Her dress was to die for."

"I did. You're right, the gown was stunning. Gemma is a beautiful woman."

"Yeah, well Hendrix is cream-your-panties gorgeous. I wonder what their kids would look like if they had any." Brynn's smile lit up her entire face. "Anyway, I digress. River and I can have a girl's weekend if I can pry the two of you apart."

I loved Brynn for helping me plan for the future when I wasn't even sure I'd have one. But the way Brynn talked calmed my fears a little.

"She'd love that. Pretty sure you're the best friend she's ever had. Thank you for being so good to her."

"River is easy to love. She's strong and resilient, Holden. Soon she'll be snuggled up to you at night again." Brynn took my hand in hers. "Where do you want to get married?"

I appreciated Brynn steering the conversation in a positive direction. It gave me something to hold onto.

"I'm not sure. We haven't traveled yet. I'd like to take her to London, Paris, Cancun, and the Caribbean. Wherever she falls in love with, that's where we'll have the ceremony. I'll buy us a vacation house, too."

"It will be fun to see her expressions and watch her explore places she's never seen before. You'll have to send a ton of pictures to me."

My eyes fluttered closed, then I snapped them open again. "I'm getting sleepy, but please keep talking. It's helping more than you'll ever know."

"What colors do you think she'll want for the wedding?"

"Lilac and a bright navy." I yawned as my body began to relax. "You'd look amazing in those colors too. Maybe you can help her meet some more female friends, so we have another person for the bridal party. You're a given. You'll be her maid of honor ..." My words faded as I gave in to the sleep that was dragging me under.

"Holden!" A small hand reached for mine, our fingers stretching to reach each other. An arm slipped around the waist of the faceless person calling my name. In seconds they were taken away. Screams and cries rang in my ears, and I curled into myself, pulling my hair in order to make it all stop.

"No!" I cried. "No!" I rocked back and forth, begging for someone to help me, but it was no use. No one was coming.

I jolted upright, trembling and searching the room. Straightening my twisted shirt, I willed myself to breathe. My heart jackhammered against my ribs, and nausea rolled in my stomach. I sucked in air as I realized Brynn was asleep next to me. The clock read four twenty-nine. I'd been comatose for almost two hours. But those fucking nightmares were showing up more and more. Jesus, what was happening to me?

Little did I know that I was about to learn so much more than my father's dark secrets, and that he would be the least of my concerns.

Chapter Thirteen

The morning sun filtered through the blinds, and I winced when I turned my head. Apparently, after my nightmare, I'd fallen back to sleep. I massaged the stiff muscles in my neck and realized Brynn was no longer next to me. She would never understand how much she'd helped me last night.

I sat up and placed my bare feet on the soft, tan rug. Scrubbing my face with my hands, a massive dose of reality slapped me silly—no River. No club. I grabbed my phone off the nightstand and checked the clock, then shoved it into the front pocket of my shorts. It was a little after nine. Time to figure some shit out.

Running my fingers through my hair, it finally dawned on me that all of my toiletries and clothes had been at the penthouse. "Fuck," I muttered. I wasn't even sure anything was salvageable. If it was, did I want to rebuild, move locations, or walk away?

I rose, wishing to hell River was with me to weigh in on the situation. I wondered if she might want a separate place to live from the club. Maybe even a log home on the water. My heart ached as I recalled her reaction to the Spokane River. She'd been elated. Happy. I longed to touch her, stroke her soft cheek with my thumb. Grief speared me in the chest. If I sat around, I was afraid the not knowing would fucking kill me, and I had to stay sane. I had to believe that she'd be back soon.

I left the bedroom and located the coffee pot. After rummaging through the cabinets, I discovered a big-ass mug and filled it to the top. As exhausted as I was, I needed an IV drip of caffeine.

"Hey, man," Chance said as he joined me in the kitchen. "Brynn said you slept for a little while. That's good."

"Yeah. She gave me a sleeping pill to help. I don't feel groggy this morning, so I guess it worked like she said it would." I sipped the steaming liquid and leaned against the counter. "Where are Brynn and Jace?"

"Jace bounced as soon as he woke up and Brynn is making a list of essentials you and River lost in the fire. I think she's going to see what she can gather for you today while you deal with other shit."

"She's the best." I eyed my friend, waiting to see if there was a hint of jealousy concerning my relationship with Brynn. I didn't see any, which didn't surprise me. Our friendships were deep, and we were connected on many levels that most people would never experience. But I suspected there were more feelings on Chance's part with Brynn. Hers too. It was time to test the water.

I leaned forward and looked him in the eye. "Does she know you're in love with her?"

Chance should have been a bodyguard because he never even flinched. I had to give him major kudos for the poker face.

Without batting an eye, he said, "No." Then he walked around me and rinsed the plate and fork he'd had in his hand. He opened the stainless-steel dishwasher and loaded it. One thing I liked about Chance was he kept shit clean, unlike Jace. Jace wouldn't load his dishes until he didn't have any clean ones left in the cabinets. He would carefully stack every bowl, cup, and piece of silverware in the sink before he finally gave in.

I nearly spilled my drink as I watched him. "I wasn't expecting that answer."

"Me either, but there it is. Sometimes I think we could make it work, but then she's dating a girl or fucking Jace and ... maybe I'm not enough for her." He focused on cleaning the black and white marble countertop instead of looking at me. This was hard for him. "Not to mention I'm pretty sure that Jace has some feelings for her, too."

"Share her. If she feels the same way about both of you, then make it work." I gave him a half-shrug as though it was the easiest thing in the world to do.

Chance faced me. "I'd be fine with it for a while. I mean as things are now, we're already with her so to speak. But I'd want to be the only one she was with, and I'm not sure she can give me that kind of commitment." Regret flashed across his features. "It's not like you and River. You both only want each other. No one else. We all literally watched you two fall in love. Every time we all hung out, we saw the feelings grow deeper. It was pretty amazing from this perspective. I want that as well. Call me a romantic, but Brynn's worth it."

Chance had always been a player. Out of the eleven years we'd been friends, this was the only conversation where I'd heard him talk about settling down. Hell, we'd all wanted Brynn for ourselves at one time or another, but this was more.

My phone vibrated, and I removed it from my pocket. A message from Pierce flashed across the screen.

Any news on the fire?

I had to appreciate Pierce's direct communication. My thumbs danced over the keyboard with a response.

No. I'm hoping to hear something soon.

Tiny black dots bounced as I waited for his reply.

Can you come over? I have some news. Before you ask, it's best not to say anything over the phone.

I glanced up at Chance. "Pierce has an update. I'm going to head over that way."

"Good luck, man. I know you could use it. I'll go with Brynn to grab you some clothes and shit. Can't have you borrowing my underwear." Chance chuckled. "Well, I guess you already are since I go commando." He nodded at the shorts I was wearing and flashed me an ornery smile.

I grinned and slapped him on the back. Maybe that would have bothered most men, but Chance and I had shared the same girl. A clean pair of shorts was nothing. "Have fun with Brynn today." I messaged Pierce that I'd be on my way shortly.

"He will," Brynn said from behind me. I whirled around to tease her about making a list for me already, but she looked like shit. Dark circles nestled beneath her eyes. She'd piled her red hair on the top of her head in a messy bun. "I bought these from Target for you this morning. Thought you might need them." Brynn held out a bag for me, and I took it from her, my gaze not leaving her for a moment longer. I'd known Brynn for as long as I'd known Chance and not once, even when she was sick, had she appeared this rough. Something wasn't right.

"Well, don't just stare at me. Look at what I got you." Brynn placed her hands on her hips and tapped her toe against the wood floor.

There she is.

I peeked in the bag and nearly groaned with joy. I rummaged through the items and smiled as I identified toothpaste, a toothbrush, hairbrush, deodorant, a package of boxer briefs, a plain T-shirt, and a pair of black basketball shorts.

"At least you won't stink like smoke," she said, scrunching up her freckled nose at me.

I wrapped her in a huge hug. "Thank you." Squeezing my eyes closed against all the bad shit that was happening, I enjoyed a moment with one of my best friends. "I'd be lost without you."

"I know," she replied, then stepped back. "Chance and I will pick some things out for you from the mall, but I figured these would get you started."

"I need to shower before I head to Pierce and Sutton's. He has some news but won't discuss it over the phone."

Brynn placed her palms together and closed her eyes. "I hope it's about River. I miss her so fucking bad," she whispered.

I stared at her. That was it, Brynn was as lost as I was without River, and it was affecting her sleep. Inwardly I groaned with relief.

"I'll update you as soon as I hear more."

Suddenly she clapped her hands a few times. "Chop, chop, Holden. Hurry your ass up! I need to know if they've found her."

I couldn't help but smile. Brynn had always been a little on the bossy side, but she was right. The clock was ticking.

Twenty minutes later, I'd replaced the thick smell of smoke with a citrus body wash. I wasn't sure how Brynn slept next to me last night. Between the body odor and fire, it wasn't a good thing.

I told everyone bye as I hurried out of the house to locate Zayne, but he was already waiting by the car.

A gentle breeze rustled the leaves on the aspen and maple trees. One thing about Chance's place that I loved was the privacy. Even though he had neighbors, it was quiet and peaceful as hell. I needed that right now.

"Morning," Zayne said as I neared the Mercedes.

"Morning. Pierce said—"

He held his hand up. "I know. It's why I've been waiting on you."

I hopped into the passenger side, then realized that my Beemer and River's Mercedes were in the club's garage. *Fuck.* We'd probably lost our vehicles.

"I'm glad you don't mind driving me around. I'm not sure if our cars survived the fire yesterday."

"You never know. If they did, you'll need to have them detailed to remove the smell of the smoke. Honestly, it might be better if they're totaled. The insurance would pay out the money at least."

I nodded as Zayne started the car, then eased out of Chance's driveway.

Zayne peered in the rearview mirror. "He's got a nice spot back here. It's secluded."

"Yeah, it is." I glanced back and realized he'd added a row of shrubs, partially obscuring the tan house. I nearly chuckled, remembering the first time he'd brought me over to see it ... before he rehabbed the fuck out of it. He'd pulled up to the garage, and I'd laughed so hard I couldn't breathe. The elderly lady that had lived there prior had painted it bright pink with green trim. It looked like a fucking dollhouse. Chance couldn't have cared less. He saw the potential of the place along with the acre of wooded property it was nestled into. A large oak tree shaded half the residence, which was perfect for Spokane's hot summers. One thing I respected about Chance, he had the ability to see beneath the surface, then turn the lump of coal into a diamond.

I appreciated that a ton since he worked for me. Sometimes I got stuck in the smaller picture. Chance could envision the larger one. We complemented each other in business well. Regardless of what happened with the club, I'd want Chance and River by my side on the next adventure.

"Holden?" Zayne asked.

"Yeah?" I reached for the sunglasses that I'd left in his car yesterday and slipped them on, blocking out some of the blaring, cheerful sunshine.

"Did Pierce mention why we're meeting them?" Zayne focused on the winding road before us, keeping his speed steady at five miles over the limit.

"He said he didn't want to discuss anything over the phone. Do you know why?"

Zayne tapped his fingers against the steering wheel. "No. Pierce is usually pretty cautious when he's discussing important shit. Phones are easily hacked. They're super convenient, but not always the safest."

"Yeah. I agree." I looked out of the passenger window, my brain throwing a million possible scenarios at me faster than I could process them. "I hope it's about River."

"Me too. Although I realize that Pierce is playing it safe, it's hard to wait when you know shit is going on." Zayne cleared his throat. "I wanted to ask you something."

"Okay, sure."

"I understand that a lot is happening, but is Brynn all right?" Zayne's dark eyebrow rose with his question.

I looked at him. "You've noticed too?"

"Yeah. I haven't been around long, but long enough to know something is definitely off. Is this her normal response to a lot of stress?"

Had I talked myself into believing she was worried about River and not anything else?

"That's a hard one to answer. I can tell you that Brynn is usually level-headed, even when shit's going down, but it's been a while since we've dealt with anything this serious."

"Just thought I'd check. I'm pretty good at reading people and Brynn is hiding something."

My mouth hung open as I scrambled for the right words to say. *Jesus, was she pregnant too?*

Chapter Fourteen

I wanted to be that insensitive fucker and ask Brynn over text if she was pregnant, but I couldn't. I would ask her when we were face-to-face. If she said no, I would insist that she take a test. Zayne was right. My plate was too full to be able to sift through the facts rationally. Brynn was exhausted, she was barely eating, and she was pale.

"I'll talk to her tonight." I shifted uneasily in my seat. If Brynn had a little one and the father wasn't interested, then her baby would have three daddies. We'd sworn years ago that we'd always take care of each other regardless, even if we were in a serious relationship with someone. Our bond was nearly impenetrable. As soon as Brynn, Jace, and Chance had accepted River, she'd been included in our pact. More than ever, I needed to find the love of my life. Not only did I need her, but her best friend did as well. Having River with us would help heal our broken hearts. She would know how to deal with the situation with Brynn. Maybe it was women's intuition, but whatever was going down, River would be able to handle it.

After what seemed like an eternity, Zayne pulled through the gates of Pierce and Sutton's property. He parked in front of the garage, and we hopped out. I'd seen a lot of beautiful places, but this one was special. Since the penthouse was most likely destroyed. I wondered if River would want a house like this or something else entirely.

"Do you need some coffee? Sutton always has a fresh pot going. I'm amazed she even sleeps." Zayne stretched, then cracked his neck and grinned at me.

"Sounds good." I could see two staircases, one on either side of the living room. The layout was pretty sweet.

Zayne led us into a chef's dream kitchen. River would flip her shit and never leave if she saw it. Stainless-steel appliances, black granite counters, a large island with drawers, a breakfast nook, and windows offering a stunning view of rolling hills.

We grabbed a fresh cup before we went upstairs.

"We're here, boss." Zayne said, poking his head into a room, then strolling in. He placed the thumb drive Tim had given me on Pierce's desk before he sat down in a black leather chair.

"Excellent. Holden, it's good to see you again. Please, have a seat." Pierce motioned for me to sit down.

My palms grew sweaty as I settled into the identical seat next to Zayne. Bookcases lined the wall with photos of Pierce and Sutton's wedding. I spotted Zayne, Vaughn, and what looked like Hendrix and Gemma from August Clover. I squinted and peered at the photo. River would lose her shit when I told her. She was a huge fan.

Rays of golden sunshine streamed through the large window directly behind Pierce's executive desk. Maple and aspen trees lined the edge of the woods, and the snow-capped mountains in the distance sparkled in the light.

I could envision River drinking her coffee in the morning and happily staring out over the acreage. Her hair would still be messy from making love the night before. Her toned legs would peek out of an oversized sleep shirt. *Fuck.* I inhaled slowly, willing my hard dick to calm down, along with my fantasies about my girlfriend who wasn't here.

"Sorry I'm late." Sutton rushed in and waved at us. "Hey, Holden. How are you holding up after the fire?" Her blonde hair was swept up into a hurried ponytail, and she smoothed her pink polo shirt with the palm of her hand. Dark circles nestled beneath her blue eyes. Sutton was most likely wired on coffee and exhausted.

I rubbed my chin, wanting to cut the chit-chat and get down to business. "Overwhelmed," I answered honestly. "Not to mention I'm about to go out of my mind over what you and Pierce have learned."

"Shit. Of course, I wasn't trying to be insensitive with the small talk. I'll let Pierce explain what we've found." She offered me a kind smile, and I immediately felt like an ass. But I couldn't wait any longer. I had to know if they'd found River.

"I'll get right to it," Pierce began. "Tim was in his car when he called you and admitted to starting the fire at 4 Play."

"Yes! We can put the bastard away, now." A grin eased across my face.

"Well, we can't. First of all, it's illegal to record without consent in the state of Washington, so it's not admissible in court. That doesn't mean I didn't turn it over to my contact at the FBI, though."

I placed my right ankle over my left knee in an attempt to keep my leg from bouncing. "So the FBI will take care of it?"

Compassion flickered to life in Pierce's gaze. "There's more." Pierce rocked back and forth in his leather office chair, and it creaked beneath his weight, breaking the silence between us. "Tim is still in the area. He didn't leave like he said he was going to."

I raised an eyebrow at him.

"Zayne updated us after your meeting with him," Pierce continued.

"Ah. That makes more sense. I knew I hadn't told you." I tapped my fingers against the sole of my tennis shoe. This was the only pair I owned now.

Mentally urging Pierce to spit it out before I had a heart attack from my pulse-pounding so fucking hard, I pressed my lips together in order to keep my mouth closed.

"Tim has made a few other calls from his car. Unfortunately, he doesn't ever say the person's name, so we're not sure who is on the other side of the conversation. But he's said a few things that lead us to believe that he's not involved with River's kidnapping."

Time screeched to a halt. Tim might not be responsible for River's disappearance, but to add to the shit show, we didn't have any other leads to go on. *Fuck! Fuck! Fuck!*

"What about Logan?" I asked, desperation clinging to my words.

"Not from what we can tell, but that doesn't mean it's a no," Sutton explained.

"Where does this leave us?" I gripped the arm of the chair as tight as I could.

"In good shape actually. Tim is aware of *who* took River."

"What? I thought he wasn't a part of her kidnapping!" I dropped my foot to the floor and scooted onto the edge of my seat.

"This is why I was late. I was transferring the recording." Sutton tapped the screen of her cell phone and set it on the desk. Tim's voice began to filter through the speaker.

"You fucking did what?" Tim asked, his dismay clear. *"What in God's name made you take River?"*

I stilled and stopped breathing, waiting to hear more.

It had to be my River he was talking about. The name was too uncommon.

"Well fucking fix it. My son is out of his goddamned mind sick with worry. This wasn't a smart move at all. You ... Jesus ... fucking fix it!"

Silence occupied the line.

"That just added another layer to why this was a horrible idea. And I'll say this, she better not be hurt when she returns home. The FBI will start sniffing around, and I'll be investigated right along with you. You'll expose my dealings right along with yours."

Silence.

"Make this right and fast. If not, you'll be in prison pretty fucking

fast, and I won't bother to visit you. Fucking take care of it, now. I don't want to have anything to do with this."

The call went dead, Tim's words ringing in my ears.

"River is alive?" I whispered as I sank to my knees. "She's alive." Tears pricked my eyes, and I stared at the floor, embarrassed that I wasn't holding my shit together. I slid back into my seat and steadied my breathing. *Oh God, she's alive.*

"*Now* Tim is involved, Holden," Pierce said. "Give us a little more time. The FBI is on it. We're going to find her."

"Do we have any idea where River is? Is she hurt? Is the baby okay?" The questions flew out of my mouth before I could stop them. I was so grateful for the news that I wasn't thinking clearly.

"Not yet. I'm hoping he'll continue to use his car for a while. He just crossed the state line into Oregon." Sutton held her phone up to me and pointed to the red dot on the map.

Pierce stood. "Holden, we're close. I know the hardest thing in the world is to wait while someone else is working on the case. But you have my word, we're on it almost every minute of the day to bring her back as fast as we can. Sutton and I are running on very little sleep. We tag team so one of us is constantly monitoring Tim. Brian at the FBI updates me daily. I'm sure this has been the longest three days of your life, but hang in there."

I nodded. "Thank you. Thank you both. I'll do anything you want me to. If I need to meet with Tim and pretend that I'm joining him, I will."

Sutton glanced at Pierce, a flicker of concern in her blue eyes.

"We're not there, yet, Holden. I want to keep you out of this as much as possible. Your meeting with Tim yesterday allowed Zayne to plant the devices. We're headed in the right direction," Pierce said. "We don't want to spook him. If he calls you, make sure you record the conversation for us."

"Okay. I will." My hands balled into tight fists. Tim was an absolute piece of shit, but if I were brutally honest with myself, I was grateful he wanted River returned to me unharmed. What did that make him, though? A little less of a monster?

My cell rang, and I pulled it out of the front pocket of my basketball shorts. The number wasn't familiar, but I chose to answer it anyway.

I held my hand up. "I have no idea who this is, but I want to take it in case it's River," I said to everyone in the room. "This is Holden."

Chapter Fifteen

I stepped into Pierce's hallway in order to focus on the call.

"Mr. Alistair, this is Officer Walters from the Fire Investigation Unit. I wanted to talk to you about 4 Play."

"Of course. Do you know if it's destroyed, or is it salvageable?" I leaned against the wall, not sure which answer would be better. They both sucked. A fresh sprinkling of hate for Tim crawled over my skin. How in the hell did he think this would draw me closer to him? Disgusted, I tried to focus on the conversation at hand.

"I'm sorry to tell you this, sir. It's destroyed. In fact, the structure isn't safe. Unfortunately, you can't even go into the building and try to salvage anything at this time. Once the flames reached the alcohol, it accelerated faster than the firefighters could control it."

I rubbed my eyes. The engagement ring was gone. Besides some clothes, my first priority was calling the designer and seeing how soon he could make another one. Since we'd designed it together, he still had the paperwork.

"What I wanted to speak to you about ... it looks like it was arson, Holden."

I nearly laughed out loud. I'd have to tell Tim that his men fucked up the job, and they left evidence.

"Arson. As in someone set the fire on purpose?" I pretended to be shocked. After all, I was good at pretending. River would have even applauded me for the performance.

"Are you aware of anyone that would do something like this intentionally?"

I pinched the bridge of my nose, willing myself not to give him Tim's whereabouts. For now, we needed the rotten bastard. If he was arrested, I had no one else on the inside to help locate my girlfriend. I had to take a gamble that the FBI hadn't reached out to the local police force yet, either. Otherwise, I'd be busted for lying to the cops.

"No, can't say that I do. I don't even think I've pissed anyone off in a while. If a name comes to mind later, I'll call you right away. I'm staying with Chance, my best friend, and the manager of 4 Play. I'll talk to him about it. Maybe he has some ideas."

"I called you from my direct number, so call me if you think of anything. We're also investigating things on our end."

"I appreciate it. I'll follow up with my insurance. Oh, do you have any idea if the cars in the parking garage were destroyed?"

"Everything. I mean everything is gone, Holden. I'm really sorry."

I rubbed my forehead, trying to collect my scattered thoughts. It wasn't about the money. It was the memories. I couldn't replace those no matter how many digits were in my bank account.

"Thanks for the information. I appreciate it. Take care." I ended the call and stared into space, wishing River was with me. I hated making decisions without her. She was my future, and I wanted her to be happy and safe when we brought her home. A long minute passed before I strolled back into Pierce's office and updated them.

"Before we head to Chance's place, I need to go by Mom's and reset the alarm to make sure that Tim no longer has access."

"You bet." Zayne stood. I hadn't realized until now that he'd changed his clothes. He had tucked his burgundy Westbrook Security polo shirt into his black slacks. He looked well-rested and alert. What I couldn't figure out was when he slept, and where.

Twenty minutes later, Zayne pulled into my mom's driveway.

"I'll come in with you and check the house," Zayne said, opening the car door.

"Thanks. Since Tim isn't far away … I don't trust him. The sooner I get him removed from the retina scanner and reset the codes, I'll feel a little better." Except that I'd see River everywhere I looked. *She's alive.* That's what I had to hold onto with every fiber of my being. Hope flickered to life inside me. A few hours ago, I didn't even have that.

I sucked it up and entered through the front door. Zayne quietly followed, then closed it behind him.

"I've only seen the foyer." His attention swept the entrance. "I'll start downstairs. Don't move. I want to look around and secure the premises."

It was strange to hear Zayne tell me to stay put in the place I'd grown up. While I waited for him, I retrieved my phone and contacted the retina scanner company. Hopefully, they could make the change quickly.

Zayne nodded as he climbed the stairs and pointed to the left side of the main floor. He continued to search the rooms while I had Tim's access revoked. Once that was done, I also reset the code on the alarm system.

Zayne finally joined me. "It's all clear."

"Thanks, man. I need a few minutes to see if there's any clothes in my old bedroom. I'll be back."

"Take your time." Zayne folded his hands in front of him, his eyes moving side to side, remaining alert.

This part of his job must suck ass. Waiting. Hell, it was about to drive me fucking insane. I'd give my right nut to have River next to me.

I hurried up the stairs and into my room. My pulse stuttered against my neck when I placed my hand against the doorframe. River's presence was still strong. All I wanted to do was crawl into bed, hold the pillow she'd slept on, and inhale her sweet scent.

Sitting on the stripped clean mattress, I closed my eyes as memories of making love to River for the first time surfaced.

River's gaze never left mine as I positioned myself at her entrance. I loved her more than she understood. I could tell her, but my actions would prove that she was the only girl for me. I was willing to be as patient as she needed me to be.

"If you want to stop, let me know," I said.

"I promise." She peered up at me, her deep blue eyes full of trust.

I slid into her slowly, almost losing it before I even started. Jesus, she felt so good. So hot, tight, and wet. I reined in my hormones and focused on her. Her heart. The way she made my pulse race when I was with her.

"I know my feelings are ahead of yours, but I love you, River. From the moment I saw you, you owned me."

Tears streamed down her cheeks as I eased in and out, and I gently kissed them away. "You're the light in my world."

I suspected that no one had loved or cherished River the way she deserved. I wanted to erase all the doubt and all the fear. River was my life. The light that had broken through my darkness when I wasn't sure I'd ever feel again.

I continued to move in a slow rhythm. River ran her hands over my back and moaned softly.

Suddenly, I paused and shuddered. I closed my eyes briefly, willing myself not to come yet. "I'm sorry. It's been a while, and it's more intense than I anticipated." I leaned my forehead against hers. "What they say is true, though. Sex is so much better when you love the person that you're with." With a strong thrust, I groaned. "God, you feel so good."

River lifted her hips, encouraging me to continue as she dug her long, manicured fingernails into my ass cheeks. Our bodies moved in sync, my climax stirring to life.

She nipped at my shoulder, then my ear. "I love you inside of me, Holden."

Her lips claimed mine, and my mouth melted into hers, moaning as her hot tongue explored.

Jolts of ecstasy rippled over me, and I growled. River broke our kiss.

"Baby, oh God." River rocked against me, picking up the pace. She was stunningly gorgeous as she orgasmed.

I would never forget the intense look of pleasure on her face. "You're so goddamn beautiful when you come." My thrusts quickened as I pushed into her a few more times. My name rolled off her tongue as I released.

I relaxed on top of her, kissing her gently as she wrapped her arms around me. "Thank you."

I lifted my head. "For what?"

Love and awe flickered in her expression. "For replacing those awful memories with something I'll cherish for the rest of my life."

My dick ached for her and was painfully hard. I missed her so goddamn much. Then the cold truth crushed my lungs, and I struggled to catch my breath. Just because she was alive right this second didn't mean she wasn't hurt or that she'd survive. I stood and headed to my closet to see what clothes I'd left behind. I realized that Brynn and Chance were buying some for me, but if there was anything here that I could use, then I'd grab it.

Walking into the nearly empty closet, I frowned. Hanging up was the football jersey that River had worn. I snatched it off the hanger and brought it to my face. Her scent was still there. I inhaled deeply, taking her in. Pain shot through my heart and my throat tightened with emotion. For the first time since she'd been taken, I felt close to her again.

"I love you, baby. Please come home," I whispered into the white material of the shirt. I gathered myself together and looked around. There were a few dress shirts and a pair of slacks, and two pairs of jeans. Removing the items from the hangers, I folded them and tossed them on our bed. Fuck. Being here was too much. I was going to lose my shit.

I dried the moisture from my eyes, collected the rest of my belongings, then hightailed it out of the room. Shutting the door behind me, I hoped like hell these weren't the only reminders I would have left of River.

My legs grew heavy as I walked down the hall, remembering River's giggles as I carried her up the stairs after her accident. The smell of her soft hair, the way she looked at me as though I was her Superman. The walls began to close in on me as the memories crushed me like a tidal wave. I had to get the hell out of here.

I hurried to the foyer where Zayne was patiently waiting. "I need to check the basement slider and windows, then I've gotta go. River is everywhere I look." I choked on my words.

"I already checked them, Holden. Everything is locked and secured. Let's leave." He opened the door and I darted past him.

The afternoon sunshine warmed my face, and the fresh, clean air carried a hint of summer. Mom's flower beds would bloom in mid-June, only a few weeks away. The front of the house would burst with color from the rose bushes, lilacs, tulips, and lilies. I'd have to ask her if I needed to call the landscaping service or if she had them scheduled already. I stared at the boxes of dirt and wondered if River would be here to smell the flowers.

I shoved the nearly debilitating heartache to the side. I opened the vehicle's back door and neatly placed my clothes on the seat—all except River's jersey, which I held in my hand. Zayne and I hopped into the car. As soon as he started the Mercedes, relief flooded through me ... until I spotted the blue recycling bin River had slept in. A savage ache spread through my chest, and I leaned my head against the back of the seat, unable to stop the tears from sneaking out.

There was only one way that I'd make it through this. It was time to talk to my best friend and plan the future. I had to stay focused and positive.

Chapter Sixteen

I waltzed through Chance's front door as though it were my house as well. After being surrounded by the memories of River at Mom's place, I couldn't live there. It was too painful. Hopefully, Chance's offer still stood.

I cringed at the irony of the song thumping through Chance's speaker system. "Fire in My Head" by Two Feet was an awesome tune. But the timing of it playing right after we lost the club, and my home, was a bit more than I could handle.

"Chance!" I yelled out to him. "I'm back. I've got news."

Chance hurried to the living room, snatched up his phone, and turned the music off. "Hey, Brynn and I were unpacking the bags of clothes she bought you." He ran his hand through his blonde hair. "I forgot how this girl can shop. Man." It wasn't like Chance hated shopping. By the looks of it, his designer jeans and blue-and-white-checked short-sleeved button-down were new. He loved looking good just as much as the rest of us.

Brynn appeared behind him and rolled her eyes. "I wanted to give you choices. Whatever you don't like, I'll take back tomorrow."

She gave a half-hearted shrug, then playfully slapped Chance on the ass.

At least she was in better spirits today. Brynn was a lot like me. We didn't do well sitting around waiting for shit to happen. We *made* shit happen.

"Oh, man!" Jace closed the door of the hall bath and waved his hand in front of his face. "I wouldn't go in there if I were you." He flashed us a mischievous grin. "That's a load off my mind for sure." He rubbed his flat stomach and snickered.

Brynn wrinkled her nose in disgust. "Jace! I don't need a play by play of your digestive system. Let's hope you didn't back up the toilet like you did on my sixteenth birthday."

"Nah, the toilet flushed fine, sweetheart. It's all good," Jace assured her and gave her a playful wink.

Jace was a total dude sometimes. Even though Brynn was used to it, as we grew older, I'd stopped making shit and fart jokes. I definitely didn't rip ass in front of her. Unable to help myself, I chuckled. Instead of everyone moping around, they tried to keep things on the lighter side, which I appreciated more than they would ever understand.

"Whatcha got, man?" Jace strolled over to the living room and sat on the couch, stretching his long legs in front of him. His Halsey concert T-shirt reminded me of the wild night we'd all had together a few years ago. We'd rented a limo, and half of the group was stoned. The other half was drunk by the time we got there. Halsey had delivered an amazing performance. When we returned to the limo later that evening, everyone was horny as hell, and the ride home had turned into an orgy. It seemed like an eternity ago that we were all that carefree. We were still naive about so many things, including who our families really were. Not anymore. I was well aware of who Tim was.

I headed to the fridge and grabbed a Dr Pepper. Chance would have to let me pay for groceries and split the utility bills while I was here. I'd pitch the idea of rent, but I assumed he would shoot down the offer. His place was mortgage-free, so his cost of living was super low. Hell, if our lives were reversed right now, I'd do the same for him. When we figured out the next step for the business, I'd give him a fat raise. He deserved it. He ran that club like it was his. Chance never missed a day and ensured everything operated smoothly.

I popped the top of the soda, the fizz shooting up over the can. Taking a big gulp, I readied myself for the conversation. I had a lot to tell them, and I definitely needed their help in order to figure out my next steps.

I joined everyone in the living room and sat on the loveseat. Brynn sat between the guys on the couch and looked at me expectantly. She looked better today, but I still wanted to talk to her about taking a pregnancy test.

"Pierce was able to record and retrieve Tim admitting that he was behind the fire." Before I could even finish, they all broke out into cheers.

I held my hand up. "Not so fast. I got excited too but the only thing happening with the confession is that it was turned over to the FBI."

Confusion flickered through their features.

"What the fuck? Why aren't they on their way to arrest him?" Chance scowled.

"Since the conversation was recorded without his knowledge or consent, it's not admissible in court. Plus, the FBI needs to continue to listen and track him." I paused momentarily. "There was another phone call," I continued to explain. "We aren't sure who Tim was talking to, but whoever was on the other end of the line has River. Or at the very least, they took her and are aware of where she's being held."

"What?" Brynn's eyes grew wide with hope and fear. "Is she okay?"

"I have no idea. I do know she's alive because Tim told whoever it was to let her go and not to hurt her. He also said he didn't want anything to do with her kidnapping."

"Holy shit. It's not Tim," Jace said, looking perplexed. "What about Logan?"

I shook my head. "No clue. Apparently, Tim wasn't lying to me after all. He had nothing to do with it."

"He's still a fucking piece of shit," Brynn said, crossing her legs. Her color had returned, but I think the emerald-green blouse she'd worn tucked into her jeans helped too. She looked more herself. Maybe I should hire her to be my personal shopper on a regular basis. It seemed to boost her spirits concerning River.

"It's been almost seventy-two hours since she was taken, and Pierce feels that we'll have her back soon."

Brynn's gaze misted over. "I hope so. Then she's never allowed out of our sight. Not even to go pee by herself. Like, ever again." Her small hands fisted at her sides.

"I'm sure she'll love that," Jace chuckled.

I glanced at Chance, who had been relatively quiet. "I realize that Tim has shady people in his life, but is the FBI or Pierce and Sutton looking at everyone he's associated with? It's now clear that Tim knows who took her."

"Pierce said he and Sutton are working around the clock, so I know they're checking into every possibility. Pierce said they take turns sleeping for a few hours in order to be able to work on River's case without a break. I'm going to check in with Pierce tonight if I haven't heard from him." I fidgeted in my seat as waves of anxiety rolled over me.

"I feel like they'll be more helpful than the police or FBI." Chance slipped his arm around Brynn as tears flowed down her cheeks.

"At least we know she's alive," I whispered. "River is alive." I stood, unable to sit still any longer. "That's what I'm holding onto. I hope like hell Tim has another conversation with whoever he was talking to. If we can even get a hint of where she's at ..." I groaned in frustration and rubbed my face with my hands. "In order not to lose my mind with worry. I need to decide what to do about 4 Play."

"Did you find out more?" Chance asked.

"Yeah, Officer Walters called me. They know it's arson."

Jace smirked. "Good, maybe they'll arrest Tim."

"I think the FBI would block that pretty quick since Tim is giving us answers without realizing it." I placed my hands on my hips. "The club, cars, penthouse ... it's all toast. I can't even get into the building to see if anything is salvageable. It's too dangerous. I'm going to call the insurance company in a few minutes and see what the next step is. Chance, is your offer still open for me to stay here? I can't live at Mom's. I went by there earlier to change the access codes and it's too much without River."

"You know it, man. After everything you've done for me ... shit, I wouldn't have this place to live or ... my life if it wasn't for you."

"This is how it's supposed to be. Family takes care of each other," Brynn said softly, her attention landing on each of us.

"Damn straight," Jace chimed in. "If you need a break from Chance, then you're welcome at my place too."

I placed my hand over my heart as an emotional lump formed in my throat. "Not to get all sentimental, but I love you guys. There's no way I'd make it through all of this without each of you."

"We've got you. Don't ever forget it," Jace replied.

"Always." Chance patted his chest.

"And forever," Brynn said, smiling gently.

"I'm going to make a call, then I'll look at the clothes you guys picked up for me. I appreciate it. I'm not a shopper unless it's for a car, which I need to do soon. The cars were totaled. At least I have Zayne for now. He's getting paid, so I might as well utilize him and his kick-ass driving skills."

"Oh, I'll search online for some ideas unless you want another BMW." Brynn chewed on her bottom lip, I suspected ideas were brewing in her beautiful head.

"Go for it. You know what I like." I hoped it would keep her occupied and her mind off River. At least for a minute.

The rest of the afternoon was chock-full of conversations and paperwork for the insurance and trying on a shit ton of items Brynn had bought for me. I'd asked her to pick up a tux for me once, and she must have jotted down my sizes because everything fit perfectly. She'd purchased eight pairs of designer jeans, polo and button-down shirts, tees, Nikes, socks, boxer-briefs, and things I hadn't even considered, including my two favorite colognes. At this point, I would only need to buy something if I had a special occasion.

I thanked her profusely and gave her a huge hug. I wondered if Chance had enjoyed his time with her or if the shopping spree had bored him to pieces.

Jace ran out and picked up dinner for all of us. We'd opted for Chinese food. My appetite was a little better since I'd at least learned that River was alive. *She was then, but she might not be now.* A chill skated down my spine with that horrible idea. I gave it a swift kick in the ass, refusing to believe that was true. River was a fighter. Strong. I refused to give up on her.

My first concern was figuring out a place for her to feel safe when she returned. Mom's house was off-limits. We needed our own space to run around naked and not wonder when Mom would walk through the front door.

It was almost eight in the evening when my cell rang. I removed it from my shorts pocket and glanced at the screen. "It's Pierce," I announced to the group before I answered. "This is Holden."

"We've got another lead," Pierce began immediately. "Normally I don't like to discuss details over the phone, but I'm going to make an exception."

I really did appreciate him getting right to the point.

"Fill me in." I paced the length of the living room, then stood in front of the window. The sun had set half an hour ago, and the city was cloaked in darkness.

"Do you know a woman named Elaine Winsor?"

I wracked my exhausted brain for the answer. "Yes! She's an investor for the club."

"You might want to sit down for this," Pierce said.

I frowned. What the fuck could be worse than what had already happened?

Chapter Seventeen

I glanced at the three eager faces that were staring at me intently.

"I'm sitting," I said to Pierce.

"Elaine Winsor isn't her real name. It's Laura Hansen."

"That's odd. Why would someone use a fake name in business?" My brain started spitting out lots of reasons why, and none of them were legal.

"Holden, she's about to be arrested for sex trafficking. She's been using your club as a poaching ground." Pierce's tone was clipped.

"What!" My cell clattered to the wood floor. "Goddammit." I snatched it back up. "Sorry. Pierce, don't tell me that you think ..." I couldn't force the words out of my mouth. "Please don't tell me that introducing River to 4 Play ... that I'm the reason she's missing." Guilt exploded inside me, ripping me to shreds in its wake. It was my fault that River had been taken.

"You can't go there, Holden. You're not responsible for another person's choices. We think that whoever Laura is working for kidnapped River. This is one of the largest international sex trafficking rings that the FBI is aware of. They auction the girls to wealthy men, hire them out at parties, and force them into prostitution. It's screwed up. They've been after them for years without a break ... until now."

"They took her to sell her to some monster?" I shouted, my chest squeezing tight as my heart hammered in my ears.

"As soon as the arrest goes down, the FBI will search the premises."

"When is that supposed to happen, and where?" My body trembled violently.

"I can't tell you where, but it will take place in the next few hours. Holden, if River is there, then you'll see her in the morning."

"If not?" Bile churned in my stomach. Tim was trying to stop River from being auctioned off to the highest bidder, but was his threat enough to save her?

Pierce cleared his throat. "Then we keep looking. We're closer. Tim is still in Oregon, too. He's clear of the trafficking, but if this raid is successful, the FBI is going after Tim and his partners. Shit's about to blow wide open."

Rage, blinding and terrifying, shook me. Tim could have told me where River was. He could have helped me, but instead, he ordered Laura to let her go unharmed and walked away from the situation. In my eyes, he was just as fucking guilty. Complicit. A monster.

"I'll reach out the minute I know something. Brian is great about keeping me in the loop when we're working a case."

"Thanks, man. I'll keep my phone charged and be ready if it's good news."

"Same. Hang tight. I'll talk to you later." Pierce disconnected the call, and I focused on my white and red Adidas tennis shoes.

"Holden?" Brynn tensed, and her brows furled together.

"There's an investor in 4 Play that is about to get arrested for sex trafficking. Pierce and the FBI think she took River to ... sell her." Black clouds rolled into my mind. *What if the FBI is too late? What if River was sold earlier today?* The air thickened and closed in, smothering me in the small space of the room. I headed for the front door, desperate to be outside in the open.

Chance was hot on my heels. "Talk to me, man." He folded his arms across his chest as we stood on the porch and stared into the thick, inky darkness.

"The FBI is planning to arrest Laura tonight. They'll sweep the property, and if River is there ..." I paused, unable to say the words. "What happens if River doesn't make it home?" I breathed out my fear along with my question. "What if it's too late and she's already been auctioned off to some disgusting pig?" My voice cracked with my heartache.

"I refuse to think that. Shit, River is probably giving them hell. Not only is she trying to make it back to you, but she's protecting your baby. Mama Bear at her best." Chance leaned against the wall of the house; his expression grim.

"Tim better hide where I can't wrap my hands around his fucking throat. He knows who has River and what Laura is planning, but he chose to walk away instead of making a simple phone call to tell me the truth. He's wrapped up in all of this too." My fists curled as white-hot fury swirled beneath my skin like I was a possessed man. Scrubbing my palms down my face, I ignored the churning in my gut that told me I was still missing something.

"What do you need me to do?"

I glanced at him. "Keep me occupied. Help me figure out what to do about 4 Play. Do I rebuild it or not? What if other sick fucks use my business for trafficking? I can't be responsible for that shit." I laced my fingers behind my head, my stomach knotting.

"Let's brainstorm. Hell, maybe there's a solution and you can still have the club if that's what you want."

My shoulders slumped in defeat. "I brought River to 4 Play. *I* invited her." Guilt stampeded across my chest. "All I wanted was to give her something better. Help her heal. But here we are. I fucked up once again."

Chance's hand gripped my shoulder. "Don't you dare take that on. I'll fucking kick your ass. Did you know that Laura or whatever her name is was a crazy bitch? No. Did you force Laura to take River? No. Did you make Laura kidnap girls and sell them? No. You *cannot* force someone to do something. Those are her choices, not yours. If you'd said that you held a gun to Laura's head and made her do these things, then we might have a different discussion. But that's not what's happened. Don't own that shit."

My heart and logic warred with each other. Logically, I knew Chance was right. But my heart ... my heart said I'd failed to protect the one person that meant more to me than my own life.

"Pierce said he'd call me when he learned something. We should get to work."

"On it. Let's fill the others in and see what they think." Chance opened the door and motioned for me to go on in.

"Sounds good." I peeked at Zayne, who had soundlessly appeared at the side of the home. For a second, he'd startled me, but then I remembered that he patrolled the entire property.

He nodded in my direction, and I assumed Pierce had updated him concerning the new development.

Over the next few hours, we talked about the club and how to make it safer. But even as we tossed out different ideas, I realized I could try my best, but there was no way to protect everyone from harm. Finally, Brynn suggested that I not make any decisions right now. We were all too emotional and on edge to think clearly.

Jace strolled into the kitchen, then returned with a beer for each of us. I constantly glanced at the clock on my phone. No matter what, I couldn't seem to distract myself.

Brynn had finally drifted off to sleep on the couch, snuggled between the guys. It had been nice to see her enjoying a few hours of her day earlier. I knew she loved to shop, but this was different. Her happiness was helping me as well. It gave her a purpose for a little while.

I rose from the chair and strolled to my new bedroom. The idea alone seemed strange. For the last several months, I'd shared a bed with River. Maybe, just maybe, she'd be with me soon.

When she was with me again, I couldn't wait to get her thoughts about the club and rebuilding. Maybe she'd still want to go to New York after she settled in. We'd bring the rest of our family and give all of us a fresh start. It was difficult planning my future because she was in it. I had no idea if she'd return whole or broken beyond repair. Regardless, I'd love her until she was able to move forward. She'd have a bodyguard full time, no compromising on that detail. If she wanted to keep the baby, then we'd shop for a house in a place where she felt safe and secure. If not, we'd discuss abortion and adoption. I'd do whatever she wanted. Nothing else mattered but her.

Stretching out, I stared at the ceiling as my hand patted the other side of the bed. Would she be next to me by tomorrow? I was afraid to hope, but at the same time, I couldn't help it.

I inhaled deeply. With the stress, I'd found myself breathing shallowly. My eyelids fluttered closed as I imagined each part of my body relaxing. *In. Out. In. Out.*

The high-pitched chirp of my phone ringing nearly shot me out of bed. I fumbled around on the nightstand, but only managed to knock the alarm clock off, sending it clattering to the floor. I swore a blue streak. It was a few minutes past three in the morning. With another attempt, I located my cell and answered.

"This is Holden." My voice was groggy.

"It's Pierce."

I sat up ramrod straight. "Did they find River?" Time screeched to a rude and abrupt halt. Silence jammed the line while the beat of my pulse pounded in my head.

"No. I'm sorry, Holden."

"Goddammit."

"They arrested Laura, but the property was clean. The FBI searched for hidden walls, basements, cellars, loose floorboards, they tore the place apart. It was a thorough search. We will see if Laura gives up her boss," Pierce explained.

His words hit me in the chest, cracking me open. Saying nothing, I waited for more from him while my stomach formed painful knots.

"Don't give up. We sure as hell aren't," Pierce said.

"Do we have any other leads?" My body trembled as the dark news seeped into the depths of my battered soul.

"They're following this one. It's all connected. As soon as the FBI learns more, or Sutton and I do, I'll call you."

"All right."

"And the thumb drive Tim gave you is authentic. It hadn't been tampered with. With the conversation we picked up from his car ... Holden, I don't think he has anything to do with it."

I ran my fingers through my hair, scrambling for any other clues I might have missed. "What about Logan?"

Papers rustled in the background. "He's still a possibility."

"Is he even with Tim?" I asked.

"Not that we can tell. The tracker is working, and Tim is still in Oregon. It's been quiet, but he'll have to get back in his car sooner or later. In the meantime, we keep moving forward."

Moving forward, ha. It seemed as though we were running in circles. Maybe Pierce thought we were getting closer, but to me, with every step ahead, we took three back. At this rate, River would be gone before we could get to her.

"Do you think ... do you think River has been sold by now?" *Just lie to me, Pierce.*

Tension snaked down my neck and shoulder blades while I waited for Pierce to reply.

"It would be awfully fast, but I don't know for sure," Pierce replied.

Suddenly, I decided that I didn't always like Pierce's direct approach. Maybe this time, I needed him to fucking sugarcoat it for me. My sanity was swinging from a thin thread, ready to break at any given moment.

"I'll keep you updated. Try to get some sleep, Holden."

"I will." I disconnected the call and rubbed the back of my neck. A ball of emotion erupted inside me. They were supposed to have found River and brought her home. I massaged my temples as I began to contemplate my next step.

My head whipped around at a soft knock, then my door opened.

"They didn't find River, did they?" Brynn asked, her chin trembling slightly.

I pursed my lips, unable to find my voice.

Tears streamed down Brynn's face as she sat next to me and took my hand in hers. "Fuck. Fuck. Fuck." She wiped the moisture from her cheeks, then she leaned against me.

I sniffled, realizing I was crying in front of Brynn for the first time since I'd met her. Men in my family didn't cry. They buried it deep, squared their shoulders, and jutted their chin up in a mental fuck you. But not this night. Not when the air I breathed had been ripped from my lungs, and my hope trampled.

"What happened?" Brynn tucked her hair behind her ear and peered up at me beneath her damp eyelashes.

I swallowed hard, attempting to share the news.

"They arrested Laura and searched the house and property, but nothing. Not a goddamn thing."

"If they don't have evidence or a confession, is there a possibility that she might walk away?" Brynn sat up, fear flickering in her eyes.

"I don't know. I wouldn't think so. Otherwise, she'd alert her boss so they ..." An idea broke through the pain. "What if they're setting her up? What if they let her go so they can follow her in order to reach the people at the top?"

Brynn nodded. "The FBI, Sutton, and Pierce do this for a living. We have to trust that they know what they're doing. Pierce will call as soon as he has information." Brynn sank her teeth into her lower lip. "This isn't over by a long shot."

I assumed Brynn was saying it for my benefit just as much as hers.

"No, it's not." I slid my arm around her shoulders and pulled her into me. Out of sheer desperation, I changed the subject. "Do you think River would want a log home on the lake? Our own little paradise?"

Brynn attempted a smile. "Holden, River doesn't care where you two live as long as you're together."

She was probably right, but at one time in River's life, hadn't she dreamed of living somewhere special?

"Pierce and Sutton's place is remarkable. I'd love to design and build one for us. I think that having a separate place to sleep away from the business would help me disconnect. Chance is more than capable of managing the club."

"Are you going to rebuild?" Brynn's face lit up with her question. "I loved 4 Play and all the perks." She smiled at me.

I nodded. "Yeah, I really think I want to. The location was right. It's prime real estate. But this time ... this time I'll know what to look for and I'll do everything in my power to make the club safe on all levels."

"Which will increase its reputation. I mean, think about it. You turned 4 Play around and ran off the drug dealers and obvious prostitution. Laura was just one sneaky bitch. Add a layer of protection, so to speak. You already run background checks on all the members, but maybe Zayne can weigh in on additional steps. Sutton could be useful as well. Shit, screw the background checks. Pay Sutton to run them. She digs way deeper." Respect flashed across Brynn's features.

"I like that idea. A lot. Let's talk to Chance and Jace in the morning and get their input on designing it. I'm not sure I need a penthouse. A smaller space to crash, if necessary, would work."

"Let's say you and River build a few hours away. It would make sense that you'd have another place to sleep. Like you two can work at home, then be at 4 Play three nights a week and Chance can take care of the rest. It's not much different than what you're doing now."

I gave her a half-shrug. "It is, but I think Chance is wanting more responsibility. Besides, if we go to New York, he's going to be running the club anyway."

Brynn's shoulders slumped. "I forgot about New York." A wistful look crossed her face. "Do you have to go? I would think River will need all of us to heal. Just ... don't go yet. Please."

What Brynn said made sense. River would need to be around people who loved her. "You can always come to New York with us. I'll hire you and pay for an apartment."

Brynn held up her hand, interrupting me. "I can pay for a place to live." She gave me an exhausted smile. "I'll think about it. It would be nice to help and have a goal other than shopping. Plus, I'd have my best friends." Brynn's face fell, a grim expression clouding her features.

"What is it?"

My earlier conversation with Zayne popped into my head. This was as good a time as any to find out what was going on. I shifted on the edge of the bed, and our gazes locked.

"What's wrong, Brynn? Why have you not been feeling well? And no bullshit story, either."

Chapter Eighteen

rynn stared at the floor, unwilling to look at me. "I can't," Brynn whispered, her words weighing heavily on my heart.

"Can't? Or won't?" I tilted her chin up, forcing her to look me in the eyes. "I don't know if Chance or Jace has noticed, but you're pale, you're exhausted, and you've lost weight. Brynn, you don't have weight to lose. I understand that the situation with River is fucking with all of us, but there's something else going on. Tell me."

Brynn shuddered and rubbed her arms as she nervously peeked at the open bedroom door. "You can't tell anyone. Not Chance, Jace, Zayne, your parents ... no one. Promise me."

Fuck. This had to be really bad if she didn't want the others to know.

"You have my word. Out with it already." Honestly, I wasn't sure I could handle anything else. My emotional plate was overflowing already. Then, I considered how Brynn was feeling. Her best friend was missing, and she was keeping a secret from us, pretending to be strong. She needed me.

"I'm sick," she said, hiccupping through her cries.

I shook my head. There was no way that I'd understood her

correctly. "Like the flu?" Before the words even left my lips, I instinctively knew it wasn't.

Her chin quivered. "No. I have ..." She shook her head and covered her face with her hands, hiding her tears. She glanced up at me and chewed on her bottom lip. "Cancer," she said, choking on the word.

Goosebumps erupted all over my body. I'd never felt so powerless, so stripped of choice until River was stolen from me ... and now Brynn.

I crushed her petite frame against me. Desperation and pain whipped through the air as we clung to each other. This was more than I could handle. She had to bring the guys into the situation. "Where? What kind?" I tried to mask the panic in my tone.

"B-Cell Lymphoma. It's in my stomach right now." She pulled away from me, fear rolling off her in waves. "It's stage three."

"What's stage three?" Chance asked from the doorway. A crease dented the smooth skin in between his eyebrows. "Brynn?" Fear danced across his features. He swallowed hard as he stared at her.

Inwardly I sighed with relief that he'd overheard her. I couldn't do this alone. Not with River too. I was running on emotional fumes.

"Chance," she said softly.

I stood and stepped out of the way as Chance charged forward, bent down, and cupped her face in his hands. He gently wiped the tears from her cheeks with the pads of his thumbs. "Is it treatable?" His voice was hoarse with grief.

"They think so," she said, grabbing his wrists.

Chance lowered his head and gently pressed his lips to hers. "What's your treatment plan?"

"Chemo for four weeks on, then a break. I start next week." Her attention darted over to me, then back to Chance.

He kissed her again, then pulled her against him. "I'll be with you every step of the way. I'll drive you to and from your appointments and take care of you."

"We all will. I'll even run errands for pot brownies or gummies," I added.

A sniffle came from the other side of the room, and we all glanced in that direction. Jace stood still, tears in his eyes and his hands shoved into his jean pockets.

"Brynn," he whispered, his lower lip shook. "This isn't allowed."

Brynn rushed over and threw her arms around Jace. He hugged her so tightly, I wondered if she could breathe.

"We're all here for you, babe." He kissed the top of her head.

"I didn't want to say anything. I'm so sorry." Brynn stepped away from Jace and wiped her damp cheeks. "Everything with River is bad enough." Brynn's shoulders shook as her sobs ripped through the room.

Jace held her while Chance and I remained quiet. I'd seen Jace fuck Brynn, Chance fuck Brynn, Sariah and Payton fuck Brynn. I'd touched her, kissed her, and fucked her myself. But this ... this was much more intimate. We saw each other emotionally, mentally, and spiritually stripped down. Exposed and vulnerable. There were no facades or egos involved—only a deep, abiding love for each other.

"Do your parents know?" I asked as I sat on the edge of the bed again.

Pulling herself together, she joined me. She fidgeted, then nodded. "Yeah. They said that they can't come in from Europe. Mom said that she and Dad would FaceTime with me, though."

I rubbed my jawline, itching to find Brynn's father and beat the shit out of him. What sorry excuse of a parent FaceTimed their daughter instead of coming home while she was fighting cancer?

"You're moving in here," Chance stated. "I can help you better if you're here. We can all go to your parent's place and pack what you'll need. You're not fucking staying there alone. You will never be alone again." Chance was barely holding it together. I could tell by the rigid set of his jaw and the tension in his shoulders.

Jace crossed his arms over his chest, anger behind his gaze. "While you're receiving treatment, I'll go by and check on your parents' house every few days. I'll water plants or whatever you need me to do. I'll even hang out a bit here and there, so it looks like someone is living there."

"Are you sure?" Her attention bounced to each one of us. "It's going to be a lot. You all have so much going on. I'd never ask—"

I barked out a laugh. "We know you, Brynn. You never ask for help. And if you honestly think that we're not going to take care of you, you're sadly mistaken. When River returns, she'll be right next to you every step of the way. We're family, Brynn." Although I meant every word I'd just said, I had no idea how mentally and physically intact River would be. But I knew River. She would move heaven and earth to be with Brynn, to support her, and to love her.

"Thank you." Her chin trembled.

"This is why you haven't been eating?" Chance asked, pain etched into his expression.

She nibbled on her thumbnail. "Yeah."

"I've got some edibles at my place. Do you want to try one?" Jace asked. "It should settle your stomach and give you the munchies." A grin eased across his face. "You've always been pretty entertaining when we've smoked."

Chance and I chuckled.

"I'm willing to try it. But if it works anything like a joint does, I might wind up emptying your refrigerator, Chance." Pink dusted her cheeks.

"Excellent, it will give me an opportunity to buy some better food for us," I joked. "You can have your own stash of munchies."

Realizing none of us were going back to sleep, we moved into the living room. The second Brynn shivered, Chance immediately grabbed her Dallas Cowboys plush blanket from his bedroom. He sat at the end of the couch and stretched one of his legs in front of him. He patted the seat between his thighs. Brynn settled between them and nestled her back against his chest.

"That's better. Thanks." She peered up at him and smiled.

We discussed treatment plans, schedules, and divided the

responsibilities. Although I hated that 4 Play was gone, maybe not working right now was actually a blessing in disguise. We could all help with Brynn. As fucked up as it was, Brynn gave me something else to think about other than what River might be living through.

I had a purpose. Help my friend live.

Once Brynn had drifted off to sleep, I rose from the chair and stretched. "I'm going to shower."

"Since it's after ten, the shop should be open. I'll pick up some edibles for Brynn," Jace said.

"Thought you had some at your place?" Chance quirked an eyebrow at him.

"Like I'd fucking eat over smoke." Jace rolled his eyes. "I was afraid she'd turn down the offer if she realized that I needed to go to a shop. But they'll be able to help me pick out what will work best for her. That's the beautiful thing about weed being legal here. You can get help and ask questions. Buying off the street is like Russian roulette, you never know what you're going to end up with."

"I'll catch you later, then." I left the living room and closed my bedroom door behind me. My jaw clenched, and I swallowed back the scream building in my throat. I had to suck it up. This wasn't about me and my feelings. River needed me to be strong. Brynn needed me to be strong.

"Goddammit," I quietly swore as I grabbed the back of my neck and rubbed. I entered the small but adequate bathroom. When River came back, it might be a tight fit, but we'd figure it out. She'd want to stay as close to Brynn as possible.

I turned on the shower and waited for the hot water to begin steaming up the bathroom. Glancing in the mirror, I ignored the circles under my eyes and rubbed a hand over the dark stubble on my chin. Shaving had been the last thing on my mind, and I honestly didn't have the energy to attempt it.

My mind wandered to the first time River and I had showered together. My cock thickened as I undressed, then stepped beneath the spray. I allowed the water to run over my body, my heart aching for her.

I fucking wanted to punch something. Pent-up rage boiled inside me, threatening to erupt. In the past, I'd had football and the sex club. Maybe I should go to school and use the gym. Even though I'd graduated early, I still had access to the workout room. I didn't care about walking across the stage, so River and I had skipped the ceremony and fucked like bunnies that night. Even then, she'd been my main priority.

My tongue flicked over my bottom lip as my dick peered up at me. "I know buddy. I miss her too." I washed my hair and soaped up, attempting to deflate the major hard-on I had. I realized it was a stress reaction, not to mention I was used to making love to River all the time. I missed her so goddamned badly. Before a big football game, I'd always spent my evenings leading up to the big day fucking my brains out in the Master's Playroom at 4 Play.

I closed my eyes. Images of River on her knees with her lips wrapped around my cock flitted through my mind.

She glanced up at me, water clinging to her eyelashes as her tongue swirled around the tip. River's hand glided up my shaft as she took me into her mouth. I moaned as I hit the back of her throat.

"Baby," I said, gripping her hair. She licked and teased me until I was about to explode, then she sucked on my balls. She continued to work my cock, and I planted my palms against the sides of the shower, losing myself in the sensation.

"Do you like that?" River asked, her innocence making me nearly come.

"Yeah." I parted my legs as she continued.

In one quick move, I gently grabbed her beneath her arms and helped her stand, then I faced her away from me. "Bend over," I ordered.

She steadied and positioned herself. I growled as her pink pussy called to me. I ran my fingers over her sweet, wet slit. "I want to fuck you so hard."

She whimpered her response.

I reached between her thighs, rubbing her swollen bud. I knelt, exploring every part of her sensitive flesh. She quivered beneath my mouth as I shoved my tongue deep inside her and wrapped my fingers around my shaft. I grinned and then sucked her clit hard when I saw her watching me stroke myself.

River's legs began to tremble, and I stood. I pushed against her entrance with the head of my cock, then slid into her nice and slow. Moving my hips in slow circles, I moaned her name as her core clenched around me.

"Holden," she gasped. She pressed her palm against the side of the shower, and I picked up momentum, thrusting deep inside of her.

"You feel so fucking amazing, baby." I gripped her hips, digging my fingers into her flesh before I massaged her clit. My pace quickened, and River pushed her ass against me.

"Harder," she cried. "Fuck me harder!"

Her slick pussy tightened around me, and I thrust into her, our cries muffled by the sound of the shower. River's climax peaked my own, and I shuddered against her.

Once I'd recovered, I planted light kisses along her back before I pulled out. I gently turned her around and cupped her cheeks with my hands. "I love you, River. Don't ever doubt it." I kissed her, pouring my heart into it.

"And I love you, baby," she said softly.

I leaned my head against the shower, my dick still screaming at me. Grabbing the soap, I lathered up and began stroking my shaft. River loved seeing me jerk off. She'd spread her legs and fuck herself with the vibrator. Her back would arch, her tits screaming for me to put my mouth on them. Watching her always made me lose my shit in record time.

My body tensed with a final stroke as I came. It was more than a physical release. It was mental and emotional. Tears pricked my eyes as the fear and grief bubbled up inside me, and I permitted myself to lose it for the second time since River had been taken.

I turned off the shower and stepped onto the black rug. Once I dried off and dressed in jeans and a plain black T-shirt, I checked my phone, but there weren't any missed calls or texts.

As much as it pained me, I had to focus on what I could control. With Brynn's news, I'd decided to rebuild 4 Play. Life was too short to ignore what made me happy, and I loved the club. I loved building the business. At least that would give us something to work on while Brynn started chemo.

Next, I wanted to find a lake property to buy. I'd considered not purchasing it without River's approval, but if she didn't like it, then I could always sell it and make a profit. There was no reason to wait.

When River came home, I'd take her to see the land and share my vision with her. I wanted a place to spend the rest of my days with her and, hopefully, raise a family.

I just had to get her back first.

Chapter Nineteen

Brynn's news had mentally and physically drained me, but I was determined not to let her know. I had no choice but to move forward, no matter what my life might look like.

Once Jace had returned with some edibles for Brynn, he'd plopped down on the couch with her and turned on a romantic comedy while he massaged her feet. I'd busied myself in the dining room, jotting down ideas for 4 Play as well as a new place to live. Their laughter floated through the area, and I was grateful that sound had replaced the tears, but the emptiness in my heart from missing River was overwhelming.

Chance and I had discussed possible layouts for the club and narrowed it down to a few ideas we were excited about. We'd agreed on a specific brand of high-end cameras and security as well. I wanted to make sure there weren't any blind spots, so they would be checked daily. It hadn't escaped me that Laura might have had someone adjust the camera at the loading dock before the furniture had been delivered.

Although I hoped Laura sang like a canary about her bosses and the organization she worked for, I realized it wasn't likely. The glimmer of hope I'd allowed myself had betrayed me and sucker punched me in the gut. Next time Pierce called with a lead, I wouldn't jump on the expectation train. I would wait until River was safe and in my arms.

By eleven that evening, Jace had headed home, and Chance and Brynn had moved to Chance's bedroom. She'd been dozing off and on all afternoon, but I hoped she would get some rest that night. If she wasn't able to sleep, I figured she'd slip into my room later to talk. The painful understanding of the sacrifice she was making to support me clawed at my chest, puncturing my already wounded and battered soul, making it even harder to breathe.

I changed into shorts to sleep in and crawled into bed, my mind still spinning with ideas for the club. Even then, River was constantly present at the edge of my thoughts. I reached for the remote, turned on the TV, and flipped through the channels, searching for a distraction from the brutal realization that River wasn't next to me.

Sitting up, I punched my pillow a few times in order to soften it up. I definitely needed to buy some of my own. I might actually wake up without a serious crick in my neck.

The Spokane news ribbon flashed across the screen, and I bolted upright. The female anchor spoke as images popped up behind her.

"Early this morning the FBI raided a house located in Deer Park along with fifteen acres of wooded property in search of several missing women. Laura Hansen, a local investor in the world-renowned club, 4 Play, that was destroyed in a fire this week, was arrested for kidnapping. Although the women weren't located, Laura is in police custody. If you've seen any of these women, please call the 800 number you see on the screen."

"Shit," I muttered as I stared at the photos. One girl looked to be about ten, another in her early twenties. Yet another looked like she was a teenager ... the pictures continued to appear, then my attention landed on River. It was the recent photo I'd provided the police. But it didn't stop with her. The images kept scrolling by, revealing the enormity of the sex ring.

My cell vibrated on the nightstand, and I answered it without checking the caller I.D. It was after eleven, but everyone knew that I stayed up until the early morning hours.

"This is Holden." My focus remained on the television.

"Hi, Holden. It's Shirley. I hope it's not too late to call."

I grabbed the remote and paused the news. "No, it's fine. I'm typically up late. How are you?"

"Pissed," she said. "That's probably not the best way to open up a conversation but it's the truth."

"No worries." I waited while the flicking of a lighter filled the line.

"Well, I've literally been stalking Josie. She came back to town a few days ago, so I figured I'd catch her at her place, you know? I had today off and figured this would be a great time to find out why she'd turned on River. Didn't want to scare her off though, so I parked a little way up the road, but close enough where I could still spot anyone coming and going from her place. Weird thing is, I didn't see any activity at all. Her car was parked there, but no one came or went." Shirley paused, inhaling deeply. "I mean, what young kid stays inside all day?"

I wanted to tell her plenty of them, if they were bingeing a Netflix show or playing video games, but I kept my mouth shut and let her talk.

"Anyway, I finally got tired of waiting and walked up to her porch. Then I noticed that her front door was cracked open a bit. I tried knocking but didn't get an answer. I mean, I get it. I normally don't answer if I don't know who it is either. I waited a bit before I opened it and yelled for Josie. That's when it hit me. The worst rank and pungent smell that's ever assaulted my nostrils. I covered my nose and called for her again. Something was horribly wrong, and I knew it. As much as I wanted to go in, I didn't. I called the police instead and reported my concerns, then I called Ed. Within the hour, Josie was rolled out in a body bag."

"Oh shit." I massaged my throbbing forehead with the news. "Do you think it was Logan or his men?"

"Hon, who the hell knows for sure? People in this town tend to get mixed up in some bad shit. Next thing you know they turn up dead. I just wish I'd been able to talk to her first. I was prepared to give her some money for whatever information she could share with me."

"Maybe this is best. I don't want you to get sucked into a dangerous situation." I stared blankly at the frozen television screen, wishing the nightmare would end.

Shirley chuckled. "You sound like Ed. Don't you go worrying about me. I grew up in rough towns where people would rather shoot you than to say good morning."

"Tough crowd."

Shirley laughed. "I can see why River fell for you."

"Oh?" I wasn't sure how Shirley could have figured that out in a few conversations, but I was curious.

"You're caring, protective, and funny."

A sad smile eased across my face. "Thanks. I'm definitely protective of the people I love. This time ... this time I failed. I even hired a bodyguard for River, but she ditched him."

"No, sir. You can't blame yourself for River running off and dodging her bodyguard. The fact that she *had* a bodyguard tells me how much you love her. That girl is strong-willed and used to figuring out life on her own."

I blew out a sigh. Talking to Shirley was helping. "I think what happened was that she ... she'd taken a pregnancy test. It was positive. She hauled ass out of the office and down the hall to the elevator. River *wanted* to ditch her bodyguard. I figure the test results scared her pretty badly."

"Jesus," Shirley whispered. "So ... whoever took her kidnapped two people."

I already understood, but hearing Shirley say it out loud sent a new jolt of fear through my veins. "Yeah. I didn't have a clue about the pregnancy until her purse was found. The test was in her handbag."

Even though I'd never met Shirley before, I imagined her eyes were wide with the new information.

"Listen to me, Holden. River has lost a lot in her young life, but she'd do everything to protect a baby. Everything."

My chest tightened, and I held my breath. "I know." And deep inside myself, I did, but that didn't mean that she was safe. I suspected the amount of stress she and the baby were under was enough to cause a miscarriage. I shoved the cloud of darkness from my mind and refused to focus on it.

"Listen, Ed just pulled into the garage. You call me if you hear anything."

"I promise." I didn't want to tell her that River's picture had been flashed all over the news minutes ago. A part of me wondered why the media hadn't released her photo earlier, but I suspected the FBI had something to do with it.

The call ended, and I placed my cell on the nightstand. The information that Shirley had given me was interesting, but not enough to make me give a shit about Josie. River and Brynn were my primary responsibilities.

I did like Shirley. A lot. Once River returned, I'd see what she thought about inviting Shirley and Ed out to stay for a few days. I'd be happy to fund the trip, since they'd been an intricate part in helping River and me meet.

Stifling a yawn, I settled in for a long night of mindless TV while my brain worked out different scenarios of how to find where River was. Tim was my best bet, but I'd told him to basically go fuck himself after he had his minions set my club on fire.

Finally, somewhere in the middle of season one of Lucifer, my eyes fluttered closed, and I fell into a fitful sleep.

"Holden. Holden, wake up," a faceless kid said.

I lifted my head, glancing around a child's room. "What is it?"

"Something bad is going to happen."

I struggled with the blankets, then sat up, rubbing my sleep-filled eyes. "Go back to bed. Everything is fine. You probably just had a bad dream."

"It wasn't a dream. Please," they begged.

I kerplunked into bed and pulled the covers up beneath my chin. My eyelids drooped closed, then snapped open again. I pointed to the door. "Out."

Feet shuffled across the floor, and the sound of the doorknob turning echoed through the otherwise silent room.

Nearly asleep again, a scream ripped through the night, and I jumped out of bed and ran to the hallway.

"Holden! Holden! Don't let them—"

"Stop!" I bolted forward, slamming into the back of the adult at the end of the hall.

"Holden!" Little fingers reached out to me.

Our hands grasped each other's, and I tugged hard in a vain attempt to free them. Losing my balance, I toppled to the floor, then a thick, inky blackness clouded my vision.

I sucked in a breath, my body visibly trembling as I flung the sheet off me. Covered in a cold sweat and nauseous, I jumped out of bed and hurried to the bathroom to splash cold water on my face. I grabbed the tan hand towel and dried off, then returned it to the circular hanger.

"What the fuck?" I stared at myself in the mirror. My nostrils flared as I attempted to control my rapid pulse. I hung my head, trying to decipher if these were nightmares or lost memories. What if the years I couldn't remember anything ...? My breath halted in my lungs. My vision blurred, and my pulse pounded in my ears.

"Hello?" Brynn's voice came from the bedroom, breaking through my panic.

I tried to pull myself together before I spoke to her. "Hey, how are you doing?" I strolled over to her as if nothing were wrong. As if I hadn't just had another fucking nightmare that twisted my stomach into knots and caused me to break out in a cold sweat.

"Chance is snoring." A sleepy smile pulled at the corner of her mouth. She tugged on her pink and white striped Victoria's Secret pajama top. It was cute that she still liked matching sleepwear. "And ..."

"And?" My forehead creased with concern.

"You were yelling. I could hear it from Chance's room."

My eyes widened in shock. "Shit. I'm sorry." I rubbed a hand over my chin, feeling like an ass for waking her.

Brynn pointed to the bed, and we crawled in. She snuggled beneath the blanket, and I remained on top of them.

"What's going on?" She stifled a yawn.

"Nothing for you to worry about." I looked at her, wondering what she was thinking. She had to be terrified about her diagnosis as well as River. There was no way that all the stress was helping her body fight off the cancer.

"Holden, I'm going to say this the nicest way I can. Fucking spill it. I can't focus on my cancer every second of the damn day. I don't want you guys to act any differently. It will help me a lot if you talk to me about your life, the club, what you're thinking. What I really need is for my best friends not to tiptoe around me. Don't change. Let's talk the way we always have."

She made sense. If I were in her place, I'd want the same from my friends. I blew out a long sigh and laced my fingers behind my head. "I've been having some really strange nightmares."

Brynn propped up on her elbow, her fist planting against her cheek. "Tell me about them."

I stared into space, attempting to collect the pieces that I could still remember. Once I woke up, they faded quickly. "I think I'm a little kid and everyone around me is faceless. I can't tell who they are. But ..." A sharp pain stabbed me in the chest, and I allowed the heartache to anchor me to the moment. "Someone keeps screaming for me to help them." I glanced at her, checking to see if she'd fallen asleep yet.

"Is it a boy or a girl?" She stifled a yawn.

"I don't know. When I'm in the nightmare the only feeling is ... terror. Like some really bad shit is going down, and I can't do anything to stop it."

"Maybe you're really dreaming about River. The subconscious is tricky. It's not always literal." She reached out and placed her hand on my forearm.

Brynn's suggestion would make sense, but I still couldn't shake the utter devastation that accompanied the nightmares.

"It's not about River. I had the same night terrors when I was younger. They stopped for a while, but they're back." I didn't want to verbalize any more to Brynn, but it was almost as though the dreams were stealing a part of my soul.

There was no way to prepare myself for what lay ahead. But the fact remained that one of the happiest days of my life would also unlock secrets that would nearly destroy me.

Chapter Twenty

The house was refreshingly quiet the following day. With no sign of Chance or Brynn yet, I texted Jace.

Plans today? I have to get the hell out of here for a while.

Black dots flickered across my screen while I waited for his response.

I need to hit something. How about we go to the college? Beat the hell out of shit, then eat.

Jace had read my mind. *Perfect. Meet you in thirty.*

Instead of texting Chance and Brynn, I scribbled them a quick note that Jace and I were heading out for the day. I wasn't sure if their phones were on, and I didn't want to risk a message waking them. Brynn needed her rest.

Once I informed Zayne of the plans, I changed into a pair of black basketball shorts and a plain white T-shirt. I slipped on my tennis shoes, grabbed my gym bag with fresh clothes, wallet, phone, and keys, then quietly left.

Zayne was waiting by the Mercedes as I hurried down the porch steps. I was hoping that we would hear something about River that day, but I desperately needed a change of scenery. Brynn's news had ambushed me. Even with the signs that she wasn't feeling well, I'd never expected to hear the word cancer.

"Hey, man." I opened the passenger door and hopped into the car. Zayne slid into the driver's side and started the engine.

"Morning." He shifted and eased out of the driveway and onto the road.

"I talked to Brynn." I reached for my sunglasses and put them on to block out some of the bright morning sun.

"How did it go?" Zayne asked, remaining focused on the curves in front of him.

A nervous knot of panic formed in my stomach and grew. *What if Brynn died?* I kicked myself in the ass for even considering that. She hadn't even started treatment yet. People survived cancer all the time.

Tears clogged my throat, choking my words off. I swallowed through the thickness, but my voice sounded strained when I finally spoke.

"She has cancer." I stared out the passenger window while my emotions snuck up on me again. Every time I thought I could have a conversation about her treatment, I lost it.

"Fuck," Zayne replied. "How bad?"

I tapped my leg impatiently. This conversation sucked. "Stage three lymphoma in her stomach."

"Fuck," Zayne said again. "Sorry, man. I don't even have the words right now. ... *fuck* ..."

I shifted in the seat, stretching my legs in front of me. "Yeah. It's more than I can handle."

"Maybe you should go to the gym more often. At least you can hit a heavy bag and not get arrested. Your anger will take over if you don't watch it."

"Why do I have the feeling you're speaking from experience?" I asked.

"Because I am. There was some really cool shit about being an Army Ranger, but some of it fucked me up. Most likely for the rest of my life. I went through a rough period, and in order to control my temper, I drank and fucked until I lost myself."

"It's easy to do." I understood all too well. When I'd started the sex club back in high school, I'd done the same as Zayne. It was Brynn who'd helped me slow down before it was too late.

"Easy" by Gino the Ghost came through the car stereo.

"Didn't peg you for rap." Apparently, I didn't know shit about this guy, but it would be interesting to dig beneath those layers and learn who Zayne, the man, was. Not the bodyguard or the one that served in the military, just Zayne.

"I like a variety of tunes. Depends on my mood actually." He tapped his fingers on the steering wheel. "Good club tune, though."

He was right. The dance floor was always jumping when this song played.

"Speaking of, are you going to rebuild 4 Play or move on?" Zayne rested a hand on his leg while he continued to drive.

"Rebuild. The clubs are my life."

Zayne's eyebrow rose. "Clubs?"

I realized my mistake, but I understood that Zayne wouldn't say shit to anyone. I desperately needed to talk to someone outside of my circle with a clear head and an unbiased opinion.

"The lower floor is a membership only sex club. I make most of my money from that and the liquor sales."

"If it's membership only, I'm guessing there's a background check along with a confidentiality agreement," Zayne said.

"Exactly. It's why I haven't ever let you in."

Zayne didn't miss a beat as he responded. "Maybe I should become a member. I could use some play time for damned sure. It's difficult to have a relationship in my line of work."

Shocked at his interest, I struggled for the right words.

"When we rebuild, you're welcome to check it out. At the last building, there were ten rooms, and you could pick your pleasure, including BDSM, voyeurism, and more." I wondered which one he'd choose first.

"Sounds about my speed. I don't have time for relationships. An hour or three of fun, I could definitely benefit from. Plus, I know you well enough to understand that, unless someone saw me, they'd never know I was a member. Not that I really give a fuck, but I do like to have some privacy."

"It's strictly confidential. It's one of the reasons I have members from all over the world. It's clean, well taken care of, and their needs are catered to. Not just sex; food and alcohol are included. It's a package deal."

"Good business move." Zayne flipped the turn signal on, and the sound of the steady *tick, tick* filled the small space of the car.

"I'll let you check it out before we reopen," I offered. "I don't need a background check on you. You work for Pierce and Sutton. That's good enough for me. Plus, you're my bodyguard. If I can't trust you with my life, then I would have fired you already."

"You almost did." Zayne rubbed his jaw.

"It wasn't your fault. I was ... losing my shit." A quick wave of guilt swept over me for accusing him of not doing his job. He had. I just hadn't had all the information concerning the locked stairwell door.

Zayne pulled into a parking space near the college gym. "You should have brought a change of clothes so you could work out with us." I climbed out of the car and closed the door.

"I have some with me." Zayne hopped out and popped the trunk. He removed a black gym bag and tossed it over his shoulder before securing and locking the Mercedes.

"I'll give you and Jace your privacy, but I'll be in the same room so I can keep an eye on things. I won't take any chances with you. Tim could have ditched his car in Oregon and be back in town by now. I don't trust him."

I screeched to a halt. "Has Sutton said anything?"

"Nope. It's my natural paranoia kicking in."

Zayne and I entered the building and headed to the workout area. Hopefully, it wouldn't be crowded since it was finals week.

I quickly spotted Jace in the corner of the room, sitting on the weight bench.

"Hey, man." I approached him. "We're going to toss our bags in the locker room, then I'll be out."

Jace eyed Zayne for a second, then nodded.

A few minutes later, I settled in near Jace and began to stretch. "How are you doing with Brynn's news?" I asked, not tiptoeing around what was fucking with both of us.

"I'm having a hell of a time wrapping my head around it, honestly. A few weeks ago she was fine, and now ..." His blue-gray eyes filled with grief. "We've got to get River back. The girls need each other. I know the doctors will help Brynn, but I think she'll do better with River by her side."

I laid down on the bench while Jace added weights and prepared to spot me. "Honestly, I'm not sure what the hell to do. I've never been so fucking lost before." I sucked in a breath and started a set of bench presses.

"You've never been in love before. Now you have someone you would die for." Jace stood at the top of the bench, watching me in case I began to fatigue. Once I'd performed a few more sets, we traded places.

"Are you in love with Brynn?" I asked. The bar started to wobble, and I prepared to catch the weights if Jace needed assistance. "Sorry, that was a bad time to ask," I admitted.

"No shit." Jace finished, then returned the weights to the bar. He sat up and looked at me. "Yeah, I love her but not the way Chance does. I don't want to settle down with her, but I'll fuck anyone over that doesn't treat her right."

I grinned. We all would. "Same. I love her but I'm not in love with her. River is the only one I want to be with."

"I love all of you guys. We've been through hell and back before, and we'll make it through all of this shit too." Jace grabbed his navy hand towel and wiped the sweat from his forehead.

I strolled over to the heavy bag and gave it a solid jab. I really needed to hit something. Talking about River and Brynn wasn't helping. It was actually making things worse.

"I agree." I landed another hit and spotted Zayne across the room. He was cool about giving us some space, and I appreciated him not hovering.

Jace stood and headed to the leg press. He settled in, then began his sets. "How do you think River will feel about 4 Play being rebuilt? I mean, she was scoped out and kidnapped from there."

My stomach plummeted to my toes. "I've wondered about that."

Jace stared at me, waiting for me to continue.

"If she struggles with my decision, then I can always sell the club. I can find some other way to earn a living. She's all that matters to me."

"That's huge, dude. Like, 4 Play has been your baby." He stood and moved to another weight machine as he talked.

"It's different now that she's in my life. Plus, I have the ability to do anything I want, including not work, but I need to have something to do. River's job was there as well. Honestly, I have no idea what life will look like hour-to-hour. I'm just desperate to think about something else."

"Hell, I get that."

I landed a few more hits to the bag, my knuckles burning. "I'm going to look at some lake property today. Do you want to come with me? Scope out an area to build a house?"

"Yeah? You're not going to rebuild the penthouse?" Curiosity flashed in Jace's eyes.

"I've thought a lot about it. I'd like to keep them separate. I'll still have a room for us to sleep, cook, shower, but not a place to live long-term. I'm hoping it will help give us some separation."

"I think that's a solid idea. And yeah, it will be fun to see some properties. I'm always considering building, too. For now, I'm fine in the place I'm in. I remodeled it, and even if I were in a serious relationship, there's plenty of space."

"That's right. I need to swing by and see the final updates." I scratched my chin, my brain wandering back to Brynn. "I wonder what will happen between Brynn and Chance now that she's ... sick." I slammed my fists as hard as I could into the heavy bag. My breathing grew jagged with the rapid-fire hits.

Zayne approached and tossed me a pair of boxing gloves. "Save your knuckles. Put them on and I'll hold the bag so you can beat the shit out of it."

Sweat trickled down the side of my face, but I ignored it. By the time I was finished, I'd be drenched. Slipping the boxing glove on, I allowed Zayne to help with the other one.

"Hit here and here." Zayne began to show me quick combinations that could take an opponent down quickly. Tim's ugly mug came to mind as I followed Zayne's instructions and imagined I was beating the hell out of my asshole father. *Take that, you sick fuck. Take that for hurting River, take that for burning down my club, and take that for not telling me who the hell has River.*

A delicious burn traveled through my muscles as Zayne continued to teach me, and I began to release the pent-up hate for Tim. Shit. I should have been working out like this from the beginning. The overcrowded thoughts in my head started to clear, and I focused on the solution, not the problem.

I stepped back and held out my hands for Zayne to remove the gloves. Once they were off, Zayne tossed me a towel to mop up the sweat that was pouring down my cheeks.

I'd definitely have to shower before we left.

A sharp ache pierced my chest. After the purge of emotions, I finally realized what I had to do. It might be the only way to find River. I just hoped like hell it wouldn't destroy me in the process.

Chapter Twenty-One

Once I'd taken a much-needed shower, I dressed in clean jeans and a tan polo shirt that Brynn had bought me as I waited for Jace and Zayne to finish. I plopped down on the weight bench and riffled through my gym bag for my phone.

A missed call from Pierce flashed across my screen. "Dammit," I mumbled. Glancing around to see if anyone else was in the gym, I decided to wait to call him back. I preferred to be tucked safely away from listening ears. At least I'd have privacy in the Mercedes. Whatever Pierce had to say, Zayne would learn as well, and I didn't have any secrets from Jace.

Ten minutes later, Zayne pulled out of the parking lot and headed north to look at a few lake properties.

I tapped my phone screen and waited for Pierce to answer.

"Hey, Holden." Papers shuffled in the background.

"Sorry I missed your call. I was in the gym."

"A workout probably did you a world of good," he responded.

"Do you have some good news?" My pulse pounded in my ears, and I held my breath.

"Sutton spent the last few days tracking Logan and digging up dirt on him. He's not involved with River's disappearance, Holden. He's deep into the manufacturing of meth and weapons. Sex trafficking isn't his gig."

Dammit. We were running out of leads. "What about Laura?"

"The police had to release her. There wasn't enough evidence for them to hold her."

"Fuck, this means she's probably running straight to her boss ... wait, which is what we want, right?" I wasn't a cop or an FBI agent, but it seemed like it might have been their plan all along. "She was bait?"

"Pretty much. Hopefully, she'll be rattled enough to lead us to her superior," Pierce added. "On the positive side, Tim is still using his car. He's not using Bluetooth, so we're still in the dark about who he's talking to. Whoever has River called him an hour ago."

I reminded myself that I had to remain calm until River was safe with me. It was imperative that I treated all leads with skepticism in order to stay sane.

"Even though Tim hasn't spoken a name, it's clear that he knows the person well. The conversation was a bit heated. He's still pushing for them to release River. He's set an ultimatum and time frame as well. They have forty-eight hours to comply," Pierce explained.

"And if they don't?"

"All Tim said was they'd regret it. I wouldn't suspect he'd go to the authorities because of his own illegal activity. He might not have a plan either. There's a possibility he's bullshitting until he's forced to make a move."

My brows knitted together. "Are we waiting on him? I mean, the good news is that she's still alive, but it's been five days." A horrible idea sucker punched me in the gut. *Fuck.* "Pierce, what if Tim is lying? What if he's fucking with us and has realized his conversations are being recorded?" I attempted to still my bouncing leg, anxiety blossoming in my chest.

"Holden, I understand how hard this is. I've lived through it myself. But Tim hasn't said anything to make us think he's aware of the tracker. He's threatening people. When he speaks, his pitch rises, and you can hear the stress in his voice. River is alive."

Shit. I wanted to believe Pierce. I needed to. "I can't keep waiting, man. I'm trying hard to let you and the FBI handle things, but … put me in. Let me work for my father and bring him and his shit-ass friends down. I have to find River."

Zayne white-knuckled the steering wheel, and Jace scowled at me and shook his head no.

I didn't need anyone else's permission, though. It was my decision, and one way or another, I was going to bring the love of my life home where she belonged.

I blew out a heavy sigh, massaging my shoulder and breaking up the tension that was turning my muscles into vicious knots while I waited for a response.

"Give me a few hours, then we'll put a plan in place. You can't go in alone. I'll reach out to the FBI and let them know that you're offering to go undercover. And for the record, I don't like it. You're a civilian and untrained, but you're probably the best bet to blowing everything wide open."

Finally, I was getting somewhere. "Thanks. I'll wait to hear from you before I call Tim and tell him I'm in."

Jace punched me in the shoulder from the backseat, glaring at me.

"You need a solid excuse, Holden. If he suspects you're in it to take him down, then it won't work."

"I understand, but I have years of experience bullshitting my father and getting away with it. Hopefully those skills will still work in my favor."

"I guess we're about to find out. Talk soon," Pierce said before he disconnected the call.

I placed my cell in my lap and blew out a breath.

"What about Brynn?" Jace asked, disbelief hanging on his words.

I turned slightly so I could see him. "What about her? I'll be around unless Tim insists I travel. You and Chance are more than capable of taking care of her. But ... under *no* circumstance is she to know what's going on. Am I clear?"

The color drained from Jace's cheeks, and he slumped in his seat. "You better fucking come back alive, man. If ..." Jace shook his head and stared out of the passenger window.

"He'll make it out alive," Zayne explained. "Tim obviously needs him for starters. Second, you never go in the field without backup. Pierce will have two men on you at all times. You'll never be alone,"

"That's all good, but it only takes a second to get shot and die," Jace added. "No one can protect you from that. I hope you've thought this through, Holden. There's no coming back to us if you're fucking dead."

Shocked by Jace's reaction, I looked him in the eye. "If it saves River, then it will be worth it," I growled. "You'd do the same, so get off my ass."

Jace's gaze narrowed, and his nostrils flared. "I'm not on board with this. Once Brynn finds out—and we both know she will—she won't be either."

What the fuck was his problem? "Brynn won't find out because if anyone tells her, they'll be recovering in the hospital." I wasn't fucking around about this. I was trying to protect both of my girls. I wasn't sure why Jace hadn't figured that out yet, but I suspected it tied in with losing his Mom. Chance, Brynn, River, and I were all he had left. At the same time, no one was asking him to go with me.

Dread bundled inside me, and nausea rolled in my gut. I'd analyzed this idea in every possible direction once we'd learned that Tim knew who took River. I'd been patient for two days. I was done waiting on other people to find her. My heart and logic played tug-of-war as I realized that Jace was right. If this went down the wrong way, I might never escape the life my father lived. Not alive, anyway.

Facing the front again, I remained quiet and looked out of the window. Since Tim had burned my club, I planned to tell him that I wouldn't be able to recoup the money fast enough, and I'd changed my mind about working for him. Once I had the capital, I could start the next club and mention that it could be a front for the weapons. He might be blinded by his ego and not suspect much. Or maybe it was foolish, thinking that he'd take me to the center of the operation right away. No sane man would do that, but I questioned Tim's sanity all the time.

Forty minutes later, Zayne parked the car on a flat section of the fifteen acres I'd found online. The view of the lake was stunning, with a variety of leafy trees. One thing I didn't like about Spokane was the abundance of pine. I wanted to see the leaves change colors in the fall, and I knew River did as well. She talked about it all the time. Montana had mountains full of autumnal colors. Even if I had to plant them myself, I wanted our property to have that too.

The stifling tension in the car had me jumping out before Zayne had turned the engine off. I needed air. I'd hoped that Jace would understand my decision, but apparently not.

A soft breeze blew over the lake, the green leaves rustling in the wind. It was peaceful and quiet. From the map, it appeared that everyone had fifteen acres, which would cut down on noise and provide a bit of privacy. I shoved my hand in my jeans pocket and continued to walk toward the water. I spotted a dock and boat slip. It needed a bit of updating, but I was fine with that. Even belonging to a wealthy family, I'd never shied away from hard work.

A boat buzzed by, and the waves lazily slapped against the shore. There was a large open area, then trees on each side of the property. The only reason I knew there was a home next to us was from the Google Earth map. I suspected there were at least five acres between us, though. The more I walked the land, the more I fell in love with it.

Jace kept his distance, obviously still angry. Zayne caught up with me after a few minutes. "Does the property have gas, water, and electrical readily available, or would you have to have it all put in?"

"Put in, but that would allow me to position the house where I want it. I'm thinking the view of the lake is what River would love the most."

"That's what I would do. I bet the sunset is stunning bouncing off the water. Don't forget internet. I remember when Pierce was building his place, providers were scarce. He ended up paying for his own fiber optic lines to be put in. You might have to do the same."

"Good to know." I focused on Jace again. "I'm not sure why he's so pissed about my plan with Tim."

Zayne arched a brow at me. "Really?"

I rubbed my stubbled jawline. "No, but my head's not in a good place so I've apparently missed something."

Zayne folded his arms across his massive chest. The guy cleared me by a few inches and was built like a fucking brick wall.

"First of all, you didn't ask how he felt about it before you made a decision. These are your people, man. It's obvious you guys are tight. More than tight. It's clear that you all have lived some life together."

"We have," I confirmed his suspicions.

"And have you really thought this through? I mean, of course you'll do everything possible to bring River back, but life rarely goes down the way we think it will. Shit happens, and you're going to be in a dangerous environment. Jace might lose you, Brynn, and River."

Anxiety pulled and tugged at my insides. "I know. If I had another idea that would work in a short time, I'd do it. I hate Tim. He should have already done the right thing and told us where she is. Instead, he's playing God. He fucking disgusts me. River is all that matters to me. Second is Brynn. That might sound shitty, but those two are my priorities."

"Cut yourself some slack and ditch the guilt. No man should choose another woman over the one they're in love with. Nothing shitty about it. Plus, she's pregnant."

Feeling the nervous tic in my jaw, I pursed my lips. "Yeah, I haven't forgotten."

Jace approached us, appearing calmer than he had been ten minutes ago. "It's peaceful out here. I think River would like the property and the lake a lot."

"I do too. We could all hang and relax, disconnect from work and the city." I was following Jace's lead, but he seemed to have cooled off.

"You better build a nice-ass deck to grill on where we can all sit outside and see the water."

I almost smiled. This was Jace's way of meeting me on common ground and calling a truce.

"I was thinking the same thing. And a boat of course." I squinted against the afternoon sun but loved the warmth of it on my skin.

"Definitely." Our gazes locked. "Zayne, we'll be back in a few."

"Stay where I can see you," Zayne ordered.

At times, having Zayne around threw me back into my childhood, when Mom warned me to stay nearby so she could keep an eye on me.

"Where are we going?" Jace asked as he walked beside me.

"Not far. I wanted to talk to you about the shit with Tim. The plan." I squinted as we headed to the lake. "I realize this isn't easy. It's not for me either. Working for Tim is a last resort."

Jace shoved his hands into his pockets, his expression serious. "I know, Holden, but I'm in danger of losing Brynn, River, and you. That's more than half of my family." His deep voice cracked, fear bleeding through.

We reached the edge of the property and stood with our backs to Zayne. "Mine too, Jace. I have Mom, but other than that ... if I lose my girls." I gulped, a swell of heartache rippling through me. "We've known each other since we were kids, Jace. You're my brother. I'd do this for you, too."

Jace rubbed his neck. "I'd do it for you as well."

We watched the water lap against the shore. "I'm sorry I ripped you a new asshole. Going after Tim scares the shit out of me, but I have to find River. I don't have any other options."

"I know. And I won't say a word to Brynn. I was just being a dick." He smirked. "Although she'd be hell to deal with even if she is sick."

I chuckled. He was right.

"Are we good then?" I asked, glancing at him.

"Yeah. We are." Jace slapped me on the back. "Buy this property, Holden. It's gorgeous."

It wasn't necessary to say anything else. Jace's approval of the property was enough.

I glanced at my watch. "I'll call and put in an offer. I'm shocked I love the first property I've seen, but when it's right, it's right."

My cell vibrated in my back pocket, and I reached for it.

"This is Holden."

"It's Pierce. You at a point you can come over and we can make a plan? Brian from the FBI is on his way."

Holy shit, this was really happening. I swallowed the fear down, squared my shoulders, and took a breath. I was going to bring my baby home if it fucking killed me.

This time Pierce and Sutton were in their living room when we all arrived. The aroma of fresh coffee tickled my nose as we exchanged hellos.

"Are you ready?" Pierce asked, sinking into the leather chair near the recliner. Instead of jeans and a Westbrook Security shirt, he'd opted for dress slacks and a navy button-down shirt.

"As ready as I'll ever be, I suspect." I sat on the couch with Jace.

Pierce glanced at his watch as Sutton set a tray on the coffee table with a white carafe and matching cups. Zayne followed her with two more, one with crackers, meat, and cheese, the other with soda. I was a little puzzled about the food, but I'd find out soon enough. Apparently, we were going to be here for a while. "I'd better use the bathroom before we get started. Looks like it might be a long meeting."

"It's down this hall, second door on the left." Sutton pointed me in the right direction. She seemed all business. Her white silk blouse was tucked into gray slacks, and her hair was piled on the top of her head in a tight bun. As I headed down the hallway, I studied the thin chinking between the logs of their house. To me, they'd found a fantastic balance of light and dark wood. Some places had log walls as well, which I didn't like. I also didn't care for a ceiling that was all wood.

I preferred a lighter wood so the interior wouldn't be so dark in the Spokane winters. If we built on the property I'd just seen, we would have a harsher winter than here. Sandpoint, Idaho, was only an hour away. It would allow for the feeling of a small town, but not too far to drive when we needed something. Plus, the club would be in the city, so it would work out well. I made a mental note to ask Sutton and Pierce questions about construction and who they'd used.

Once I located the bathroom, I relieved myself and continued to study the design. They'd gone for a more contemporary fixture style instead of rustic. I was finding that our tastes were similar. I couldn't wait to talk to River about the ideas.

I washed and dried my hands, then gave myself a good, hard look in the mirror. I shoved my fingers through my hair and blew out a sigh. I was ready to make a plan to take Tim down.

I opened the door, and voices floated down the hall. Realizing someone else had arrived, I hurried to the living room. Once I rounded the corner, I screeched to a halt. I rubbed my eyes in hopes of clearing my vision, but nothing changed. The same fucking scene was in front of me.

The room fell into a hush, and everyone's attention landed on me. "What in God's name is happening right now?" I placed my hands on my hips, shock coursing through my veins, fueling my anger.

"Hello, Holden."

"What the hell are you doing here?" I growled.

Chapter Twenty-Two

"Holden, I'm Brian Donovan with the FBI. This is my colleague, Michelle Hunter." Brian extended his hand to me, and I shook it. Brian's dark hair was thinning even though he appeared to be in his early forties. I assumed the premature loss of hair was associated with his job. All of the stress probably screwed with Brian's sleep and aging. His stern expression softened momentarily, then slipped back into place, his alert gaze assessing me. I didn't blame him. I was the son of a criminal.

I balked. "Michelle, huh? You're with the FBI?" Peering at Jace, I realized he was in as much shock as me. She looked exactly like the Becky we all knew, except that she was dressed in gray slacks and a white shirt that was nearly buttoned up to her neck. Her blonde hair was swept up in a tight ponytail. She fit the FBI tight-ass idea that I'd always had in my head.

"That's Becky, her name isn't Michelle," Jace explained as though the FBI had no fucking clue what her real name was.

"I'm sorry, Holden." Michelle stepped forward, her gaze unapologetic. "Your family was an assignment."

Static hummed in my brain. This wasn't happening. How the

hell had I invited an FBI agent into my life? My nostrils flared and I narrowed my eyes. "That's why you cut my girlfriend's neck?" I shook my head. "I'm not working with her. She attacked River right in front of me at my house." I folded my arms, standing firm with my decision.

"The cut to River's neck was an accident. She fought back and I cut her. For that, I'm sorry. I was trying to warn her, but you came up the stairs and I ran out of time."

"Warn her? This gets better by the minute," I said, glaring at her.

"Holden, I know this is difficult for you, but I've been undercover looking into Tim. And Hannah's murder," Michelle said.

The room tilted on its side, and I scrambled to understand what was happening. "Pierce, did you know about this?"

"No. I'm on a need-to-know basis with Brian when we're working a case together. That's it. I had no idea about Michelle or Hannah's case."

I believed him. He made sense.

Hannah. Her name finally registered in my overloaded brain. "Wait, what? Hannah was *murdered?*" A ball of intense emotions lodged in my chest—rage, relief, curiosity, and grief.

I remained standing as Sutton slipped into the room and sat in the recliner. "Hi Brian. Michelle," she said, flashing a warm smile at them.

"Michelle will be difficult to adjust to." My forehead creased in a frown. "So let me get this straight. I screwed an FBI agent and let you into my home and business?"

I was acting like a straight-up ass, but I was fucking pissed.

Crimson crawled up Michelle's neck and cheeks. "I'm sorry, Holden. I will say that you're not in any kind of trouble. Your club was run very well."

I snorted. "Except for Laura." Raising my hands in the air, I called a truce. "Whatever. It's in the past. I need to find River." I reminded myself that my pregnant girlfriend was the reason I was here. The same reason that Michelle and Brian were. In my head, I gave Michelle a nickname to help me feel a little better ... Bitch Becky Michelle. I decided I'd deal with her later.

"Let's get down to business, then," Brian suggested.

I crossed the room and sat down next to Jace. He leaned over and whispered, "That's some fucked up shit, man." He nodded at Michelle.

Shaking my head, I attempted to clear the dark cloud from my mind. "Is someone going to fill me in about my sister? How did the investigation start? I tried multiple times to get the police involved, but it was swept under the rug."

Michelle and Brian sat down in the additional chairs, their eyes trained on me.

"One of the men at the station did look into the case right before it was closed. He just kept quiet about it. Once he found a few leads, he looped us in, and we took over. We're still investigating, Holden. However, we can say with absolute certainty that Hannah was definitely murdered," Brian explained in a matter-of-fact tone.

"Do you have any suspects?" I fidgeted in my seat as my pulse kicked up a notch. All this time, I'd thought no one had listened to me.

"I was looking into your father when I was with you," Michelle said.

Shock slammed into me like a hellbent MMA wrestler, and my mouth gaped. "Tim? Do you have anything confirming this, or is it a hunch you're following?"

"Both. If he didn't kill her, then we suspect that he knows who did," Michelle explained.

The shit just kept rolling downhill. "I guess you're hoping that my working for him will solve multiple problems."

"That's the idea, at least," Brian added.

"What's the first step?" I listened intently while Brian explained the plan and the backup I'd have. Instead of wearing a tap, I'd have a device on my phone that would record everything between Tim and me. All I had to do was press the button located on the side of my cell. To Tim, it would appear as though I were putting my cell to sleep instead of activating the device.

"I think it would make sense if I called and told him that I wouldn't be able to rebuild the club fast enough and need money now. Since the insurance will take a while to pay out, I figured this would be the easiest conversation to stick to. It's all true except that I don't want to work with him. In my mind, the fewer lies I have to tell, the better chance I have of pulling this off."

"Exactly. I'll help you keep everything straight," Pierce added, taking a sip of his coffee.

I nodded, relieved to have Pierce guiding me along as well.

"When should I call Tim?" I asked.

"We were thinking right now. Put your phone on speaker," Brian said.

I inhaled deeply as my heart thundered in my chest. I hoped like hell this would work. I removed my phone from my back pocket and pulled up Tim's number. I glanced at Pierce, and he nodded.

Jace patted me on the back. "You've got this, man."

Once Jace had processed through my decision to work for Tim, he'd come to terms with it, and had been supportive.

I tapped the screen, and his phone rang through my speaker.

"Son," Tim answered.

I couldn't dial in his tone yet. Was he surprised that I called, or was he expecting it?

"Are you in town?" I asked, knowing full well that he was in Oregon.

"No, but I'll be back late tonight."

"Okay. Um ... I've been thinking about your offer. The club is going to take a long time to rebuild, and I need money now."

Tim chuckled, and I could picture a cocky sneer on his face. The same expression I wanted to punch until he was unrecognizable.

"I knew you'd come around once you understood the insurance process. Tell you what, I'll cover the entire cost of the club being rebuilt if you join me."

I cringed. No way in hell did I want his dirty fucking money tied to my club. "Well, it was your fault, so I'll accept. It will allow me to get on my feet financially." I already was, but he didn't know that. I had never shared my finances with my parents. I was grown, and it wasn't any of their business.

"It's the least I can do since I was behind it in the first place," he said, a smile in his voice.

The sorry bastard found the situation entertaining.

"When can I start?" I wanted to move this along as quickly as possible.

"Let's have an early lunch at Riverfront Park. We'll be able to talk openly there," Tim said.

"What time?" I massaged my aching neck, once again wishing this nightmare was already over.

"Let's meet at ten in the morning. I have a busy day ahead of me," Tim explained.

"Sounds like a plan." I was ready to end the call when he asked the question I'd hoped to avoid.

"And Holden? Are you planning on leaving River alone?" His tone was no-nonsense. He wasn't fucking with me.

I ground my molars together, preparing to lie my ass off. "On one condition." I didn't dare look at Brian, Michelle, or Pierce. This hadn't been planned.

"What's that?"

"If you know who is involved with her disappearance, tell them to release her. Once she's safely returned, I'll leave her alone for good. She's pregnant, Dad. I need my baby to be safe."

A heavy silence hung on the line, and I held my breath, wondering if I'd fucked everything up.

"I'll ask around to see if I can find anything out. No promises, though. As I've said before, I didn't have anything to do with her disappearance and neither did Logan."

"I understand. Plus, the thumb drive proved it as well," I added.

"Well, I'm glad we've moved past that at least. I'll see you tomorrow morning."

"All right." I disconnected the call and my gaze swept over the faces staring at me.

"That was risky, Holden," Pierce said, speaking first.

"I know, but I was thinking that he might call—" Multiple pings filled the room.

Sutton glanced at her phone. "It's Tim. He's making a call." She tapped her screen a few times, then his voice came through loud and clear.

"It's me. What the hell are you doing? Did you know that River is pregnant with Holden's kid?"

Silence.

"Your plan won't work now. Let her fucking go. If anything happens and you're busted, you'll go down for not only River, but the baby too. Stop being so goddamned stupid and get her back to Spokane or I'm coming after her myself."

The pause was longer this time, then Tim barked out a laugh.

"When I have my men behind me you won't think it's so funny. You have twenty-four hours. I won't tell you again." Tim disconnected the call, and we all stared at each other with hopeful expressions.

"That's what I was hoping for when I told him she was pregnant." I pointed to Sutton's phone.

"It was a gamble, but it worked. He obviously knows this person well because he never announces who he is. They're familiar enough with each other that they have each other's numbers on their cells, too," Brian said.

"So, we're set for ten tomorrow morning." I rose from my seat, anxiety coursing through my veins with every beat of my heart. "I hope to hell this works before I get in too deep."

"Me too," Jace said quietly. "Me too."

Over the next hour, Brian and Pierce went over all the details for my morning meeting. One thing was for sure, taking action was helping me not to fixate on River as much. Even though this was all about rescuing her, it gave my tormented mind something else to focus on: the solution.

It was almost three in the afternoon when Zayne parked in front of Chance's place. I was eager to fill Brynn and Chance in, as well as grab a beer.

I closed the front door behind me as Jace and I entered the house. Brynn was in the kitchen with a big bag of cheddar Ruffles in her hand. A playful smile eased across her features. "The edible worked." She wiggled her brows at us.

"Excellent." Jace strolled over to her and gave her a big hug and a kiss on the corner of her lips.

"I'm happy to cook something for dinner. What sounds good?" I placed my phone on the kitchen counter, then wrapped her up in my arms. "I'm glad you're eating." I kissed the top of her head, then rummaged through the fridge for ideas on what to make.

"Do you know what sounds good?" She hopped up on the counter and swung her legs just like she used to when she was a little girl.

"What?" Chance said, joining us. He snatched a chip out of Brynn's hand and grinned at her before he loudly chomped on it.

Brynn's lower lip jutted out. "Those are mine. I'm not sharing."

"I'll buy you as many bags as you want. I promise." Chance slipped his arm around her, and she leaned her head against his shoulder.

"What was I saying? I keep forgetting." Brynn giggled.

I straightened and flung some cabinets open, assessing the options.

"Steak. A big-ass steak and a baked potato ... with butter, sour cream, bacon bits, and chives." She popped another chip into her mouth. "Oh, and roasted Brussels sprouts ... and rolls! Yeast rolls! Big, fat, buttery, fresh ones straight out of the oven. Then, for dessert, some chocolate. Like Death by Chocolate from Bennigan's. Wait. Is Bennigan's even open anymore? Well, it doesn't matter. Something similar would work, too." Brynn rubbed her flat tummy.

I snickered, then everyone burst into laughter. Brynn was definitely stoned, but I'd make anything she wanted as long as she ate. She desperately needed to put on weight before she started chemo.

"How about dinner on the deck then? I'll clean the grill," Chance said, grinning at her.

"I'll call in a steak order at Eggers and pick it up," Jace offered.

"Oh, yes!" Brynn's eyes widened. "Wagyu ribeye for me, please. Oh my God, they're so good. I don't even need a knife to cut the meat, and it melts on your tongue. I could almost orgasm from the first bite."

We all chuckled. Whatever Jace had picked up for her was working better than expected. It seemed like our girl was ready to play as well.

"As far as the orgasm. I'm happy to help you with that," Jace said.

"And?" Brynn looked up at Chance.

"I'm in," Chance said, smiling at her.

"I feel like it's been a hot minute since I've had both of you." Her green eyes raked up and down Jace's body.

"I'll find something else to do while you all have some fun. Just take it into Chance's room so I can prepare dinner."

Jace called in the order and scheduled to pick it up in a few hours. He slapped me on the back as he followed Chance and Brynn to Chance's bedroom.

I leaned against the counter, my head hanging down. My cock was so fucking hard it hurt. River's beautiful, naked body flashed through my mind, and I considered taking a shower to relieve the pressure.

The doorbell interrupted my fantasy, and I hurried to the front door. Peering through the peephole, I swung the door open.

"What the hell are you doing here?" I said, my tone sharp and bordering on rude.

Chapter Twenty-Three

"It's against my nature to apologize, but here I am. Can we talk?" Michelle asked, her eyes pleading with me.

I stepped onto the porch and closed the door behind me. No wonder Zayne didn't let me know who was here. The FBI could apparently do whatever they wanted ... without anyone's consent.

"What do you want?" I didn't waste any time and cut straight to the chase. The summer breeze blew hot and humid as I waited for her reply.

"First, to offer my congratulations to you and River. I didn't realize she was pregnant." Michelle sat down òn one of the burgundy chairs.

"Neither did I. The test was in her purse. I found it after she was taken." I leaned against the square pole and crossed my ankles.

Michelle fidgeted in her seat and focused on Zayne's Mercedes.

"Why are you here, Bec ... Michelle? I thought we worked through this in the meeting at Pierce's."

"I never meant to hurt her that night. I swear. She's strong and tough. She caught me off guard and my hand slipped. You have no idea how awful I felt." Michelle's attention landed on Zayne, who had reappeared from the side of the house. He was obviously making his way around the property.

"Fine." I stared at her, not giving a rat's ass what her excuse was. "Anything else?"

"I wanted to explain and make sure you understand that I'm on your side." She tucked a blonde wisp of hair behind her ear.

"Well, it doesn't seem like I have much of a choice. You're FBI and pulling rank on me." I emphasized my words with air quotes.

"Look, Holden, you can believe what you want, but this is the honest truth. I was assigned to look into your father for suspected weapons dealing, but while I was there, I learned that he might be connected to Hannah's death. I'd dated you long enough that I realized you were oblivious to what Tim was involved in. You were never on the FBI's radar, but you're Tim's son, so I had to keep my eye on you as well." She pressed her lips together, then darted her eyes away, scanning the area around us.

"So that's why you fucked me a few times a day? To keep an eye on me?" I smirked as her cheeks flushed a bright pink. Michelle was into rough sex, and I doubted she'd shared that tidbit with many people. She also preferred it up the ass. I'd been happy to accommodate anything she wanted as long as I had verbal consent and a safe word. I'd even taken it a step further and recorded a conversation with her giving consent. Rough sex can leave marks, and no way in hell would I be accused of something I wasn't guilty of, especially if it wasn't even my idea.

"To be honest, it was hands down the best sex of my life, and I started falling for you." She looked away, embarrassed she'd admitted her feelings.

I chuckled and stared up into the crystal-blue cloudless sky. "Glad it wasn't too difficult for you." I focused on her, and my gaze narrowed. "I can let that piece go. Sex is sex, it meant nothing to me. You weren't my type, I just kept you around for a distraction. But ..." I pointed at her. "You betrayed me when I let you into the lower level of the club. I brought you in and trusted that it was all confidential.

There wasn't even a hint of concern on your face. That's what I'm pissed about. And how you warned River about my family was completely uncalled for. You could have found another way."

My gut clenched at the next realization. "You really were jealous, weren't you?" I chuckled and turned away from her. Spotting Zayne near the car, I trained my attention on him so I wouldn't lose my shit and yell at Michelle. She was hiding behind her job, and it wasn't going to fly with me. I turned to her again.

"I left all of the details of the lower level out of my report. The only thing the FBI knows is that we were sleeping together for me to get closer to you and gather information," she said, obviously proud of herself for keeping my secret, but mostly hers. Once I'd introduced her to the bottom floor, and the different rooms, all she wanted to do was play. The BDSM room sure as hell didn't hold any secrets concerning Tim's weapons deals or Hannah's murder.

An unsettling energy buzzed through me. I clenched my jaw, willing myself not to tear her a new one. "Did you find out anything that could help me with Tim tomorrow?"

She stood and smoothed her gray slacks. "I'm hoping his threat will bring River home, but whoever took her is playing hard ball. I wouldn't count on it."

Michelle didn't have to say that aloud. I was thinking the same thing. "I'm not either. I would like to make Tim slip up, though. He's at his weakest when he's frustrated, so it's my job to rattle him. The best way I can do that is to tell him what I know without sharing how I learned it. It's super risky because he could figure out his car is tapped, and we'd lose our only connection to finding my girlfriend." *Girlfriend. She should be my fiancée.*

"If you have to play that card, come up with a reason when he asks how you know," she suggested.

"I saw a ton of papers on his desk and his laptop was unlocked. It's how I found out that he deals weapons." I looked at her. This time I actually wanted a response.

"It should work. We don't want him to be suspicious of your true motives." She glanced up at me and fluttered her lashes like she did when we were dating. I doubted a playful, sultry expression was part of her job.

"I'll feel it out tomorrow morning then." I shoved my hand into my jeans pocket and stared at her. I wanted to see her face for this next part. "Were you shocked when Tim admitted to burning down 4 Play?"

She nodded. "He totally took me off guard."

I shook my head. "I know that feeling. He called me while I was standing in the parking lot watching my business burn to the goddamned ground. So, believe me when I say that I'll do anything to take this motherfucker down. And I won't even lie about it. I'll enjoy every beautiful second of seeing him fall."

"Who else knows about this? Brian didn't mention the club at all. Today is the first I've heard of his involvement with the arson."

"Just my friends, Pierce, Sutton, and Zayne. I trust them to keep their mouths closed. I'm hoping that you'll do the same. Use the information only when you absolutely need to in order to put the son of a bitch away for the rest of his life." I propped my elbows up on the railing and leaned over.

"I'll sit on it until the right time. But what I don't understand is why? Why would your father do that to you?" Surprise laced her words.

"He wanted to make sure I would work for him. He made the offer earlier that day, then after our breakfast, I got the call that the building was on fire. I rushed over to 4 Play and Tim called me while I was there. He flat out admitted to me that he was behind it. The cops know it was arson, but not who is responsible for it."

"He's obviously used to getting his way." Michelle put her hand on my arm, and I glared at her, moving out of her reach.

Disappointment registered on her features, and she pulled away. "Please be careful when you talk to him tomorrow. Use your instincts. They're good."

I huffed. "Apparently not. They were shit when it came to you."

She raised her hands. "I deserve that, but it's my job. If I worried about hurting someone's feelings every time I turned around, I wouldn't get anything done. So please understand this, Holden. I apologized and kept your secret about the club safe. If you want my help, you'll stop acting like a total asshole and focus on working together. I'm damn good at what I do, and I have to deal with egotistical men all fucking day long. Do us both a favor and cut the shit."

And there it was. Shades of Becky at her finest. "*If* I want your help?" I scoffed. "I'm not the one that showed up at the door to apologize and talk. This conversation never needed to happen. I think you're simply enjoying the scenery and wanted to have a trip down memory lane. Maybe even hoping to have one last fuck before River is back?"

Michelle stepped away and shook her head. "Good luck, Holden. I hope I won't be attending your funeral soon."

With that, she hopped down the stairs and stomped to her vehicle. She started the car and peeled out of Chance's driveway.

Zayne arched a brow and joined me on the porch, a slight grin pulling at the corner of his lips. "Should I ask?"

I dragged my fingers along my stubbled jaw. "Michelle's a piece of work. Watch your back with her. I don't give a fuck if she's FBI or related to the most powerful family in the world. She's mentally unstable."

"That bad, huh?"

"Worse. She came over to tell me she never told the FBI about the lower level of the club and the membership." I gave a half-shrug. "It's not illegal, so I'm not sure why she was making a point of pretending like she helped. She invaded my life and lied to me. She didn't do me a solid."

"It might not be illegal, but you don't want to be on their radar either. They could shut 4 Play down and investigate for years and tie up your funds. A lot of similar places are wrapped up in sex rings, drugs, and prostitution. Hell, the FBI might have shut you down permanently because they didn't like the way you smiled." Zayne ran his hand through his hair. "So, I'm not telling you to like what she did overall, but in that area, she did you a favor." Zayne grinned at me. "On top of it, she came over to tell you, so you didn't stick your foot in your mouth."

"Why are you smiling about it?" I stared at him, trying to figure out what was going through his head.

"Apparently you're one hell of a fuck." Zayne chuckled. "Women don't do favors like that unless they want something in return."

I massaged the back of my neck. "You gathered that from what I shared with you?"

"Nope. I got it from her body language and the way she looked at you. You could have taken her straight to your bed if you'd wanted to. I saw the whole thing. You made it very clear that you're in love with River and you refused to cross the line with Michelle or anyone else. I don't think you'll have any more trouble from her."

"Let's hope not. I'm not interested in Michelle at all. The only reason I'm putting up with her is for River, which is ironic because, when River learns about all of this, I'll probably have to restrain her from hunting Michelle down and beating her ass."

Zayne laughed. "Might be fun to watch."

The front door flung open, interrupting our chat.

"Holden, it's Brynn!" The color had drained from Chance's cheeks, and he looked scared as hell. "I've called the ambulance," he said.

I flew past him and into the house, searching for her. I darted to Chance's bedroom and gasped.

"Brynn?" I swear to God, my heart stopped beating.

Chapter Twenty-Four

Chills coasted over my skin as I focused on a very pale Brynn. Her eyes were closed. "Brynn?" I ran over to her as her eyelids fluttered open, her breathing labored. I glanced at her stomach and swore. She looked like she was six months pregnant.

Crawling onto the bed, I took her limp hand in mine and kissed her knuckles. "Hang on, hon. Help is on the way. Stay with us."

Fear danced across Brynn's face as she attempted to take a deep breath.

"It's okay. The ambulance will be here soon," I promised.

"What the fuck happened? I don't understand." I asked Jace while I continued to brush her red hair off her clammy forehead, willing her to be all right. Tears clouded my vision while I spoke softly to her.

Jace bowed his head, and his body shuddered with a shaky breath. He held her other hand as we waited for the paramedics. "I think her stomach is pushing on her lungs."

Sirens filled the air and grew louder with each passing second, then the EMTs filed into the house. A firm grip on my shoulder tugged me away from Brynn.

"Holden, you have to move and allow them to get to her," Zayne ordered.

I stared at him blankly, then hopped off the bed. Jace backed up against the wall, panic-stricken. Zayne and I joined him while we waited for Chance to explain Brynn's condition to the paramedics. He appeared calm, but I knew better since his hands were shaking.

I helplessly watched as they checked her vitals and loaded her on the gurney. "Come on, Brynn. Hang in there," I whispered. Sweat trickled down my spine and forehead.

My back slid down the wall as I crumpled to the floor. This wasn't good. In a matter of hours, Brynn's stomach had transformed. The doctors had to help her, or she wouldn't even make it to her first chemo treatment.

"Who is riding with her?" One of the EMTs called out.

"Chance is her husband," I said before I realized it. One of us had to pretend to be. Her fucking parents were in Europe. The hospital wouldn't talk to us about her medical options, but they could speak with Chance since I'd offered him up as her spouse. He was the best one out of the three of us. Plus, he was madly in love with her. I had to meet with my sorry excuse of a father tomorrow. Jace was a great guy, but he always cracked under pressure. Chance had a consistent, steady head on his shoulders, even in a crisis.

The place cleared out as fast as it had filled up with the medical team. Chance waved at us, then hurried after her. I spotted his wallet on the nightstand along with his phone. I snatched them up and hauled ass behind him.

"Chance!" I waved the items in the air right before they closed the ambulance doors. "He needs his wallet and cell."

The EMT opened the door again, and I ran over, handing Chance his belongings. "Call us as soon as they have her stable with a room number." I wanted to go with him, but Jace and I would just sit in the waiting area. Since Chance was Brynn's fictional husband, he'd be able to stay with her until she was stabilized. Plus, if Pierce learned anything about River, I needed to be available to help. Not to mention that I didn't trust Tim to not show up in Washington unannounced. I didn't want him anywhere near Brynn, and the best way to protect her was to keep my distance until she felt better.

He nodded, his face twisted with fear as I backed up so they could rush her to the hospital.

I stood rooted to the ground in Chance's front yard as I watched them drive away, the sirens piercing the humid summer air. Returning to the porch, I sank down on the steps. Sighing hard and giving into the hot wash of uncontrollable emotions, I rested my chin on my knees and lost my shit.

The porch creaked behind me, but I remained still. I couldn't handle looking at anyone. My heart couldn't take anymore. First River, and now Brynn. What if the doctors couldn't help Brynn? What if she died, and this was the last time we would see her alive? Jesus. How the hell would I be able to tell River that Brynn had passed away while she was gone? I flexed my fingers, then clenched them into a tight fist. None of this shit was okay. It wasn't right. We'd been through enough.

The small thread that was left of my sanity snapped, and my anger was quickly redirected toward my bastard of a father. Fuck Tim. I wanted answers, goddammit.

I rose and hurried down the steps. Even though I hadn't seen him, Zayne's presence was right behind me.

I stopped abruptly, then spun on my heel. "Can you give me some space for now?"

"A little." Compassion filled his green eyes.

I stomped off like a two-year-old that hadn't gotten his way. Any ounce of maturity had checked out the second Brynn had left the property. Seeing her like that fucking gutted me. I couldn't imagine how hard this was going to hit Chance when he had time to catch his breath.

Reaching the end of the driveway, I turned right and walked

down the road. I had no idea where I was headed, but I had to walk. Hell, I wasn't even sure I could go back to Chance's after seeing Brynn struggling to breathe. Too much had happened in the last few days for it not to hang over my head like a black storm cloud that had the potential to kick up a tornado and rip right through me at any given second. I was definitely about to lose my mind.

I wasn't sure how long I'd been walking, but the sun had begun its descent, leaving streaks of purple and gold in its wake. A part of me wondered if River could see the sky. If so, did she know that I was thinking about her? Finally, I came to a stop and turned back toward Chance's place.

Zayne had kept true to his word. Although I could see him, he hadn't smothered me. My head cleared enough to realize that I'd left Jace by himself. Maybe he needed the time alone, too.

Zayne waited, then fell in step beside me. "Brynn's alive. That's what you need to focus on."

"Yeah, like you have any fucking clue of what that did to me today," I snapped.

Zayne's expression didn't change. "I lost someone. There wasn't any hope of a recovery. So, yeah, I understand what you're going through. Brynn is still alive."

Shit. I'd been a total ass.

"I'm sorry I lashed out at you . . . and that you lost someone." A part of me wanted to ask what had happened, but I couldn't. I was doing my best not to spiral out.

"I know my advice will be difficult, but focus on River. Meet with Tim, see if you can get him to slip up. Control the things that you can, Holden. Brynn will have an entire medical team at her disposal. I'm not trying to be a dick, but there isn't shit you can do for her. She'll have doctors and nurses around the clock checking on her constantly. The best thing you can do for Brynn is to bring River home. She needs some hope. Not only has it been too much for her physically, but mentally as well."

I blew out a huge sigh. "It fucked me up seeing Brynn struggling to breathe like that."

"I'm sure it fucked everyone up." Zayne continued to look straight ahead as he spoke.

Guilt elbowed me in the side, and I winced. I hadn't even checked on Jace. I'd stormed out of the house and left him behind. "I need to talk to Jace."

Without another word, we walked the rest of the way back. By the time I climbed the steps of Chance's porch, the darkness had settled in for the evening. Crickets softly chirped, the only noise in the otherwise silent neighborhood.

I entered the living room and nodded at Zayne before I closed the door. Jace was sitting on the couch, staring at the television. A single lamp softly lit the space.

"You realize the TV isn't on, right?" I asked him as I sank wearily into the chair.

"Yeah. It's just the focal point, I guess." He looked at me.

Jace's eyes were swollen and red-rimmed. I was glad he'd been able to let it out. It sucked when the emotion sat on your chest like a stubborn elephant unwilling to move.

"Any word from Chance?" I fidgeted in my seat.

"No. I assumed he'd call you first." He ran his hands through his hair and propped his foot up on the coffee table in front of him.

"Have you eaten anything?" I stood, ready to at least grab a beer.

"No ..." Jace glanced at me. "The last thing I tasted was Brynn's lips. I don't want to lose that. Not yet." He touched his fingertips to his mouth.

"I get it." I made my way to the kitchen. Pulling the refrigerator door open, I moved out of the way as a bag of Brynn's Ruffles toppled to the wood floor. I snatched them up and placed them on the counter. "She still puts her chips on top of the fridge." I shook my head. "Strangest place for them." I peeked at Jace, who had a silly grin on his face.

"She's done that since we were in middle school. I guess I'd forgotten because she rarely eats chips these days." He sat up straight. "Do you think she's going to make it, Holden?"

It was definitely time for a Heineken. I twisted the top off and took a long drink. "Yeah. I do." Returning to my chair, I plopped down. "I'm not sure what happened today, but she's a fighter. She's not any more ready to leave us than we are for her to go." I picked at the corner of the label that was wrapped around the green bottle.

"Maybe we overdid it in the bedroom earlier." His brows tugged low, shadowing his blue eyes.

I couldn't help but grin. Brynn could definitely hold her own with these two. "It probably made her feel alive and took her mind off her cancer. You guys did her a favor. Don't give it a second thought."

"You're right. I'm trying to figure out what the fuck happened. One minute she was ... not fine, obviously, but eating. The next ... she was struggling to breathe."

"What happened, exactly?" I asked, propping my elbows on my knees. "I just realized I have no clue of how it all went down."

Jace stared out of the window and shook his head. "I don't know. After we were done playing, she dozed off. There was still an hour before I had to pick up the steaks, so I came out here and turned on the television. Chance flew out of his room a little later, fear written all over his face. He told me to stay with Brynn. I hauled ass to get to her, but I stopped once I saw her. The sound of her gasping for air was the worst thing I've ever heard in my entire life." His shoulders slumped forward, and he wiped moisture from his cheeks. "It was fucked up. Her stomach ..."

Silence fell between us. It was heavy and loud, or maybe it was all in my head. "You should crash here tonight. That way if we can see Brynn, Zayne can take us straight to the hospital." Jace reached over and grabbed the remote control and finally turned the television on.

I removed my phone from my back pocket and held onto it. "Yeah, okay. Sounds good."

It was nice to hear a sound other than the beating of my broken heart.

My cell rang at nearly two in the morning. Chance's name flashed across the screen, and I answered quickly, jackknifing up in the bed.

"Hey, how's she doing?" I glanced over at Jace, who had stretched out on the couch and fallen asleep.

"She's finally resting. It's been a flurry of nurses, doctors, tests, questions, and more tests. Bottom line is her cancer is much worse than they realized. Her stomach was distended from the fluid and tumors erupting inside her. There are so many of them, Holden."

"Holy shit." I stood, needing to pace while he updated me. "Can they operate or ... " I had no fucking clue what that treatment even looked like.

"They can't. There's too many and they're small. The doctors called and the Knight Center at OHSU in Portland, Oregon has a bed for her. She's going to be transferred by medical flight in the next few hours or so." Exhaustion lingered in his tone.

"The hospital has an amazing reputation and cutting-edge treatment and technologies that other places in the country don't have." A classmate had landed a job there while she was pre-med. She loved to talk about how amazing the Knight Center was.

"Yeah, I've heard the same thing. By the way, thanks for telling them I was her husband. I wasn't thinking fast enough."

"You're the best person to be with her, Chance. I have to deal with Tim and ... Jace will help me stay sane. Plus, well, she loves you. I'm not sure she's figured it out yet. What I do know is that you have a pretty level head and can understand the doctors, since your parents are both surgeons."

"I've always resented them for putting their careers before me, but now ... Now I'm grateful I can throw their names around a little bit. I think it got Brynn taken care of faster."

"Then toss the husband card around like a motherfucker."

"Hey, man...can you pack a bag for me and Brynn and bring it to the hospital? I'll see if you and Jace can see her. It looks like it might be a while before we come back to Spokane." Chance's voice cracked. "I have no idea what to expect."

My throat tightened with dread. "Just focus on being there with her. I can fly down any weekend to see her and I'll bring clean clothes. Jace too. Whatever it takes, you know we're all in this together."

"Thanks, man. I'll see you when you get here."

I disconnected the call, then gently shook Jace awake. "Hey, Brynn is going to be transported to the Knight Center at OHSU in Portland. Chance is going with her. I need to pack them a bag, and we'll take it to him. We might be able to see her for a minute before she's transferred."

Jace blinked at me a few times, then sat up slowly. "Okay. What do you need me to do?"

"I'll pack their clothes. Why don't you grab their toothbrushes and deodorant and stuff? It'll be quicker if we do it together."

Jace stood and stretched. "On it."

I hurried to the front door and searched for Zayne, but I didn't see him. Fishing for my phone in my back pocket, I typed out a quick message that we'd need to head to the hospital in a few minutes.

Chapter Twenty-Five

Zayne sped to Sacred Heart as quickly as possible. I was grateful it wasn't winter. The hill leading up to the main building was a bitch when ice covered the road. Spokane kept it as clear as possible, but there were still spots of black ice. If you hit a patch, not even studded tires would help.

Forty minutes later, we were directed to Brynn's room. I suspected we weren't supposed to actually go in and see her, but we'd planned on being discreet.

"Chance," I quietly said as we approached. The scent of disinfectant and sickness curdled my stomach.

Chance spun around and gave us a solemn wave. Since it was in the middle of the night and most patients were sleeping, I tried to be extra quiet.

Jace had his hands shoved into his front pockets, his shoulders rigid with tension. Zayne silently walked a few steps behind us. I wondered if the hospital brought up Zayne's memories of everything he'd gone through.

Chance hugged Jace and me, then I handed him his black leather duffel bag. His long-sleeved white button-down shirt was rolled up to his forearms but untucked from his jeans. Dark circles shadowed his eyes, and he nervously ran his hand over his blonde hair. "We crammed everything possible in it, including stuff for Brynn." I flashed him a sad smile. It wouldn't be the same without Brynn and Chance around. Hopefully, they would be home soon. "Thanks, man. I really appreciate it."

"Can we see her?" Jace asked.

"You've got to be quick and quiet, but yeah. She was asleep the last I checked on her," Chance explained.

"Go on in, man." I patted Jace on the back.

"I'll make it fast." He slipped through the crack of her door and disappeared.

I assessed Chance. "How are you holding up?" I asked, folding my arms over my chest.

"It's going to be a long, hard road. I had no idea things were this bad." Chance swallowed, his Adam's apple bobbing up and down.

"Don't forget to take care of yourself too. Watch funny shit on TV, listen to your favorite podcasts, try to sleep, and definitely remember to eat. You're a bastard when you're hangry." We both chuckled. "I'll expect an update at least twice daily. Maybe we can FaceTime, that way we're all able to look at each other."

"She's going to need to see both of you, so I'll make it happen."

We kept the conversation light. Neither of us wanted to admit that this might be goodbye with Brynn. The second the idea slammed into me, I shook it off. I couldn't ... I wouldn't entertain the possibility that she might not make it through this.

A few minutes later, Jace slipped back into the hallway. "She's awake." He nodded at me to get in there.

My hands trembled slightly, and I fisted my fingers. She didn't need to see how scared I was. I poked my head into her room and willed my mouth not to hang open. Her stomach had grown even more. She was pale and hooked up to oxygen. Images of seeing Emerson in the hospital bombarded my mind and my palms grew clammy. I reminded myself that this situation was different. Brynn would return home.

"Hey, babe." She grinned at me and rubbed her tummy. "This is what I'd look like if I ever got pregnant."

"You're beautiful. I can't wait for you and River to have little ones together."

Brynn struggled to sit up, and I hurried to help her.

"I'm so fucking weak. I hate it."

I fluffed her pillows and helped her get as comfortable as possible in the hospital bed.

"It will get better. It's only temporary. Try to keep that in mind." I took her hand in mine and sat on the edge of the mattress. "You scared us pretty bad."

Brynn sniffled. "I'm so sorry. I'm sorry I'm putting you all through this. As soon as River gets home, she's going to have to put up with me being sick." She rolled her eyes. "Not much of a welcome home party, huh?"

I kissed her knuckles. "Don't even think twice about it." I smoothed her hair off her forehead. "Are you in pain?"

"Some, but I didn't want any drugs. The edible was enough."

"I snuck you in a bag of Ruffles. It's in Chance's duffel bag."

Her face lit up with her smile. "Really?"

I chuckled. "Yup." Shifting on the bed, I stared at her. "I hope it was okay that I told the EMTs that Chance was your husband. It just flew out of my mouth. All I could think about was that your stupid parents weren't here, and we had to have a way to help with decisions and information."

"It's fine. I would have done the same if I could have breathed well enough to talk. No offense to the two of you, but Chance has the most level head. Plus, his mom and dad have a lot of pull in the medical community."

"Excellent, sounds like I made the right call." I offered her a warm smile, trying my best to assure her that she was in good hands.

Brynn leaned her head back against the pillow. "I'm scared, Holden. I won't admit it to anyone else, but I'm fucking terrified."

Our gazes connected. "We all are. Chance will be with you in Oregon, and Jace and I will fly down on the weekends. We're only a FaceTime away, so call us whenever."

She nodded and tightly gripped my hand. "Do you think River would mind if I asked you for a kiss? In case it's the last time ..." Her words stuck in her throat, and her body trembled.

"If River were here, she'd kiss you too. I think she'll understand." I ran my fingertips over Brynn's cheek. "You know I love you, right?" I whispered, preparing myself for goodbye. This could be the last time I might ever see her.

Tears flowed down her cheeks as she nodded. "I love you, too. You've been my rock for years. All three of you have. And for the record, I don't regret any of it. Even the fucked-up parts." She wiped her face and gave me a brave smile. "Just so you know. I plan on kicking the cancer's pathetic ass, so tell River I'll see her soon."

"I will." A lump lodged itself in my throat. "You say the word, and I'll be with you too."

Brynn shook her head. "You find River. The second she's in your arms, please text. Or even better, call."

"I promise. I should go. Chance said to keep it short." We stared at each other, my brain imprinting this moment in my mind for the rest of my life. I leaned over and gently touched my lips to hers and tried to tell her all the things I couldn't say. This kiss wasn't like any I'd ever had before. The desperation, the passion, the drive that fueled all of the previous kisses we shared, all of that was gone, and what was left in its place was the purest kind of love. "I love you, Brynn."

"I love you too. See you soon." She gave my hand one last squeeze, then let me go.

Reaching the door, I glanced over my shoulder and silently told her goodbye. I kept my head down as I left her room. I cleared my throat, then looked at Jace and Chance. Tears streamed down my cheeks. "You take good care of her, man." I pulled Chance in for a huge hug. "Say the word and we'll be in Oregon in a few hours." I smacked him on the shoulder.

"I will. I'll FaceTime you guys as soon as she gets settled in." Chance dropped his arms, then embraced Jace. "You guys are my family. I can't make it through this without you."

Jace sniffled. "Same." He stepped back and sucked in a breath. "Talk to you later."

I gave Chance a small wave as I walked away.

"We're going to fucking see her again goddammit." Jace hunched over, staring at the floor as we trudged down the hall.

"Fuck yeah, we are." I wished I could have believed my own words. Deep down, I realized I was leaving a part of my heart with Brynn. A piece that I might never get back.

Chapter Twenty-Six

I had time to shower and change into fresh clothes before meeting Tim for lunch. One look at me and he'd know something else was wrong. I'd struggled with the idea of telling him about Brynn, but I was on the fence, flopping back and forth like a fish on dry land. Tim had known her since we were in sixth grade when her family moved into the neighborhood. My mom had warmed up to her immediately, which Brynn needed since her parents were gone more than mine. Even with two daughters, Mom had taken Brynn under her wing, nurtured her, loved her, and guided her. That was the reason I knew she'd take to River, too.

It was always Mom, Mallory, and Hannah who took Brynn shopping for school clothes. My mom attended parent-teacher conferences and made sure she was keeping her grades up. Sometimes she'd stay at our house, but her parents were weird and wanted her to be at home with the nanny most of the time. Brynn got along with her, but said we felt more like her real family. I understood that feeling all too well.

I grabbed my wallet and cell phone, mentally preparing myself to meet Tim. Jace had planned on heading to his place after I returned to Chance's and updated him. Even though we'd not said it out loud, I think we both needed some space. Grief was strange. It pulled you in so many different directions. It was difficult to know what you wanted from minute to minute.

It had been a long time since I'd been to Riverfront Park. If shit weren't so fucking serious, it would have been a perfect day for it. There wasn't a single cloud in the sky, and the water was calmer than usual.

An hour later, Zayne drove into an empty parking lot a few blocks away from where Tim and I would meet. The FBI didn't want Zayne to go in with me, so he'd drop me off, and I'd walk the rest of the way. I needed to give Tim the impression that I trusted him enough to be alone with him.

"Are you ready?" Zayne asked.

"I'm ready to end this bullshit. Once the FBI has River in custody, I'm done with this son of a bitch."

"Hang in there. We're getting closer. I'm sure it doesn't feel like it, but we are." Zayne rolled up the sleeves of his white button-down, revealing his muscular forearms. "Don't forget to keep your phone on the table and start the recording. You won't see me, but I'll be close and so will Michelle."

I groaned. "Better watch out. She'll be all over you next." I quirked an eyebrow at him.

Zayne rubbed his chin, his gaze hiding behind his Ray-Bans. "She's not my type. Brynn is."

My mouth gaped slightly. "I'll keep that in mind if you join the lower-level club when we reopen. I might have someone for you to release some of that stress." I grinned. My man was human, after all.

"Good luck. We'll have eyes on you the entire time."

"Thanks. I have a feeling I'm going to need all the help I can get." I climbed out of the car and adjusted my Ray-Ban sunglasses, still squinting against the early afternoon sunshine. I reached the side-walk, and two pretty girls stopped and stared as I walked by. Their giggles floated through the summer air. I was glad River wasn't flirty and giggly. I loved hearing her laugh, but it was genuine, not a ploy to get me into her bed. It was funny. Once I'd spent some time with her, I'd realized how much the immature behavior of some women grated on my last nerve. Bitch Becky Michelle immediately came to mind.

I located Tim exactly where he said he'd be, by the food truck. He sat at one of the outdoor tables, his attention on the newspaper in front of him.

I drew in a sharp breath and shoved a hand in my jeans pocket. Brian had talked to me about defensive posture and what to avoid. Clearing my throat, I approached Tim. "Dad." Bile churned in my stomach at the mere idea that he was my dad. Maybe after this was finished, I'd change my last name, so I'd no longer be associated with a sick and twisted criminal.

"Son. It's good to see you." He chewed on a French fry and grinned. "Do you want a burger?"

I pulled the chair out, the metal feet scraping against the cement patio. "No, thanks. I'm not hungry."

Once everyone was out of earshot, he leaned back in his seat, studying me intently. "You look like fucking shit. What's going on?"

Taken off guard, I blanched. I set my phone on the table and activated the recording device. He glanced at it, and my heart pounded, but he didn't say anything, just removed his sunglasses.

"Holden, this profession is very dangerous. There's no room for a personal life. Your emotions will trip you up and get you killed."

"I understand." I attempted to relax, Brian's voice and coaching ringing through my head.

"Then what can I do to help, so we can get down to business?" Tim took a large bite of his hamburger, then wiped his mouth with the thin paper napkin.

A large glass of ice water was placed before me, and I took a drink, stalling momentarily. I had to play this just right. "As I mentioned on the phone, River is pregnant ... with your grandkid. She needs medical care and a safe environment. Once she's home, I'll let her know that I'll help with the baby, but that we're over. I'm on your terms after that. Whatever you want, wherever you need me, I'll be a hundred percent committed."

Tim stared at me, his eyes searching my face. "I have no idea where she is."

I propped my elbow on the table and continued to hold his gaze. "The one thing I know about you, Dad, is that your connections are limitless. You can pull a string from across the world, and it will ripple all the way to Washington state. You're powerful. I assume you have men that work for you, guard you, and obey your every command." I hoped feeding his ego would help my case.

"I do." He stopped eating. I had his undivided attention.

"If you don't know where she is, I'm betting that you know *who* has her, and why. Bring her back here safe and sound and I'll do anything you want. You'll own my fucking soul, old man."

If Tim had peacock feathers, he'd be strutting around the park. I'd finally realized that he didn't see people as human beings. They were nothing more than possessions to him, and I was playing into that, hoping like hell he'd take the bait.

Tim lifted his chin and narrowed his eyes. I wondered if he was attempting to determine if I was on the up-and-up or jerking him around.

He cleared his throat. "I have the perfect job for you. We fly to Monte Carlo in three days. Don't tell anyone. Don't talk to anyone about working for me. Keep your mouth shut." Tim stood and slipped on his sunglasses again.

"What about River?" I asked as I rose from my seat. "We don't have a deal unless she's returned safe and sound."

"I heard you, son. Wait by your phone." With that, he turned and walked away.

"Fuck," I muttered. What the hell did all of that mean? I picked up my cell and pushed the side button, ending the recording. Shoving it in my back pocket, I began to leave the same way I arrived. Once I was out of sight, Zayne fell in several steps behind me. This time he was wearing a gray baseball hat that shaded and hid part of his face.

"Keep walking. Don't look at me," he said in a hushed tone. "Tim has armed men all over the park. Take a left up here and head to the gift shop. A guy named Tad will pick you up. He's one of Pierce's employees and drives a black Mercedes with tinted windows just like mine. He has red hair and blue eyes. Get in and pretend that nothing is happening around you."

My heart hammered against my chest. Tim had weapons trained on me. What the actual fuck?

Purposefully relaxing my shoulders, I continued to walk the park like I didn't have a care in the world. I followed Zayne's instructions to the letter.

Minutes later, I reached the gift shop, and a Mercedes rolled up. I opened the door and identified Tad before I hopped in.

"Do you have any idea what's going on?" I asked as I fastened my seatbelt.

"Tim has men trained on you, Holden. He's waiting for one wrong move," Tad explained. He pulled onto the main road and headed in the opposite direction.

I turned to him, my gut twisting into painful knots. "It was a precaution, right? He's testing me?"

Tad cleared his throat. "I hope that's what it was. Either that or he's onto you."

I scrubbed my face with my hands, adrenaline pumping through my veins. "How will I know?"

"You won't until you hear from him again." Tad flipped on his turn signal and waited for the traffic to clear.

"I have no fucking clue what the hell happened out there." I blew out a sigh and stared out of the passenger window as the trees and buildings passed by.

Tad's cell rang, and he answered from his steering wheel.

"Holden, it's Sutton. Hang on, Tim is making a call. I wanted to loop you in," she explained.

My entire body went rigid with tension. If I believed in prayer,

I'd be on my knees begging like a little bitch for a break in River's case. But I wasn't. I'd stopped believing a long time ago.

"The clock is ticking," Tim said, still not using his Bluetooth.

What the hell was up with that? I pursed my lips together, and my chest burned with a combination of hope and fear. *You owe me, you fucker. Where is River?*

"In order not to risk anything, I'll send someone else to pick her up at the designated location at ten tomorrow night."

Confusion lines creased my forehead. I couldn't tell if he was talking about River or someone else.

"Later," Tim said, then disconnected the call.

"Dammit. That didn't tell us a fucking thing. Holden, I'll keep monitoring his calls. I have no idea if he was talking about River or not." Silence filled the line. "Are you all right?"

"That depends on what your definition of all right is," I responded.

"Learning that your father has men with weapons surrounding you has to be a little nerve-wracking." The sound of paper shuffling in the background reached my ears. "You did well. Brian, Pierce, and I have already listened to the recording of your meeting with Tim. I'm guessing that the armed men were precautionary. Tim can't trust anyone in his type of work, and that includes his son. This won't be the last time, I'm sure."

"I appreciate all the safety measures." It hadn't occurred to me that Tim lived his life constantly on-edge, but it made sense.

"Using yourself as bait isn't something to take lightly. Hopefully, Tim will call soon with some news about River," Sutton said.

"He knows the deal, so if he wants me to work for him, he has to deliver her beforehand." I ran my fingers through my hair, irritated that the bastard hadn't said anything that would help us locate River.

"Zayne will meet you at Chance's place. He's already on the way," Sutton said.

"Us, too. Talk to you soon."

Tad ended the call, and I provided him with Chance's address.

We rode the rest of the way without talking, my brain working double-time as I tried to figure out Tim's weak spot. He had to have one. Everyone did. It wasn't money or women ... an idea suddenly occurred to me. I'd talk to Zayne as soon as I saw him. He'd know what to do.

Chapter Twenty-Seven

Zayne was waiting patiently for me on the front porch. "I'm going to search the place before you go in."

I unlocked the door and waited with Tad as Zayne secured the premises. Since he'd beat us there, I assumed he'd already patrolled the property.

I entered Chance's place and called out for Jace, but there was no response. Before I'd left to meet Tim, Jace mentioned he had some errands to run, and he'd see me when he got back.

An eerie silence filled the home as I walked over to the windows. My thoughts took a dark turn to Brynn. Chance hadn't given us an exact time that Brynn would be transported to Oregon, but I realized he'd let me know when they were in transit.

The front door opened, and Zayne strolled back inside. "Tad is going to take over for me while I talk to you."

"Was that normal today?" I asked, eyeing Zayne.

"Can be. Powerful people have a lot of enemies, so it's not out of the ordinary. What bothered us was that a few of his men had their weapons directly trained on you. Every move you made, so did they."

I folded my arms over my chest. "So, Tim was ready to strike if I screwed up."

"It appeared that way. The possibility that he'd take his own son down is disturbing." Zayne placed his hands on his hips and stared at me.

"I don't fucking care. He won't shoot me. I basically offered him my soul in exchange for River." I shook my head in disbelief that any of this was happening. Maybe my idea from earlier would work, though. "He knows my weak point. Her. Now I need to figure out his." I glanced at Zayne. "Did Sutton ever learn whose house Tim was at the other day? The one with the blonde headed lady and the little girl?"

So much had happened in the last few days. I'd forgotten all about it.

Zayne removed his cell from the front pocket of his black slacks. He tapped the screen a few times, then a phone began to ring.

"Hey, Zayne," Sutton answered.

"Holden is with me and you're on speaker."

"Hey, Holden," she said.

I laced my fingers behind my head, anxiety skipping through my body. "Hey, I was wondering if you'd been able to check out the address I gave you?"

"Not yet. We've had higher priorities, so it got moved down on the list," she explained.

"On the way here, I realized I don't know what Tim's weak spot is, where he's blinded." I glanced at Zayne, who continued to stare out of the window at Chance's tree line.

"You're wondering if this lady and little girl are his?"

"Maybe. Honestly, I'm not sure that fucker even has human emotion, which means he doesn't have a blind spot. Anyone that aims guns at his son is seriously fucked up."

"I agree with you. At the same time, I'm not surprised. Pierce considered mentioning the possibility to you, but Brian said no. He didn't want you to go in spooked. You were already nervous, and there was no need to stress you out any further with a *possible* scenario."

"Yeah, good call. That would have messed with me." I squeezed the bridge of my nose, willing the looming headache to go away. "What do you think? Can we check into the woman and little girl he saw that night? Maybe they're his kryptonite."

"I'm meeting with Pierce and Brian in a few minutes. I'll dive into it as soon as that's done. I'll keep you posted."

"Thanks, Sutton. I appreciate it. Maybe we'll luck out."

"Fingers crossed," she said before she ended the conversation.

The second the call ended, my phone rang. I pulled it out of my pocket and glanced at the screen.

I answered and placed it on speaker.

"Hey, Chance. How's Brynn?" I sat on the arm of the couch, suddenly overwhelmed and exhausted.

"They're preparing for her to fly down. They drained her stomach, and it looks a lot better."

"Hopefully she's a little more comfortable now. How's she doing otherwise?"

"She's apologizing and crying a lot," Chance said softly. "She's really scared, man. So am I."

My heart stuttered. "When will they start treatment?"

"Tomorrow morning. They'll get her settled this evening." Chance sighed. "Never in a million years did I think we'd all be here right now."

"Me either." My shoulders slumped with the weight of the world pushing down on them. I wasn't even sure how to support Chance when I was so mentally fucked up. Between River and Brynn, I couldn't see straight.

"Will you be able to stay with her in the room?" I asked, glancing up at Zayne.

"Yeah. I'm pretty sure she'd beat the hell out of anyone that told me I had to leave." Chance chuckled. "She's still feisty when she needs to be. They're running a ton of tests and she's feeling like a pin cushion. When the last nurse came in, Brynn yelled at her."

I winced. Brynn could be vicious on occasion. "Was the nurse okay?"

Chance and I laughed. Not that it was funny, but at this point, we were trying to keep our heads above water.

"I think she's used to it."

Muffled voices came through the line. "They're ready. I'll try and FaceTime you guys tonight. She said she misses everyone and wants to see your ugly mugs."

I grinned. "She didn't say that."

"Nope, I did." At least Chance was attempting to keep his spirits up.

"Jace will be back at some point, so text me when you two have a few minutes and we'll make it happen. Give her a kiss for us."

"I plan on it."

"Later, man." I tapped the red button on my screen and realized Zayne was staring at me, his hand covering his chin.

"What's that look for?" I tossed my cell on the couch and stretched out. I was running on only a few hours of sleep for the last several nights, and it was starting to kick my ass.

"Are ... you, Chance, Jace, and Brynn. Are you all together?" Zayne's tone twinged with a hint of curiosity, but was completely free of judgment.

I propped my head on the throw pillow. "Not anymore. We ..." I played with the idea of how much to tell him. Honestly, I got the feeling that Zayne wouldn't give a shit how close we really were, but it wasn't just about me, and I had to respect everyone's wishes.

"I think we've all been in love with Brynn at one point. We all grew up together. And, yeah, we've all been together and done shit, but I stopped almost a year ago."

"Hmm. I didn't see it at first. Then your conversation with Chance tipped me off. I've noticed how Brynn looks at each of you. I'm not sure she could choose who she loves more."

"Chance," I said, helping him out a little bit. "He's fucking balls-deep in love with her too. They've just never discussed his feelings." I chewed the inside of my cheek before I continued. "I suspect that's all about to change."

"An illness like cancer can change a lot of shit fast." Zayne leaned up against the wall and crossed his legs at the ankles.

I sat up, eyeing him suspiciously. "Are you into Brynn? I mean, I don't know a red-blooded male that isn't. She's stunning, smart, and has a huge heart. She doesn't let many people get close to her."

"She's made it clear she wouldn't say no if I wanted to spend some time with her. That was before her diagnosis though. I suspect by the time she's better, her focus will be elsewhere."

"Yeah, I agree. If you're simply needing to fuck, then I can hook you up with some beautiful women. One, two, three, whatever your pleasure is."

"I can tell you're used to dealing with clients," Zayne chuckled. "A night of fun would be good. Before Vaughn met Claire and Pierce and Sutton got back together, we had some wild nights." A grin pulled at the corner of his mouth.

"Together?" I asked, suddenly curious.

"We definitely shared and watched," Zayne folded his arms across his chest. "Now that they've settled down, and I haven't ..."

"If you met the right woman, would you?" I asked, sticking my nose where it really didn't belong.

"That's not on my radar right now."

"Can Tad stay on duty tonight? Let me treat you to an evening of fun." I grabbed my phone and texted Sutton.

Can Tad stay for the next twenty-four hours? I'd like to treat Zayne to a night out. He needs it.

I assumed Pierce was working since I hadn't spoken to him all day. Sutton's response came quickly.

Let me check the schedule, and you're probably right. Z never takes time off, so it would do him some good.

While I waited for Sutton's response, I grinned at Zayne. "What's your poison?"

"Scotch."

"Blonde? Brunette? Redhead?" I scrolled through my contacts, searching for the right girls for him.

"All of the above."

I chuckled. If Zayne and I had met under different circumstances, we would have become friends.

Sutton's message popped up on my screen.

Yeah, I can move the guys around. I'll let Zayne know.

I held my cell up. "Looks like you're going to have one hell of a night." I grinned.

Seconds later, Zayne's phone pinged with a text. "I'm ready. I'm going to head to my place and get cleaned up."

"I'll text in a bit with details. I need to check on availability first."

"Thanks again." Zayne shook my hand and patted me on the back before he left.

Half an hour later I'd reserved the Davenport Grand Penthouse Suite for Zayne and two ladies. Alcohol, food, and plenty of toys would be waiting for him when he arrived. Jamie and Nicky would take damn good care of him, too.

I stretched out on the couch again, my thoughts reeling with what to do about Tim. If he suspected me, he didn't show any signs. Well, other than his armed men following my every move.

Stifling a yawn, I realized that I was alone for the second time since River had been taken. Finally, the silence lulled me into a restless sleep.

"What are they talking about?"

I peeked through the crack of the door and slapped a hand over the mouth of the faceless kid next to me. I held a finger up, hushing them. If we got caught, we'd get our asses beat. Again.

A man lifted the woman's dress, his hand disappearing between her parted thighs. She moaned and sank her teeth into her red-painted lip.

"Are you ready?" the guy growled, the bulge in his slacks growing.

"Yes," she panted.

He snapped his fingers. Seconds later, a muscular young man with light scruff on his face showed up and dropped to his knees. He buried his head between the woman's legs. Her back arched as the man unzipped his pants and grabbed his dick in his hand, stroking himself as the woman moaned.

She lowered the front of her dress, revealing her tits. The young man on the floor began rolling her nipples between his fingertips.

"Hurry up, boy." The man growled at him. "It's my turn."

"Oh, yes, Robert. You know I love to watch him suck you off." She jerked the young man by his hair and pulled his head away from her glistening pussy. "I'll be waiting." She winked at him.

He crawled on the floor, his shoulders down as if the shame was too much to bear. The man jerked the guy by his arm, then forced him on his knees and demanded he open his mouth.

I scrambled backward, tugging the shirt of the faceless person next to me.

"Holden?" his voice was full of fear.

"Shut the fuck up," I snarled. "We aren't supposed to see this."

Groans and moans of pleasure escaped the room as I stood and tiptoed down the hall, the faceless kid right behind me.

What the hell had I just seen?

A small hand took mine. "I'm scared."

"It's okay. Let's go back to bed. We'll be safe there."

I landed on the floor with a thud, the impact jerking me out of my dream. My breaths came in short, jagged bursts, and sweat trickled down my forehead. Realizing that my entire body was trembling, I swallowed, attempting to calm my galloping heartbeat. Nausea rocked my stomach, and I remained still until I was sure I wasn't about to puke everywhere.

What the hell was that? I stood slowly and grabbed the arm of the couch, testing my balance.

The door opened, and Jace entered the house, freezing in place the second he saw me.

"Dude, are you okay?"

Chapter Twenty-Eight

I shook my head. "Can you bring me some water?"

Jace hurried to the kitchen, then over to the couch where I'd finally had the good sense to sit down. I took the glass from him and sipped the cool liquid, unsure if my stomach would rebel.

"You're not as pale." Jace's intense gaze remained on me as I took another drink. "What happened?"

I swallowed a few times. "A nightmare." My voice was hoarse, scratchy, and sounded strange to my own ears.

"Must have been one fucked up dream. I don't think I've ever seen you like this."

"They've been happening more lately, but this ..." The bitter and sour taste of bile burned the back of my throat as pieces of the dream flickered through my mind like an old black and white movie with lousy reception.

"Do you want to talk about it?" Jace sat on the edge of the chair and looked at me.

I sank back into my seat and stared at the floor. Maybe talking about it would minimize the horrible feelings that were coursing through me.

"There's always someone with me. We're young. Even though I'm just a boy, I have the mind of an adult, so I understand what's happening." I slammed my eyes closed, then back open. "I'm just a little kid, but whoever is with me is always faceless. It's eerie as fuck."

"What else can you remember?"

"There was sex. We were watching." I gulped as my head started to spin.

"Um, that's not a bad dream. I think you're simply stressed to the fucking max." Jace took my glass from me and set it on the coffee table.

"It wasn't like that. There was a young man, and he was being forced against his will." I shook my head in disbelief, and my hand flew up in front of my chest, indicating that I couldn't talk about it anymore. "Forget it. Obviously, my subconscious is messing with me." Even though the words came out of my mouth, I couldn't shake the horrible feeling that clung to me.

"Who was forcing him?" Jace pressed.

I glared at him. "A couple. A man and a woman, but no one I recognized."

"Are you writing all of this down?" Jace asked.

I snarled at him. "What are you, my fucking shrink?" Guilt washed over me the second the words left my lips. "Shit, I'm sorry. I'm stressed."

Jace shrugged it off. "I was simply trying to help. It's hard not to ask questions when you've been raised by a psychiatrist. I didn't mean to get all up in your business."

I glanced at Jace, his expression masking his real feelings. He'd learned at a young age to never show what he was thinking. Ever. It wasn't worth being analyzed and dissected.

"I know." Desperately needing to change the subject, I let Jace know that Zayne was off duty tonight, and Tad was with us.

"Zayne works all the time. He probably needs to get his brains fucked out. Relax a little." Jace grinned at me.

"I set him up at the Davenport with a few of the girls that entertain clients when they're in town."

Jace's laugh filled the living room. "You're a good man, Holden. If he's still with you during the holidays, that would be a damned good Christmas bonus too."

He had a point. "Hopefully, I won't need a bodyguard by then, but that's probably wishful thinking."

My cell rang, and I searched around for it. I snatched it off the floor and answered Sutton's call.

"This is Holden."

"You were right. The lady with the little girl is important." Sutton had nipped the polite chit chat in the bud this time.

I scooted to the edge of my seat. "Who are they?"

"To protect you, I'm going to leave some names out of our conversation," Sutton explained.

Jace sank into a chair, his gaze connecting with mine. I mouthed that it was Sutton, and he nodded.

"The woman's name is Autumn Foster. She kept her married name, but she's divorced. She and Tim don't try to hide their relationship either."

"Okay?" I wasn't sure why this was important information.

"Her father is the one that brought Tim into the weapons business. Autumn and Tim have had an off-and-on relationship for the last three years," Sutton said.

"So, the little girl ...?" I clenched my jaw together, adding the years to try to determine if I had a half-sister.

"She's Tim's daughter, Holden."

I closed my eyes and massaged my temple. The nightmare was still lingering around the edges of my mind. "What's her name?"

"Waverly."

Images of the little girl running to Tim and throwing her arms around his neck haunted me. She was adorable and innocent, but she belonged to not only one monster, but her grandfather probably made Tim look like he had a halo and angel wings.

"I want to meet her." My throat felt dry as the words left my lips. "She's my sister. I've lost one already, I would love to have a relationship with this one."

"I understand. She is adorable. But Holden, maybe wait until River is back before you mention this to Tim. He'll know you were checking up on him. I don't want to take any chances."

"I won't say a word, but I wonder if Mom knows."

"Again, I wouldn't say anything. She could go straight to Tim and mess up all of our hard work."

I leaned back on the couch. "Guess Mom and I will have plenty to talk about soon."

"Let's hope so. The clock is ticking with your demand for Tim to bring River home. Don't think we're waiting around, though. We're hoping Laura will expose her bosses."

"She's still the only lead we have, huh?" I picked at an imaginary ball of lint on my jeaned thigh.

"I suspect, by the end of the day, we'll have more. It's just a hunch, but I'm usually pretty good at those."

My stomach flip-flopped. "I hope so."

"I'll call you as soon as I know something. Oh, and Holden?"

"Yeah?"

"Thanks for taking care of Zayne. It's difficult for him now that Vaughn and Claire are engaged, and Pierce and I are married. A night of fun will do him some good."

My eyes widened. "He told you?"

Sutton laughed. "We're like you, Brynn, Chance, and Jace. We share everything with each other. We're family."

I doubted they'd all fucked Sutton, but I had no intention of revealing that part of our relationship to her.

"Hopefully he'll enjoy himself." I wasn't sure how he couldn't. The girls were gorgeous and definitely knew how to show a guy a fun time.

"Have a good night. I'll call as soon as I have an update," Sutton said.

"Thanks. You, too." I disconnected the phone and shook my head before I looked at Jace. "Tim's secrets just keep coming."

"Do I want to know?" Jace stood from his chair and headed for the kitchen. He grabbed a few beers and Brynn's chips. "I'm starving. I haven't been eating right since River, and now Brynn ..." He twisted a cap off and handed me a bottle.

"Me too. We should order some food since nothing is cooked and I'm not really up to it."

Once we decided on dinner from PF Chang's, I updated him on my new sibling.

"Honestly, I'm not surprised." Jace popped a chip into his mouth. "I swear, the older we get, the more we learn how our reality and family don't line up. Our families for sure weren't who we thought they were. I mean we knew Tim as a good guy."

"No shit." It was insane how fast my perception had changed.

Jace and I ate and watched television. I doubted either of us was really paying attention to the show, but it was noise. It was nearly ten in the evening when Chance texted me.

You guys want to FaceTime?

"Jace, Chance wants to know if we want to FaceTime with him and Brynn."

"Hell, yeah." He scooted closer to me on the couch and ran his hands through his hair. He was as nervous as I was to see her. The sight of her struggling to breathe had fucked us both up.

Chance's video call came through, and I positioned the phone to include Jace and me on the camera. I tapped the accept button, then Chance's face filled the screen.

"Hey, guys. How's it going there?"

"Good. We haven't destroyed your house yet." Jace grinned, trying to lighten an intense situation. "How are you and Brynn?"

Chance angled his iPhone and brought Brynn into view.

"Hey," she offered us a brave smile and waved. "I miss you guys."

"We miss you, too," I said. "How are you feeling?"

"Better than yesterday, that's for sure." She laid a hand on her much smaller stomach. "I start chemo tomorrow. They have an entire cancer treatment wing here with the best specialists in the country. Try not to worry as much. I'm in good hands."

I paused, scrambling for the right thing to say. "You're going to beat this, Brynn." I clutched the cell tighter than necessary, but I meant it. She was coming home. Both of our girls were.

"Any update on River?" Her voice held a hint of hope.

Jace pointed at me. "Nope, but he's got a new little sister."

I rolled my eyes. "Thanks, asshole."

"What?" Brynn asked as she sat up in bed a little straighter.

"Her name is Waverly. Tim and his girlfriend, Autumn ..." I blew out a sigh. "They've been off and on for several years. I'm hoping to meet her soon."

"Oh, Holden, this could be a really good thing. Do you have pictures of her? How old is she?"

It was a relief to see color in Brynn's cheeks and hear her sounding more like herself. "No, but I'll see if Sutton found some online. I think she's probably around five years old. Blonde hair and big blue eyes. She's a doll." And one that deserved to be protected from her family at all costs.

"She sounds adorable. I can't wait to learn more. Might be fun to have a little one running around. I'm pretty sure we would all spoil her rotten."

I loved Brynn's enthusiasm, but I wasn't so sure Waverly's parents would allow us anywhere near her.

Brynn leaned her head back on the pillow, and Chance crawled into bed beside her so we could all see each other better.

"So ..." I rubbed my chin, a mischievous smile easing across my face. "I hooked Zayne up with a hotel room and a few ladies. Dude needed to blow off some steam."

Brynn giggled. "If only I was there." She wiggled her eyebrows at us.

"Maybe something to look forward to after you're all better. He seems like he might be up for the idea at least."

Brynn frowned. "I'm lost. You talked to Zayne about me?" Her voice held a note of warning.

"He asked how you were doing. One thing led to another, then he asked about membership to the club once it was rebuilt."

Brynn bit her lip. "Like the lower floor membership?"

"Yeah. He said now that his buddies are engaged or married, it's been difficult to go out and have some fun by himself. I told him as soon as things were back in business, I'd let him know."

"Oh, this could be fun." Brynn grinned, then peeked at Chance, her smile faltering.

Jace discreetly nudged me. He'd noticed Chance's change in expression as well. Most of the time, we all discussed the club and who we wanted to fuck, but our lives were changing. I suspected Brynn was attempting to hold onto anything that helped and gave her a bit of hope. She needed something to hold onto ... we all did.

Brynn took Chance's hand in hers and squeezed it.

"Brynn's chemo is scheduled for nine in the morning," Chance said.

My stomach clenched as a dark cloud hovered over our conversation again.

"Will you check in once she's done? Let us know how it's going?" I asked Chance.

"Yeah. Maybe we should also try and connect with each other this time every night unless she's not feeling well." Chance peeked at her.

"Sounds good," Jace said. "It will give me something to look forward to. Holden's a drag these days." Jace chuckled.

My gaze connected with Brynn's, and a quiet understanding was exchanged between us. I nodded slightly and mentally promised I'd take care of Chance if anything happened to her.

Chapter Twenty-Nine

Once again, I was afraid to close my eyes at night. My subconscious spewed nightmares at me about River, or Brynn's sunken, pale face begging me for help. It was too fucking much.

After Jace had left to go to his place, I connected my cell through Chance's stereo system and turned on Spotify. "Home" by Edith Whiskers filled the house. I scrolled through my phone, intending to catch up on emails, but my mind continued to return to River. Was she asleep or awake right now? Had those monsters hurt her? Was our baby okay? Pure fear shot down my spine.

One thing was for sure: I'd end Tim once he returned her. He was just as responsible as the person who took River. Regret nudged me. She'd come so far in the months she'd been here. The only person I knew of that had been after her was Logan, but Sutton and Pierce had cleared him. Even Tim hadn't been a part of the plan.

What I couldn't figure out, though, was why River? She had moved in with me and put her life together. Hell, she didn't even know anyone here other than Jace, Chance, and Brynn. She'd met a few of the club employees but hadn't developed any kind of friendships yet.

I massaged my temples, willing my brain to work. As much as I hated them, I had to focus on the nightmares. There was something there. I could sense it. I shuddered, almost able to feel the ghost of a small hand on my arm. "Goddammit," I said to absolutely no one. Since Jace left an hour ago, I was floundering in the brutal silence and hazy memories. But ... "Focus, Holden."

When Chance, Jace, and I were sophomores in high school, I'd decided to skip school one day. Everyone else was down with the idea, and we ended up hanging out at Jace's place. Jace thought it would be funny to imitate his mom, so we all gathered in her office. He whipped out a notebook and pen and pretended to psychoanalyze us. It was all fun and games until he stumbled on an experimental hypnosis technique his mom was studying. More like perfecting.

Brynn snatched the notes out of Jace's hand and started to read the process. Laughter floated through the room until we realized Brynn's expression had grown serious and intrigued. Chance suggested that we try it. We were rich, bored kids that were willing to try anything at least once.

Since Jace's mom was gone for the week, we had the house to ourselves and decided to go for it. What we hadn't planned on was that it would actually work. Not to mention it was dangerous as hell.

I'd volunteered to go first. Then again. And again. Until I went under so deeply, Brynn couldn't bring me out of the trance and back to reality. Jace and Chance had hightailed it to the basement and grabbed bags of ice that Jace's mom stored for parties. When they returned, they dumped it into the bathwater I was submerged in. After that, they made me swear I'd never do it again. But now ...

It had been a long time since I'd tried it, but if I could connect with the part of myself that had answers, it would be worth the risk.

I hopped off the couch and glanced at the clock on the wall. The second hand ticked methodically, the only sound in the room. I could do this.

Quickly typing a message to Jace, I let him know that I was going to try the experimental method.

His reply was quick, and in all caps.

Dude, no way. It's too intense. You remember what happened last time.

I blew out a quick breath, toying with the idea of backing out.

I'll figure out how to do it without you if you don't want to help.

His response came almost immediately.

Fuck that. I'm on my way. Be there in fifteen.

I scolded myself for being stupid and willing to try the process without someone experienced with me. The last time I'd gone under had been disastrous, and I'd nearly not been able to break the hypnosis. It wasn't something that I took lightly, but I was bound and determined to find River. And regardless, if I wanted to admit it or not, somewhere buried in my memories, I had the answers. I just had to risk everything in order to get them.

"This is fucked up, Holden. If Brynn finds out about this, she'll beat your ass." Jace leaned against the bathroom counter with his mom's black, hardcover book in his hands.

I slipped my tennis shoes off and climbed into the bathtub with my jeans and shirt on. "It's been two weeks since River was taken. I can't wait any longer. Plus, we have a plan in case I get stuck."

Jace's gaze narrowed at me. "Don't get stuck. Just don't." He ran his hand through his hair, obviously nervous. "I'm pretty sure that I already know what your answer will be, but are you sure, Holden?"

I glared at him. "I don't have a choice." I sat in the tub and stretched my legs in front of me. If Jace couldn't bring me out of the trance, then he knew what to do. I began to run the warm water.

"Are you ready?" A grim expression settled over Jace's features. "If anything happens ... love ya, man."

Jesus, Jace was really spooked. I took a minute and stared at him. "You, too." My pulse spiked as I realized where he was coming from. My focus was finding River and figuring out the fucking nightmares, but we were at risk of losing almost everyone we loved. And here I was, risking my own life as well.

I closed my eyes, listening to the thump-thump of my heart in my ears. One after the other, I blocked out the fear, the anger, the images that had been assaulting my mind. I blocked out River and Brynn. *Breathe in. Breathe out. Breathe in. Breathe out.*

Jace guided me, and each part of my body began to relax. All of the tension eased from my limbs while I sank deeper. Deeper. Deeper.

A sweet voice reached my ears. I peeked at the cute redhead that had knocked on our front door.

"I'm Brynn." She smiled, her front tooth a little crooked, but I liked it. It gave her character.

"Hi, I'm Holden." I offered her a wave. She was pretty, and I suddenly felt shy.

I glanced around at my living room as Mom and Brynn's mother got acquainted.

"Do you wanna go to the game room?" I asked, already bored of the adult chit-chat.

Brynn's face flickered in and out before she answered in my memory. Suddenly everything shifted, and I stared at the white light that pierced the darkness. I walked slowly toward it, voices filling my head.

"Cupcake, honey?" Mom asked, smiling warmly at me. Hannah shoved one in her mouth, and we all laughed as a blob of icing dotted her nose.

I continued to walk down the hall, images of my past popping up on either side of me. Mallory and Hannah playing outside, Christmas morning with all of us gathered around the tree, my football games, Hannah's volleyball games, and Mallory's plays.

With each memory that presented itself, I was no longer convinced that my nightmares were connected. Our family was happy. We had meals together until they began to travel. Mom and Tim were active in our lives until I was around ten years old. Even then, when Mom was back, she took care of Brynn and us.

Darkness fell. Desperately, I glanced around. Where was I? A door creaked open, and moonlight spilled into the hall. I took a tentative step closer.

"Holden?" I froze. It was the same voice that had haunted my dreams.

"Yeah?" Glancing down at my hands, I realized I was only four or five years old again.

"It's happening."

Confusion clouded my mind. I didn't understand. "Where are you?"

"Holden?" The voice was peppered with fear.

"I'm here, but I can't find you." I hurried through the door, searching for who was calling my name.

The room spun, and I grabbed my hair. "No. No. No."

I forced myself to breathe and focus on what was in front of me.

Faceless adults were talking and laughing. Jazz music floated in the air as moans of pleasure reached my ears. Images grew clearer as I gaped. Even though my body was young, my mind was an adult.

Horror ripped through me as I watched a naked young woman crawl on her hands and knees as a man led her around by a leash. He set a bowl of food on the floor and forced her to eat like a dog. I tore my gaze away, my eyes burning with tears.

Young men were lined up against a wall. Adult women and men alike were pacing in front of them, assessing their manhood. With a single motion, each guy was selected and led out of the room.

"Holden?" The voice began to fade. "Help me."

Frantic, I ran through the crowd, searching. Searching. Searching.

A scream reached my eardrums, and I whirled around, the room changing into a long hallway. "No!" I ran after the faceless kid as they cried and screamed my name. "Stop!" "What's your name? Please. Tell me." My questions were only met with sobs. Frigid cold seeped into my bones, and I shivered. Then everything disappeared.

I gasped for air. Freezing water dripped from my cheeks, and I wiped my eyes as I attempted to ground myself in the present. Spitting and sputtering, I grabbed the side of the tub and finally recognized a panicked Jace.

"Jesus, Holden," he said through a clenched jaw. He gripped my hand and helped me stand. "This better have been worth it because I'm not sure I can bring you back again."

I draped my arm around his shoulder as he steadied me. It took all my willpower to pick up one leg, then the other. My teeth chattered, and I glanced at the water in the tub. Chunks of ice floated on the top.

Jace handed me a plush, beige towel, and I dried my hair, still reeling from the session.

"Goddammit." He guided me to the toilet and flipped the lid down. I gratefully sat on top, my pulse still pounding in my ears.

"Dude, do you know how many people never made it back to reality with this kind of bullshit hypnosis therapy?" He stammered, his brows furrowed together as he waved his hands around. "Tell me what happened before it fades completely." He collected the pen and notebook from the counter and sat on the edge of the tub. "Thank God I remembered to bring a few bags of ice. It's been a long-ass time, and I'd almost forgotten how we brought you out years ago." He flipped the pages, pulled the cap off the pen with his teeth, then slipped it on the end. "Spill. Now."

I folded my hands in my lap and closed my eyes.

"At first, I was the age I am now, then I started to walk down a corridor toward a light. With each step I was a little younger. I saw Dad, Mom, Mallory, Hannah, and Brynn at different times in their lives. I saw Christmas and cupcakes ... Everything went black, then a light came through a crack in the door. The same voice from my nightmares called for me. It definitely belongs to a young kid. By the time I arrived, I was young—maybe four or five. I have no idea whose house it was. It wasn't familiar."

Drops of water fell from my hair onto my cheeks, and I wiped them off with the back of my hand. I pushed myself to continue.

"So many kids. My guess is they were around eighteen, but I couldn't tell for sure." I choked, panic and grief punching me in the chest. "Naked. One young lady was forced to crawl around on all fours and eat out of a dog bowl." I gripped the counter, my knuckles turning white, as my breathing became labored. "Young men lined one of the walls as adults selected them like they were candy at a store. Jesus." My words lit a fire in my gut that burned up my throat, and I clung to reality.

"I don't understand," Jace said softly. "Tell me everything." He jotted down notes as I tried to continue.

"I can't." I shook my head. "I can't."

"Holden, this might be your last chance. Hang in there. Take some deep breaths and tell me what happened."

Tears burned my eyes as I looked at my best friend. My brain was still trying to process what I'd seen and where I was. More importantly, who was calling my name.

I scrubbed my face with the towel, then slowly looked at him.

"I ... they ..."

Chapter Thirty

"Those people were sex slaves, Jace." I jumped off the toilet, flipped the lid open, and lost my dinner.

"What do you need? I think Chance has some ginger ale in the kitchen." Jace stood and hurried out of the bathroom before I could answer him. I flushed the commode and pulled myself off the floor. My limbs trembled as though the weight of the confession had rendered me nearly immobile.

He returned and popped open the can, the hiss of the carbonation breaking the silence of the quiet room.

Once I washed my face and brushed my teeth, I felt a little more human. More grounded to the present instead of the visions from the hypnosis.

"I'm good. I'm going to head into the living room."

Jace frowned and eyed me suspiciously. "You're definitely not okay." He grabbed the notebook and pen and nodded at my clothes. "You need to change first. Chance will kick your ass if you trail water all over his house."

"Shit. I'm still so out of it I didn't notice."

"I'll give you a minute." Jace left my bedroom, and I tossed the towel on the carpet near the dresser so I could stand on it without making a big mess. I opened the drawer and removed a pair of black boxer-briefs and red basketball shorts. Images plagued me as I removed my wet shirt and jeans. My stomach clenched again as I recalled the hollow look in the girl's eyes as she was led around on a leash. I nearly gagged. As I dried my body off, it dawned on me that she might have been drugged. Everything happened so fast that I couldn't tell for sure.

After I'd rolled my clothes in the towel, I placed it on the counter. I slipped into the dry clothes and flipped the lever that allowed the tub to drain. A chill skated over my skin, and I decided to wear a long-sleeved shirt. I was fucking freezing.

Once I'd cleaned and dried the floor, I collected the bundle and ginger ale, then grabbed the black and white throw off the foot of my bed. I threw it over my shoulder and headed to the living room. I tossed the blanket on the end of the couch, then located Chance's washing machine and threw the wet items in. Once I started the small load, I settled in on the sofa.

"Are you doing better?" Jace propped his elbows against his knees, his expression flickering with concern.

"I think so." I ran my hand through my wet hair and pulled the cover over me. "Thanks for your help. I don't know why I thought I could do that without anyone."

Jace's hand trembled. I wasn't the only one who was trying to keep his shit together. The hypnosis had really fucked him up, too.

I looked at my feet. "Someone is always calling me for help but ... whoever it is never has a face. Not in my dreams and not during the hypnosis. I don't know who it is and it's fucking with me bad." I tugged a loose thread at the corner of the blanket.

"Young? Old? Male? Female?" Jace had his pen poised and ready for any information that might help us connect the dots.

I stilled, attempting to access that deeper part of myself that I trusted had the answers. "I can't tell. Definitely young. And someone close to me. In some of the dreams they come into my bedroom and wake me up."

"Why the fuck haven't you told me about this before, dude?" Jace looked as if he wanted to punch me. "This is serious shit. Whatever your subconscious is trying to tell you, it's fucking big."

I took a sip of my drink, the carbonated bubbles dotting my upper lip. "I told Brynn. She heard me yelling in my sleep one night."

Jace frowned. "As in after the fire when you moved in with Chance?"

I nodded. Although I realized that Jace had my best interests at heart, I wasn't in the mood for a lecture. I should have told him before, but it wasn't something I liked to talk about.

"Do you remember how we got into the hypnosis?" I leaned my head against the back of the sofa and looked at him.

He nodded. "We were young and stupid." He paused. "I'm not sure that's changed." He raised a judgmental eyebrow at me.

I rubbed my chin, recalling the times we'd experimented with the hypnosis. "We were in tenth grade. We were definitely young and stupid."

"I still don't know what possessed us to dig through my mom's confidential information." Jace tapped the pen against the arm of his chair.

"We were bored as hell with too much time on our hands. Wasn't it actually Brynn's idea to snoop?" I couldn't help but grin. "Your mom was at a psychiatry conference, and no one was at your place, so we decided to hang there."

"Brynn was always the adventurous one." Jace's face fell. "Except that time. She wanted to be the one to guide the hypnosis session instead of going under."

My fingertips tapped against the ginger ale can as Jace and I revisited the first time I'd used the experimental method.

"Mom's notes mentioned that some people were more susceptible than others, and that the hypnosis was dangerous. We thought she was being overly cautious." He shook his head. "Man, she wasn't kidding." He laced his fingers behind his neck. "We almost weren't able to bring you back from going under back then either." He shook his head. "Why do you keep tempting fate? The percentage of people being stuck in that reality is too high to risk it. Like, you do understand that you'd be mentally fucked up for the rest of your days, right?"

I ran my hand over my hair, water droplets flicking onto my shirt and face. "I'm desperate to find River, Jace." I bowed my head, willing myself not to come unglued. Between the session, River, and Brynn, I was barely holding on.

"Holden?" Jace scooted to the edge of his seat. "Do you remember what you saw the first time we did this?"

Dryness seized my throat, and I attempted to swallow. "Fuck." We stared at each other speechless. "That I was in a weird house with kids, and someone was screaming my name."

"I have the notes at my place. Let's go." Jace stood and patted his pockets, ensuring that he had his phone and wallet.

"Tad will need to take me," I reminded him. "If you're coming back, then just leave your car here."

Jace walked to the door and paused. "Better yet... We need a change of scenery. We're staying at my place, so grab whatever you need. We're going to figure this shit out once and for all." Conviction weaved through his words.

"I'm in. No matter what happens, I'm all in." I darted into the bedroom and quickly tossed some clothes and toiletries into a grocery bag. It was funny how I'd taken even the little things like a duffel bag for granted. I met him at the front door and looked at him. "Thanks, man. You have no idea what this means to me."

"I've always got your back." He squeezed my shoulder before we left.

Each time I'd fucked with fate, I'd walked away unscathed. But this time? Fate would have the last laugh, and fuck with me.

Chapter Thirty-One

Tad never questioned us as we let him know that we were headed to Jace's. It was nearly one-thirty in the morning, and at this point, neither Jace nor I had any plans to sleep.

We waited on the porch of his bungalow-style house, since Tad had insisted that he search the property.

Jace had recently updated the siding to a light sage with white trim. The lower half of the home offered a great stone contrast.

"Clear," Tad said, his voice deep and hushed. He held the front door open for us, then slipped out.

Jace closed and locked the door behind us. "Make yourself comfortable. You know where the guest bedroom and bath are."

"I guess it's been a while since I've been over." I toed off my tennis shoes and placed them near the entrance. Following Jace into the living room, I made myself comfortable on his brown leather sofa. Apparently, Jace had been busier than I'd realized. Not only had the outside of the place had a facelift, but he'd also remodeled the inside. The overhead light gleamed on sections of the shiny, light-colored wood floors. A black and brown silk rug covered the majority of the area. The stone around the gas fireplace matched the exterior, pulling the elements together. A curved flat screen television was mounted to the opposite wall. His brown leather furniture was complemented by an iron coffee table and two end tables.

"You've done a lot of work to the house. It looks good."

"Thanks. It's kept me busy in a good way, if that makes sense."

It did. Since Chance and I had the club, Jace had been forced to come up with other ways to occupy his time. Belonging to the wealthiest families in the Pacific Northwest had its perks. None of us had to work, but there was also way too much downtime. Even though we'd all attended college, Jace hadn't finished. His world had been turned upside down a few years ago when he'd lost his mom, and he'd struggled to find his way afterward.

Jace opened the drawer of the end table. He rummaged around until he produced a notepad and pen, then he settled in and flipped through the pages. "Found it."

I eyed him suspiciously. "I can't believe that you kept those notes all of these years."

"I read them over and over again. Apparently, you're not the only one obsessed with the technique. Mom definitely was, and I guess I was for a long time, too. I finally forced myself to leave it alone." He looked around the living room, sadly, and sighed. "I still miss her."

His words were so quiet I almost didn't hear him. "I know, man."

"Sometimes I think I hear her calling my name from the office. That probably sounds crazy, but in a twisted way it comforts me."

"Is that why you decided to remodel? To help you process?" I'd made it a point never to tell him he'd heal and move on. There was no moving on after you lost a parent or sibling.

He reclined and propped his feet up. "Yeah. I was on the fence about selling for a while, but at least for now, this is where I want to be."

I hesitated before I asked my next question. "Are you still toying with the idea of becoming a psychologist? It's obviously still your passion. Don't turn away from it because of what happened with your mom."

Jace glanced at the papers in front of him. "I'm not going to rush into making any decisions. If I can help you, maybe I'll consider it." He smirked at me. "Not sure anyone can help you, though."

I grabbed a magazine off the coffee table and chucked it at his head. "Asshole." We laughed, then settled down and focused.

"What do the notes say?" I willed the corded muscles in my neck and shoulders to relax.

He frowned and thumbed through a few pages before he started. "There's mention of a house and someone crying for you. You were searching through the rooms and checked a bathroom. When you saw your reflection in the mirror you panicked. We never did understand why it freaked you out."

My hands grew clammy, and a shiver shot through me. "I remember now. It wasn't that I saw my reflection, it was the eerie-as-fuck feeling I had when it happened. Like, I was seeing a different part of myself." I stood, an overwhelming sense of deja vu slamming into me.

"Dreams aren't often cut and dry. There's a lot of symbolism, but this ... this was hypnosis so I'm not sure if the same rules apply." Jace hopped out of his chair and ran upstairs where the bedrooms were located. When he reappeared, he held up his MacBook in his right hand. "Let's see what we can find."

"Poor Brynn was so freaked out she never wanted to talk about it again." I placed my hands on my hips, suddenly wondering how she was doing. I wished like hell I could be with her, but I had to stay focused on River while I waited to see if Tim would come through. "If this is connected with River in anyway, I have no fucking clue how." I stretched, my body aching from sitting too much.

Jace flipped open his laptop, and his fingers flew across the keys. "Mirrors, mirrors. Got it."

His gaze narrowed as he stared at the screen. "Hmm, no that doesn't fit. Bingo." He peeked up at me. "Mirrors symbolize the imagination and the link between the conscious and subconscious."

"But we already know that." Frustration seeped into my words. "I mean, we know I have a block of time where I can't remember shit. I've lost memories, and they're buried in my subconscious. I can't shake the feeling it all ties into River's disappearance."

"It just confirms that whatever is going on with your nightmares and the hypnosis is definitely something that you experienced."

I could literally feel the color drain from my face. "No fucking way." My stomach squeezed tight, and I was ready to vomit again. I took long, deep breaths. "There's no way I witnessed teenagers as sex slaves. It has to mean something else." I sank onto the sofa. "Right?"

Jace and I stared at each other, a heartbreaking silence hovering over the room. "I don't know, Holden. I want to tell you that it's symbolism, but ..." Compassion flickered across his expression. "After everything with my mom ... you probably saved my life. Maybe this is my opportunity to help you in return. Regardless of what we learn, I've got your back. And you know Brynn and Chance will do everything in their power to help you get through whatever this is as well."

I threaded my hand through my hair, tugging the strands in frustration. "How the hell did we get here?" I glanced at him.

"It doesn't matter. We have to stay focused on finding the answers."

He was right, but there was only one solution that I could think of. "Goddammit. I need to go under again."

Jace closed his computer. "You can't. We have to give it some time. You're running on fumes and your nerves are fucking shot. I won't help you do this. Not until you get some rest."

A sharp ache spread through my chest. "What if we're too late, Jace? What if River never makes it back?" Fear, grief, and anxiety swirled in the pit of my gut.

"She will. I don't know how this will play out, but River is one strong woman. Plus," he tapped the side of his head with emphasis, "she's fucking smart. Street smart on top of it. I damn-well guarantee you that she's figuring out a way to make it back here."

Dawn sunlight trickled over the wood floors, etching a wide band of honey colored red light into the foyer.

Wherever River was, I hoped she could see the same sunrise. *I love you, babe.*

"I'm going to make some coffee and breakfast. Why don't you raid my fridge and see what you want to eat?"

It would be useless to argue with him, but if I was going to talk him into hypnotizing me again, I had to feed my body and mind.

Following Jace, I halted once we reached the kitchen. "Shit, this looks amazing." I ran my fingertips over the black marble countertops. The white marble backsplash brightened the space, providing a wide-open feel. The stainless-steel hood hung over the new matching stove. The dishwasher and refrigerator were spotless, which led me to think they were smudge-proof.

"It came together really nicely." Jace busied himself with starting some coffee while I rummaged through his food. "What sounds good? Pancakes? An omelet?"

I stopped searching his fridge and looked at him. "That's what I made for River the morning I found her in my recycling bin."

Shock registered in his expression, and he nearly tripped over his feet. "I'm sorry, what? Like the big blue trash container?"

"Oh, that's right. When you guys met her, I introduced her as my cousin. I never told you how we really met." I couldn't help but smile at the memory of meeting her that day.

"You gotta fill me in."

I removed the milk, eggs, cheese, green onions, mushrooms, and a can of biscuits and placed them on the counter.

"Bacon," Jace said, nodding as he pulled the package of pancake mix down from the cabinet.

I glanced at the ingredients. "Shit. I must be hungry."

"Good. Now quit stalling and tell me how you really met River."

I retrieved a small pan for the gravy and set it on one of the five burners. "Becky had just left." My lip curled in a snarl. "Michelle," I corrected myself. "Anyway, she went out the front door, thank God. Oh, and that bitch can say whatever the fuck she wants, I know she is jealous of River."

"Agreed," Jace said, whipping up the pancake batter.

"I needed to take the trash to the curb for pickup, but when I approached the canisters, one of them was laying on its side. All I could see was a pair of black, worn-out Converse poking out of the recycling bin. I gently shook a foot and backed up, not wanting to spook anyone."

"What the hell was she doing sleeping in your container? It was winter."

"It was below freezing, too. I was worried maybe someone had frozen to death, so I tugged on her ankles." A chuckle rumbled through my chest. "Then I met the tip of her knife."

Jace barked out a laugh. "Who was startled more? You or River?"

"I definitely scared her more. It took me a while to talk her into coming inside so I could make her some breakfast." I scanned the ingredients that were in front of me. "She was terrified, dirty, and exhausted. All I wanted to do was help her."

"I think any decent human being would have." Jace tossed the bacon in the pan, then started the pancakes as we continued to talk.

"She wouldn't come into the house. It took me forever to convince her that I wasn't trying to hurt her. Eventually, she finally came in and stood next to the sliding glass door. I tried to reassure her that she was safe, but I had no idea what she'd just lived through. She agreed to some food and ate it all. River was even open to more, but as she approached the kitchen, she accidentally dropped the plate and it shattered all over the floor." I shook my head as the events played out in my mind. "Dan must have done a real number on her because she bolted. I almost caught up to her when she jumped over a lawn chair and tripped."

"Is that how she really broke her leg?" Jace poured the smooth, thick batter into the pan.

I popped open the can of biscuits and placed them on the cookie sheet. "Nope. She shot up and high-tailed it out of the backyard and into the alley. She was fucking fast, too." I tossed the empty container in the trash. "I tried to stop her, but she ran in front of a car."

"You saw it all go down, huh?" Jace stepped out of the way and opened the oven door, and I slid the pan of biscuits in.

"Yeah, Maxwell was driving, and he about shit himself," I snickered.

"Oh man. He's a weaselly fuck, but I wouldn't wish hitting a person with your car on anyone."

"It's funny how those seconds changed my entire life." I opened the white cabinet and removed a few plates. "I hate that she got hurt, but I'd do anything to have that time with her again." Grief wrapped its fingers around my heart and squeezed. A second wind of determination followed, and once again, I swore that I'd move heaven and earth to bring the love of my life home.

Chapter Thirty-Two

Once breakfast was over, Chance texted that Brynn had started her chemo. I hoped like hell the treatment worked.

I stretched out on the couch and dozed off and on while Jace buried himself in research. We'd always been upfront with each other, but this time I felt like there was something he wasn't telling me. I wasn't positive, but I had a strong hunch that it was a detail from the first time I was hypnotized.

The morning crawled by at a turtle's pace. I should have gone to bed, but I was a fucking chicken. Jace was wrong. My nightmares and visions couldn't be a part of my past. What I struggled with even more was how this might tie into River. Or was I fishing for anything that might make sense of her disappearance? Logan and Tim were ruled out. Laura was the only suspect that we had, and she'd not been helpful at all.

Anger pulsed through my veins. Laura had used 4 Play to lure young women into a sex ring. The pair of balls on this bitch were insane. If she had River ... was it Laura's idea or her boss's? *How fucking dare she?* Even worse, I should have known what was happening in my club. Guilt toyed with me, making me second-guess my intuition and the choice to rebuild.

Questions spun in a million directions as I scrambled to put the pieces together. Even though Pierce and the FBI suspected Laura, it could still be a dead end. No one was sure that we were even on the right path.

I rubbed my eyes, trying to connect the dots between my nightmares and Laura.

"I can literally see the wheels turning in your head," Jace said, glancing up from his mother's notes.

"You can probably hear them, too." I sat up. "I'm just trying to see how Laura fits into my nightmares. Or does she?"

"I think we have to look at the common thread. Sex trafficking. If Laura does have River, then I'm pretty sure the goal is to either sell her or make her a sex slave."

I winced. "You didn't have to say it out loud, Jace."

Jace set the book down on the end table. "I'm not trying to be insensitive, Holden. But the more we talk about it, the more likely it is that your brain is going to kick in at some point and it's all going to fall into place. Don't forget, Tim is working to get River back, too."

"I don't trust the son of a bitch," I growled. "If he were really on my side, he would have already told me where she was."

"There's no way I can disagree with you on that one."

My phone vibrated against the glass of the coffee table in front of me. "It's Chance."

I accepted the FaceTime call. The second I saw Chance's face, I immediately knew something was horribly wrong.

Jace joined me on the couch, then gave me a sideways glance.

"Hey, man. How is everyone doing?"

The overhead hospital lights shone on Chance's cheeks and showcased his tears.

"Dude, talk. What's going on?" I ordered.

He shook his head. "You guys need to fly down. She had an allergic reaction to the chemo. They had to induce a coma and she's on a ventilator." Chance stared at the floor. "It's not good. You guys should get down here in case this is goodbye."

I shot off the couch, my heart splintering. We couldn't lose her. No way. It wasn't fucking allowed.

"Jace will book us a flight, and I'll start packing. Is there anything we need to bring down for you?"

Chance shook his head. "No. Just get down here."

"We're on it. And if anything changes ..."

"You'll be the first call I make," he assured me.

Chance disconnected the video, and I stared at Jace.

"I'm already on it." He returned to the recliner and grabbed his Mac.

An unexplainable calm enveloped me as I pushed all the fear and negativity down into the darkest part of myself. I had to keep a level head.

Jace looked up from his computer. "We can be on the next flight if we can make it in two hours."

"Yes. That gives us an hour to get clothes and shit together. I packed to stay here for a few days, so I'm already set."

The sound of Jace typing was the only sound in the room. "Booked." He closed the laptop and hopped out of the chair. "I'll be ready in ten."

"What can I do to help?" I asked as my pulse throbbed in my head.

"Whatever bodyguard is outside, let them know."

"Oh shit. I bet Zayne is back." I hurried to the front door and searched the premises.

"Hey, man." I waved at Zayne in the front yard. "I'll explain on the way, but we gotta head to the airport in ten minutes." I closed the door before he could reply.

I ran up the stairs to Jace's room. "Zayne's back. I've seen him drive in an emergency. He'll get us there on time."

"Excellent." Jace ran his hands over his hair and searched the room with a blank expression.

"A few pairs of clothes, toothbrush, shower and shaving shit, and your MacBook. Oh, and chargers for phones and headphones," I rattled off the list.

Jace pointed at me. "Thanks." He darted to the bathroom, scooped the necessary items into his arms, then tucked them into his suitcase.

"Is that your phone charger?" I removed it from the wall anyway and tossed it on top of his clothes.

"Yeah. My Mac cord is over there." He tilted his head in the opposite direction.

I snatched it up and helped him finish packing. Since I hadn't even unpacked my reusable grocery bag, I was already set.

"Ready?" Jace heaved the strap over his shoulder. "I have extra clothes in case you need to borrow a shirt or something."

"Good idea. We can always shop if we have too ... but I doubt we will want to leave Brynn's side unless they force us."

"Keys, wallet, phone ... I'm good. You?" Jace patted his front pocket, then scooted by me and into the hall.

Mentally, I double-checked that I had my shit as well.

The sound of our socked feet smacking the wood stairs echoed through the house. I grabbed my belongings that were still in the entry way and flung the front door open. Jace locked up, and we hurried to the car. Zayne was already in the driver's seat. As soon as we were settled in and buckled up, he shifted into drive.

"Brynn had an allergic reaction to her chemo. She's on the vent. Chance said to hurry ... we might have to say goodbye." My words clogged my throat, and I struggled to breathe.

Without a word, Zayne tapped the phone button on the steering wheel as he pulled out of Jace's driveway.

"Zayne. What's going on?" Pierce's voice came through the Bluetooth system.

"Is your plane available? We have a medical emergency in Portland." Zayne's gaze cut over to me.

"I can have it ready by the time you reach the airport. Is Holden all right?"

"It's Brynn," I chimed in. "She's at OHSU for ... she has cancer." I wasn't sure if Zayne had filled him in or not. "She had a reaction to her chemo and she ... we don't know if she's going to live." My words trailed off.

"Shit," Pierce said. "Yeah, it will be ready to go. Plus, my plane will get you down there a lot faster."

I glanced over my shoulder at Jace in the back seat.

"Thanks, Pierce," I said.

"Zayne, you know where to go. Keep me posted. Hang in there, guys. If you need anything, and I mean anything, I'm only a phone call away." Pierce's words were genuine and heartfelt.

"Find River," I whispered beneath my breath. There wasn't any reason for me to say it out loud. I knew Pierce and Sutton were working their asses off.

Zayne disconnected the call, and I slumped into my seat.

"You're a fucking life saver, Zayne. Thanks, man. I'll let Chance know when we'll be there."

"Good thing I booked refundable tickets." Jace removed his phone from his pocket and canceled our flights.

Once we were on the way to the airport, Jace leaned forward. "How was last night, Zayne?"

"Oh shit, that's right." I glanced at my bodyguard, who I was quickly considering a friend.

"Exactly what I needed." A corner of his mouth turned up. "Stress release in the best form."

"Hell, yeah it is." Jace slapped him on his shoulder.

"I'm glad it helped." A flicker of jealousy reared its ugly head. I wasn't jealous of Zayne being single. I just missed sex with River. My gut twisted into painful knots. I'd never realized that missing River would be this fucking intense.

The flight was quick and painless. Not only had Pierce flown us down, but he also had a company Mercedes waiting for us. Zayne had explained that Pierce and Sutton owned a penthouse in Portland, and some of his men worked here. Regardless, the trip was seamless, and we were at the Knight Center before noon.

Stopping at the front desk, the sweet, elderly lady provided Brynn's room number for us while Jace called Chance and let him know we'd arrived.

Zayne, Jace, and I remained quiet as we rode the elevator up to Brynn's floor. The center was huge, and my chest squeezed tight as I realized the only reason it was that big was because of the overwhelming need. Cancer was a bitch. I stared at my shoes and attempted to brace myself for what was ahead, but nothing in this world could have prepared me for what shitshow came next.

The elevator doors slid open, and Zayne held the door as Jace and I entered the hallway. Hospital employees hustled and bustled at the nurse's station as we walked by. A few heads turned, and I nearly laughed. Jace was definitely a good-looking guy, but if I had to make a bet on who the ladies were drooling over, it would be on Zayne. He was GQ magazine cover quality, for damned sure.

I spotted Chance stepping into the hall from Brynn's room. He shoved his hands in his pockets and met us halfway. He hugged us tightly, then led the way to her room. Zayne took his post at her door.

"Any changes?" I asked while I slipped inside. My mouth gaped, and I slammed it closed. "Shit." I turned away in an attempt to collect myself.

Jace cleared his throat, tears welling in his eyes as he stared at her.

Machines beeped and whooshed as the ventilator forced her body to breathe. The color had drained from her cheeks, and they appeared even paler against the white and green hospital gown. Blue chairs lined the wall, and we each grabbed one. As far as hospital rooms went, this one had the standard boring interior, but it was much larger.

"No. If her vitals are stable in a few days, then they'll bring her out of the coma." Chance folded his arms over his chest and shook his head. "It all went wrong so fucking fast."

Finally, I walked over and took her hand in mine. "Hey, sweet girl. Jace and I are here with Chance." I kissed the back of her hand as she remained motionless. Her eyelids didn't flutter open, and her gorgeous green eyes didn't gaze at me. I sat in the chair closest to her. A part of me wondered if she could hear me, or if I was simply making a fool out of myself. Honestly, it didn't matter. I had to try.

"Hey, babe." Jace kissed her forehead and sat in the chair on the other side of her. He took her hand in his.

"Do her parents know?" I asked Chance.

"Yeah. They're finally on the way from Europe, so there's that." He sighed and sat in one of the chairs against the wall, stretching his long legs in front of him. I hadn't noticed the dark circles beneath his eyes until now. He looked like shit.

"You brushed her hair?" Jace asked Chance.

"Yeah. If she comes out of this, she'll lose most of it with chemo. I wanted her to ..." He rubbed his nose and sniffled. "To feel beautiful for a little longer."

Shit. Chance was head-over-heels for her. Brynn deserved someone who loved her fully and completely. There's no way that she could go wrong with Chance. He loved her the way I loved River.

"If River were here, she'd crawl in bed with her." I smiled sadly. "They're small so they'd both fit."

We all stared at each other. It was fucked up not having any clue of what my life would look like a few hours from now. Fate had grabbed me by the balls and refused to let go. *Fuck fate.*

I glanced at Jace and shifted in the seat. "So ... Jace and I used the experimental hypnosis this morning," I said to Chance.

Shock registered on his features. "Fuck. Why?"

"He's a glutton for punishment," Jace added, frowning at me. "Brynn would have never allowed it."

I stroked the back of her hand with the pad of my thumb, willing her to wake up and glare at me. Maybe if we talked about it, it would fire her up, and those green eyes would narrow in my direction.

"I had to use the ice again." Jace kissed Brynn's knuckles.

"Did it help? I mean the hypnosis, not the ice. That too, but we had to use that last time." Chance leaned over and propped his elbows on his knees.

Dryness seized my throat. I wasn't sure I wanted to discuss all the details in front of Brynn, but if she could understand what we were saying, she'd kick me if I didn't continue.

Brynn's heart monitor beeped in the background as the tension in the room grew. I was so fucking exhausted I wasn't sure how I was functioning.

"Jace can tell you." I nodded at Jace.

"I found my notes from the first time Holden went under. It was a similar experience, but this time there was a lot more detail."

A frown creased Chance's forehead. "It's been a while. I don't remember what happened the first time, other than we couldn't pull him out until we tossed buckets of ice into the bathwater."

Goosebumps peppered my skin as I recalled the eerie feeling of the last hypnosis.

"A house, someone calling his name, and he saw himself in a mirror," Jace reminded him.

"So you saw all of that again, Holden?" Chance seemed more alert now that we were talking about it.

"Worse. And the nightmares are the same as what I saw when I went under again," I confessed.

"You're having nightmares? Dude, when were you going to clue me in?" Irritation weaved through Chance's tone.

Jace shot me an 'I told you so' look, and I mouthed a 'fuck you' at him. I followed it up with a half-cocked smile. He already knew how grateful I was for his help.

"Brynn knew," Jace added.

"You're just trying to get me into trouble, aren't you?" I laughed softly.

"Hell yeah. I've got to entertain our girl somehow." Jace leaned back in his chair as his gaze flitted to an unmoving Brynn.

"Man, I wish I'd been there," Chance said quietly.

"You don't. The shit that I said afterward was fucked up."

Jace nodded. "Very."

"Well quit pretending this is a suspense novel and fucking spill." Exasperation clouded Chance's features.

I gently squeezed Brynn's hand. It was nice to touch her again. I'd missed her horribly while she'd been at OHSU. "I have a hunch that my nightmares are telling me something about River. That's the only reason I asked Jace to help me. There's something I'm missing." With a shake of my head to clear away the memories, I took a deep breath. "The same little voice calls my name in the nightmares as while I'm hypnotized. It's a little kid. I'm not sure if it's a boy or a girl, but they're terrified, screaming for me to help."

"Fuck," Chance said softly.

"This time I walked down a hall and saw different memories of Brynn, Mom, Mallory, Tim, and Hannah, then I reached a door. Once I pushed it open, everything changed. I didn't recognize the room or the people. But ..." I coughed in an attempt to hide the gut-wrenching emotion that had lodged itself in my throat. "Adults were abusing boys and girls in their late teens. Sexually. It was a party, and they selected their preference." I covered my mouth with my hand. "I saw one girl being led around by a leash. She was naked and crawling on all fours."

"Shit. That's some vivid recollection." He gave me a clipped nod, but a storm brewed in his expression.

"We're still trying to figure out how it might relate to River," Jace said.

"What's startling is that your nightmares are similar. I mean, dreams are pretty symbolic. Just because you see a lot of money in a dream doesn't mean you're going to be rich. But with the hypnosis." Chance's voice trailed off. "Holden, those are memories that you've repressed."

"Exactly," Jace added.

Bile churned in my stomach, burning a trail up my throat. I wished like hell Brynn and River were here to share their thoughts.

"I hadn't had the nightmares in a while, then when I met River, they were nonexistent until she disappeared," I explained.

"That's why you think they're connected to her?" Chance shook his head in dismay.

"Yeah."

Jace's attention bounced between Chance and me as he spoke. "Ya know, I'd have to agree with you. I mean what's the probability? I think your subconscious is trying to tell you where she is or who has her."

"I made a deal with Tim, too. Since he knows who has River and hasn't told me ..." I ground my molars together as a white-hot fury licked through me. "I told him unless he brings her home, I won't work for him. His time is definitely running out." My shoulders slumped. "I'm not sure I'm a big enough bargaining chip, but I gave it a shot."

"Well, does he know where she is? That could put a kink in his plan if he doesn't know where she is," Chance pointed out.

"Dammit. With everything going on, that possibility hadn't crossed my mind." My heart plummeted to my toes. "He might not be able to do anything at all."

"Days can seem like a fucking eternity, but let's see what happens," Jace said.

Chance stared at me, but his expression was unreadable. "I remember when we were stoned in high school—"

"Which time?" Jace asked, chuckling.

"The time Holden got all serious on us and mentioned that he felt like something was wrong with him. He'd never felt complete."

"Oh shit. I'd forgotten about that," I muttered.

"Of course, you did. We were all stoned." Jace grinned at us. "We had some fun days."

I gently squeezed Brynn's hand, mentally hearing her soft laugh as we reminisced. "It was a strange feeling, one that I've had most of my life. It's hard to explain."

"In that same high-as-a-kite conversation, you also mentioned that you didn't have any memories from the ages of three to five." Chance's gaze narrowed as if he were pondering the world's problems. "Your memories, Holden." He didn't finish. He didn't fucking have to.

A long screeching beep filled the room, and I froze. "Brynn?" I shook her shoulder as nurses and doctors rushed into the room.

"Code Blue!"

Chapter Thirty-Three

"What's happening?" Chance yelled as we were ushered into the hallway.

"Get out of the room please!" A nurse said, her tone nonnegotiable.

"Coming through!" Another nurse flew past us and straight to Brynn.

"Please wait outside," someone said before she closed the door on us.

"She's dead," I whispered, disbelief and agony warring inside of me. I glanced at Zayne as I sank to the tiled floor and covered my face with my hands.

Jace knelt beside me, and he rested his forehead on the wall. "Come on, Brynn. It's not your fucking time yet."

Chance paced the hall, his fingers locked behind his head. A tear landed on his black tennis shoe.

Jesus. What just happened? My shoulders shook as a sob choked me—Brynn's laughter, her smile, her big heart ... never again. A low groan escaped me as I quietly fell apart. She was only twenty-one. She was too full of life and too young to die. I clenched my hands into tight fists, suppressing the scream that clawed its way up my throat. How the fuck was I supposed to tell River that Brynn was gone? She'd lost too much already. We all had.

Jace sat down and pulled his knees to his chest, rocking back and forth. He buried his head as his own tears escaped. Our best friend was gone. Forever. I'd never talk to her until the early hours of the morning again. She wouldn't see River in her wedding gown or throw her a bachelorette party.

The sound of the door broke through my grief, but I didn't dare glance at them. I couldn't look at the team that had failed Brynn. Deep down, I knew it wasn't their fault, but I hated them. I hated the treatment that killed her. I hated this goddamned hospital.

"Guys?" a soft female voice said. "We got her back. Brynn's alive."

I nearly gave myself whiplash from turning my head to see who was talking—a *doctor*. A small smile eased across her face. She tucked strands of salt-and-pepper-colored hair into her ponytail.

I scrambled to my feet and gave Jace a hand up. My legs wobbled beneath me as I took a step forward. "She's alive?" I repeated to make sure I hadn't been hallucinating. With the stress I'd been under, it wouldn't surprise me.

"Yeah. We're monitoring her closely. The reaction was pretty bad, but if she makes it through tonight, then our girl has a fighting chance."

"Can we?" I pointed to the door.

Her expression softened. "She needs to rest. There are a lot of studies that show that a person in a coma can hear everything that's said. I think under the circumstances, she shouldn't have any visitors."

"Can we see her before we leave?" Realizing my nose was running, I swiped at it with the heel of my hand.

"One at a time. Talk to her, tell her she's going to make it and for her to get some rest. That's it. Nothing else." Her dark eyebrow arched at us.

"Promise," we said in unison.

"There's a hotel less than a mile away. Be sure that we have all of your phone numbers in case we can't reach you. Feel free to check in every few hours, too."

"I'll handle the contact information," Zayne said quietly. I glanced over at him. His face was still full of grief.

"Chance, go on in." I squeezed his shoulder before he left Jace and me in the hall. I watched Zayne stroll down toward the nurse's station. I nearly chuckled as four nurses rushed over to help him. They were all smiles and fluttering hands as he began to talk to them. Typically, I would have been rolling on the floor laughing, but Brynn had just died. Flatlined. Coded.

I grabbed Jace in a huge hug. "Love ya, man," I croaked out.

"You, too." Jace gripped my shirt, and we clung to each other for several seconds.

One thing about Jace, Chance, and me, we weren't afraid to hug or say we loved each other. Hell, we'd seen each other fuck the girls in the club. This was nothing. This was raw and honest, and I hadn't found what I had with them in any other friends. We'd covered up secrets, lied for each other, cried, and laughed together. And now, we'd lost both our girls and were grieving together.

The door opened, and Chance left her room. "Can I go next?" Jace asked me.

"Of course." I squeezed his shoulder before he joined Brynn.

"I won't ask if you're okay. I'm not. I'm still reeling." I eyed my best friend.

"I've never told her how much I love her. Not that I love her, but I'm so fucking in love with her it's eating me up. What if I never have that opportunity?" He leaned against the wall as tears fell down his cheeks.

"Then you fucking get back in there and tell her, Chance. You fucking tell her. You heard the doctor. They think Brynn can hear us."

He looked up at the ceiling and blinked several times.

"Let me go in and tell her I love her and as soon as she's better she can help River pick out her wedding gown. Then, I'll get right back out here, and we'll sneak you in. You can't leave without telling her how you feel, Chance. Besides, your voice should be the last she hears today. You telling her how much you love her should be the words she's left with for the night."

Jace joined us in the hall. "Stay close and sneak in as soon as I'm done. The nurses can see us from their station. Jace will block their view as much as possible."

Confusion flickered in Jace's gaze.

"Chance needs to talk to her before we're kicked out," I explained.

Chance stood next to Brynn's door, and Jace stood in front of him. Jace's shoulders were broader, and he cleared Chance by an inch, so hopefully, our plan would work.

I slipped in, my attention landing on Brynn. The soft beep of the heart monitor told me she was with us again.

"Hey, hon." I approached her bed and took her hand in mine. "I love you." I brushed the strands of red hair off her forehead. "Don't forget that you promised to take River shopping for her wedding gown. You're going to be an amazing maid of honor." I leaned over and kissed her on the side of her head. "Get some rest and I'll be back later."

Her frail fingers fell from mine as I walked away, begging God or anyone who might listen to me not to take her yet. She had to make it through the night.

I stepped into the hall and held the door open as Chance scurried in. I folded my arms over my chest and stood in front of the room. I could at least talk shit long enough to a doctor or nurse if they came over and wanted to make him leave. He only needed a minute or two.

"They have all of our cell numbers," Zayne said. "I booked the penthouse at the Hyatt. There's three bedrooms."

"Thanks. Maybe you can get some sleep, too. I think we're all running on fumes."

"I only need a few hours. We'll work it out. With Tim in Oregon, I'm not taking any chances."

I cringed. "Fuck, I forgot about all of that shit."

Chance reappeared and nodded at me.

"Let's get some rest so we can be here the second they call," I said.

The four of us fell into step and passed the nurse's station.

"That is one lucky girl," one of them said.

I glanced over my shoulder to find five women watching us as we walked away. Brynn would have laughed her ass off. I could imagine Brynn throwing her head back, her laughter floating on the air, then grinning and agreeing with them.

I hoped like hell she would have the opportunity to do just that.

The city view from the penthouse was stunning, but all it did was make me miss River even more. The space was tastefully decorated with beige and white striped wallpaper that carried into the other rooms. A Victorian sofa and four chairs filled the living area. A large, flatscreen television rested on a dark brown entertainment cabinet. At first, I'd been concerned that we wouldn't have any privacy if we needed to have a breakdown, but there was plenty of space.

Chance and Jace had picked a bedroom and shut their doors. I was bone-weary tired, but I couldn't fucking sleep. Not yet. My mind was racing with possibilities for River and Brynn.

I checked my phone several times and ensured the volume was up. I'd contemplated reaching out to Tim about Brynn, but I wasn't sure Zayne would appreciate it. I didn't see the difference since Tim usually knew where I was anyway. If he'd wanted to hurt me, he would have done it by now.

I smashed the palm of my hand against the glass window. It took me a few minutes of silence to realize I needed to call Mom. I wasn't sure if she was still in London or somewhere else, but I checked the time on my cell. It was a little after two in the afternoon. To my knowledge, she was eight hours ahead of me.

Grabbing my phone out of my shorts pocket, I pulled up her number and placed the call.

"Hi, honey." Mom sounded tired, but happy to hear from me.

"Hey. How's your trip going?" I leaned my forehead against the window, watching the Portland traffic come to a standstill on the streets below.

"Exhausting, but good. I'm accomplishing so much more than I'd anticipated. How about you? I hope you're calling with some good news about River."

I counted my next four heartbeats before I answered. "Nothing yet. But the guys and I are in Portland right now."

"Oh? Is there a lead you're chasing there?" Mom asked.

"Not exactly."

"Well, why would you leave town? What if there's a break in the case and you're not there? How would River feel if she's rescued and you're in another state?"

Mom was smart and didn't miss much.

"I wouldn't have. Mom, Brynn was diagnosed with stage three lymphoma. They transferred her to the OHSU Knight Cancer Center. She started chemo today and she had a fucked-up reaction. She ... she coded a little while ago, but they revived her." I ground my molars together in an attempt to keep my emotions in check while on the phone.

"What? Holden, if this is some kind of sick joke ...I—"

"I'd never play with you like that, Mom." My chest heaved as I battled the tears again. "She's resting now. Jace, Chance, and I had to leave the center. I'll call and check in soon."

"Okay. Okay. Okay." Her voice trembled.

I closed my burning eyes and gave Mom a minute to process. "I'll cancel the rest of my meetings and be on the first flight to Portland. Are her parents there?" She sniffled.

"They're flying in from somewhere in Europe. I have no idea

when they'll be here. They knew about the cancer and didn't bother to come home," I said through clenched teeth.

"I made that mistake once with Hannah, and I'll never do it again. Brynn is like another daughter to me. I'll contact the hospital and ensure she has the best care possible."

I wasn't sure what to say. Mom rarely mentioned Hannah. She'd held her ground about cutting ties with her after Hannah's continuous drug use. I was so angry with her that it hadn't occurred to me that Mom had gone through hell and had never shared her grief with me. She just kept pushing me away, and I hadn't understood her behavior. At seventeen, I'd thought I had the entire world figured out. Hearing Mom's reaction that afternoon was a wake-up call. It wasn't that Mom hadn't cared about Hannah. She simply grieved differently. I lost a sister, but Mom lost a daughter.

A smile eased across my face. I should have called Mom sooner. She was a fucking force to be reckoned with when she wanted shit done.

"I'm going to pack and schedule my flight. I'll send you the details shortly. I'll fly into Portland and rent a car. Where are you staying?" The sounds in the background told me she was most likely running around, throwing shit in a suitcase.

"I'm at the Hyatt. We have the penthouse, but I'm guessing you won't want to stay with a bunch of guys."

"Can you book a room for me at the same hotel? I'll email you as soon as I have the flight details." Her phone clattered to the floor. "I'm sorry, Holden. I'm so rattled, I'm trying to talk on my phone and pack instead of using the speaker."

"I understand." I took a step away from the window and headed to the bar. I could definitely use a drink later to knock the edge off. For now, I'd see what was available.

"I guess it won't help that I'm packed if I don't have a flight yet." Mom sighed. "She's too young to leave us, Holden. Brynn's a fighter. She has her entire life ahead of her." Mom hiccupped through her tears. "But I'm sure as hell not helping her any by blubbering on the phone. I'll send you my flight details."

"Okay. I'll see you soon. I'll update you with any news."

"Thanks, honey."

"Hey, Mom?"

"Yes?"

"I love you."

I waited through Mom's tears for her response.

"I love you, too. And for the record, you've always been my favorite. You have such a wonderful heart."

I blinked the moisture off my eyelashes. Mom's words had reached through the phone and wrapped me in her arms. Apparently, I would always need my mom, no matter how old I was.

An hour later, I had flight details and had booked Mom's room for tomorrow. Exhausted, I made my way to the bedroom and closed the door. I stripped down to my boxer-briefs and crawled beneath the blankets. My eyes fluttered closed, then shot open again. I hoped like hell I wouldn't have another nightmare. But the harder I tried to stay awake, the heavier my eyelids grew. The sound of my breathing filled the room as I drifted off to sleep.

The most beautiful girl I'd ever seen stood in front of me, terrified.

I reached out to smooth the hair from her cheek. "I love you so goddamned much, River."

She pushed up on her tiptoes and pressed her mouth against mine. "I love you, too, baby." Her blue eyes gazed into mine, and I lost myself in her. This girl owned every part of me.

I slowly unbuttoned her new, baby blue silk blouse. A hint of black lace peeked out. Slipping off her shirt, my cock pushed against the zipper of my black suit pants. I couldn't wait to have her under me, my name on her beautiful, full lips.

I nipped her ear, then trailed soft kisses down her neck. Her nipples hardened against the fabric of her bra, and I eased the straps off her shoulders, never taking my attention off her.

I knelt in front of her as I freed her breasts. I kissed my way down her flat stomach and to her waistband. When she'd shown up at the club in tight jeans, a blouse, and black boots, I'd nearly come just looking at her.

I flipped the button open and lowered her zipper. Tugging on her jeans, I pulled them over her hips and down her thighs, revealing a lace G-string. I nipped her hip bone as she held onto my shoulders and stepped out of her pants. I placed my palms against her lower back and ass cheek, then pressed my nose against the thin material. Jesus, I couldn't wait to taste her.

I pulled her panties down in a quick move and gently bit the tender skin on her lower belly. So much for waiting. I had no control with her. All I wanted to do was fuck her with my tongue until she came all over my face. Her sweet little pussy was the only thing I'd thought about all night.

"Lay down," I growled, unzipping my slacks, and freeing my cock. I wrapped my hands around the shaft and stroked it.

River's teeth sank into her bottom lip as she parted her legs for me.

"Do you like this?" I stood and moved my feet farther apart.

Her attention was on my dick as I rubbed it for her. A small whimper escaped her as she watched me massage a drop of precum into my skin. Her tongue darted over her lower lip, and her core glistened from desire.

"Yeah." Heat traveled up her neck and cheeks. She was so fucking hot when she looked up at me beneath her dark eyelashes, naive and willing.

I knelt on the floor and pulled her to the edge of my bed. I placed a leg over each of my shoulders, then licked her swollen clit. She sucked in a breath and arched her back, her perfect tits on full display. I ran my finger up her wet slit as I continued to lick her bundle of nerves. River sank into the bed and bucked her hips.

Losing any restraint, I shoved my tongue into her.

"You taste so fucking good." I glanced up at her, then devoured every inch of her.

She dug her fingers into my hair, tugging slightly as she moaned and fucked my face.

I eased a finger into her, then curled it. She gasped and clutched the bedspread.

"Holden ... Oh God."

She writhed beneath me, and my dick begged to be buried deep inside her slick walls. "That's it, baby."

I was on fire. My entire being hummed with expectation and need. My tongue probed deeper, possessing every part of her as she released.

I hopped off the floor and slid my cock into her before she had time to recover. Her eyes widened as she dug her fingernails into my ass cheeks and rocked against me.

"Harder," she panted. A frown creased her brow, then her mouth gaped in pleasure. She quickly rolled over and pinned me beneath her. I sucked on her nipple, biting it gently as she threw her head back and picked up speed.

I lifted her, then brought her down on my cock again. She was stunning as she moaned with pleasure, her tits bouncing to the same rhythm that I fucked her. I wanted to come all over them.

She eased up and down my dick, and I slipped my hand between her legs, massaging her clit. "That's it, baby. Fuck me hard. Take what you need."

I lifted her up again and again until my balls tightened. Jolts of pleasure shot through me as I released inside of her. Seconds later, her core clenched around me as she came undone in the best way.

She collapsed against me, breathing hard and glistening with sweat. I kissed the top of her head and rubbed her back. I never wanted this to end. I never wanted to let her go.

I woke out of a sound sleep, the taste of River still on my lips. My cock was painfully hard, and I slid my hand into my boxer-briefs. With a few long, firm strokes, I released onto my stomach, my body jerking with thoughts of being buried deep inside her.

I shuddered, then stared blankly at the scene in front of me ... alone with a limp dick in my hand. My heart ached. It had been a sweet dream, but heavy, unshakable defeat followed quickly. I couldn't seem to kick the nagging feeling that I might not ever make love to River again.

Chapter Thirty-Four

I'm not sure what got into me, but after the dream, I stopped thinking clearly. It was most likely the death and revival of my best friend and fear of never kissing River again that propelled my decision.

I grabbed my cell off the nightstand and texted Tim.

I'm in Portland. Brynn has cancer. She coded today, but they revived her. But that's not why I'm reaching out. I need to have some kind of decision about my offer—River for me.

I stared at the phone, willing the black dots to flicker across my screen. Nothing. After another few minutes, I tossed it onto the nightstand. I needed a shower to clear my head.

My stomach growled as I washed my hair and body. I was out in record time, eager to see if Tim had replied. I toweled off as I walked over to retrieve my phone. I snatched the cell up and swiped, activating the face recognition. Nothing.

"Fuck him," I muttered. Who didn't message after the news that someone they knew had died? Granted, Brynn was alive, but we weren't out of the woods yet. I wasn't sure why I kept hoping that I'd reach some speck of humanity that was buried inside of his cold, hardened heart. The hopes of that idea faded, and I dressed in a clean pair of jeans and a black polo shirt. It was funny that I missed wearing a suit and working at the club. I missed the excitement, the people, and partnering with River.

Ignoring the fury uncurling inside me, I stayed focused and left the bedroom. Jace and Chance were in the living area with the television on low. I didn't bother to speak. Instead, I headed straight to the bar. Grabbing a glass and a bottle of scotch, I poured myself a healthy dose. I slammed the alcohol back and grimaced as it burned a trail down my throat. A warm sensation followed, and I rolled my shoulders before I filled the glass again.

"You might want to slow down in case we can see Brynn again today," Chance suggested gently.

"No. I can't, man." I usually wasn't much for getting plastered, but I couldn't get any fucking mental or emotional relief. Every time I closed my eyes, I dreamed of kids being abused, or of River. She should be here with me, with all of us as we nursed Brynn back to health and kicked cancer's pathetic ass. I hated this. I hated that I couldn't find River when I knew deep down inside that she was being hurt by whoever had her.

I poured another drink, then set the bottle down. Unadulterated hatred flickered to life inside me, catching fire and spreading through my entire being. I fucking hated Tim for what he'd done to my girlfriend. For what he'd done to me. Memories from the day River had been taken snapped through my mind. Every nerve in my body stood on end, and I curled my fingers around my glass. "As soon as Brynn is past the dangerous part, I'm going to hunt my father down and fucking end him."

Jace hopped off the couch and joined Chance and me at the bar. "I'm in."

My attention zeroed in on Chance. "You know I'm here for it. Whatever it takes to bring that son of a bitch down, I'm in." I took another drink and wondered if Zayne would want to help. Probably not, but I bet he had some badass skills I could use from his Army Ranger days.

Chance's phone rang, and he snatched it out of his back pocket. Fear twisted his features.

"Hello?" His attention bounced between Jace and me. "Okay, that's good, right?"

Anxiety pulled and tugged at my insides. From the way Chance was talking, I was guessing it was the hospital.

"Thank you." Chance disconnected the call. "Brynn's doing okay. No more scares. They still want to keep a close eye on her, and they think we shouldn't visit until the morning. The nurse mentioned that her blood pressure and heart rate had finally settled down. The doctor didn't want her to get excited at the sound of our voices."

I released the breath I hadn't realized I was holding. "So, our girl is hanging in there?" I clenched my jaw in order not to lose my shit again.

"So far so good. We'll know more in the morning." Chance eyed the scotch and grabbed the bottle. "Maybe we should just chill tonight. If the hospital calls, Zayne will drive us. I need to fucking unwind."

Jace collected a few glasses and held them up while Chance poured the amber-colored liquid.

I raised mine.

"To Brynn's full recovery and River's return," Jace said.

"Cheers." The clinking from the edge of our glasses echoed through the room.

Instead of slamming down the double shot, I took a small drink. "I'm not trying to be an insensitive ass, but I need to talk about something other than sad shit."

"Same," Jace chimed in. He strolled over to the couch and plopped down, stretching his legs out in front of him.

"What's on your mind?" Chance settled into one of the chairs, and I sank into the other.

"I miss the club." A weight lifted off my chest as I spoke the words.

"And?" Jace took another drink, then rested his tumbler on his jeaned thigh.

"If ... if things don't turn out how I hope they will." I swallowed hard. "I have to figure out how to pick myself up and rebuild my life."

"Dude, that's some dark shit. I thought you didn't want to talk about anything fucked up?" Jace's brows knitted together.

"I'm simply telling you where I'm coming from. I need to rebuild 4 Play." My hold on the glass tightened. "I have to plan ahead, or I'm going to go insane."

"Did you ever call the realtor about the property in Sandpoint?" Jace took another drink, tilted his head back, then cracked his neck.

"No. It slipped my mind with all the shit going down." I rubbed my chin. "Being on the water made me think, though. What if I built the club on the Spokane River? There's several pieces of property for sale."

"Too bad you can't build over the river." Chance crossed his legs. "Imagine what that would be like if you were dancing on a glass floor."

"I like that idea, but I don't think it would be a pleasant experience if people were drunk. Which, most of the time they are. Holden would be cleaning up chunks all night long." Jace flinched at the disgusting idea.

"Gross." I raised the glass to my lips and sipped the scotch. I took a moment to taste the alcohol as it rolled over my tongue and down my throat. The first few drinks, I hadn't given a shit what it tasted like. I just wanted to numb some of the unbearable pain. It was the only time-out that was available. I grinned. "Well, I wouldn't be cleaning it up, but Chance would if we were low on staff that night."

"Not happening. I make the bartenders do it on slow nights." Chance grinned as if he was really proud of himself.

"I think near the water would be pretty amazing. You could offer a closed-in balcony with an open roof for people to get some air. The last thing you want is someone wandering down to the river and falling in," Jace suggested.

I frowned. "Dammit. Maybe that location isn't the best idea. It sounds like more of a liability. One death and I'd be sued for every penny I have."

"Fuck that." Chance pressed the rim of the glass against his lips, then took a drink.

"Where's the prime area? Where do businesses boom?" Jace asked.

"Where I was at or on the river." My leg bounced as I pondered different options.

"Are you going to rebuild the Master's Playroom?" Chance asked.

"Oh yeah. And with the clientele that we currently have, I'll expand the lower floor too. I'm thinking we could easily add and book ten additional rooms."

Jace rubbed his fingertips together. "Major money."

"It will be a nice bump." I rolled my head, the stress easing from my neck and shoulders.

"So, you've decided to rebuild 4 Play. The only question is where? I'd pick out three places and list the pros and cons. It should be an easy choice after that," Chance suggested.

"That's a great idea." Unwilling to drop the subject yet, I grabbed a notepad and pen from the end table next to me. "Okay, so I can build where we were before the fire, on the river, or ..." I tapped the pen against the arm of the chair. "The water won't work. We've ruled that out. I guess I have some research to do."

"That should keep you busy. Plus, what if there's an existing building for sale? You can do a full reno. That would be cheaper than building from the ground up." I must have made a face because Jace followed up with, "I mean, don't immediately dismiss the idea." He stared at me. "Decisions made out of desperation never end well."

He was right. "I won't decide anything yet. I need something else to think about." I shifted in my chair. "What I want to do is go under hypnosis again."

"That has disaster written all over it." Jace shook his head. "Why now? I mean, Brynn almost left us, and you've been drinking."

"Exactly. I'm fucking exhausted and my barriers are down. I'm finally a bit numb. My thoughts aren't tapping on my skull every fucking second of the day."

"I get that. I do." Jace stood from the couch and topped off his drink. "It's already risky with your guard up. I'm almost afraid of what you'd see while you're like this."

We stared at each other in silence for a long moment.

Chance rose from his chair, pinning me with an intense gaze. His forehead creased. "I don't like it, but you'll do it with or without my approval." He placed his hands on his hips. "I know we need to find River, so I'll see if we have access to enough ice."

"Just call the front desk and ask for a few bags. And salt," I said, excited about the possibility of being able to connect the memories. "I did some research, and if you add salt to cold water, it lowers the temperature faster."

"Huh, I didn't realize that," Chance said, downing his drink.

Ten minutes later, Jace produced his mom's black book of notes and flipped it open. He heaved a sigh. "Are you sure, man?"

Jace was nervous. I didn't blame him. I hadn't ever gone under hypnosis after drinking. "Yeah. I've got to get some closure." I wouldn't admit it, but that's exactly what I was after. My entire life was open-ended, hanging on a shred of hope that something good would happen. I had to take control again, in whatever way I could.

I stepped out of my shoes and crawled into the bathtub, fully clothed. Chance threw a few hotel towels on the floor so I wouldn't bust my ass getting out of the tub soaking wet. Two more were ready for me on the towel warmer.

This was a huge risk, and I realized Jace and Chance understood it, but I needed to make sure they knew something first. "If anything happens. I love you guys. Take care of River and Brynn."

"Fuck off," Chance said. "If we lose you, I'm going to jerk you out of the tub and beat you until you snap back to reality." Chance cracked his knuckles. "Just saying."

I grinned at him. "Asshole."

No additional words were necessary as we stared at each other for a minute. "Let's do this."

I sank into the tub and willed myself to relax. Jace began to read from his mom's notes, and I slipped further and further away. I focused on my rhythmic breathing. In. Out. In. Out.

"Hello?" I called out. I was in the hall again, but there wasn't a white light this time. It was pitch fucking black. I put my hands up in front of me, attempting to feel for a wall. I inched forward and chewed on my bottom lip. An overhead light came on, and my eyes struggled to adjust to the harsh brightness.

The young lady I'd seen before with the leash around her neck was curled up in the corner of a cell, naked and shivering. I looked around the room, but we were alone. She peered up at me. Dirt covered her legs and knees. Her dark hair was matted to the side of her head.

"Are you alone?" I asked, approaching tentatively.

"Who sent you?" she asked, her teeth chattering. "What do you want?"

"I want to help. Why are you here?" I wrapped my fingers around the bars of her cell.

"You're here to hurt me." She drew her legs tighter against herself.

"What's your name? I'm ..." I suddenly realized I shouldn't give her my real name just in case she told someone that I'd been down here. Wherever down here was. "Steven."

She stared at me. Her dark eyes were clearer than when I'd seen her at the party.

I glanced at the lock, but it needed a key. It wasn't as if I could sneak down here and set her free. Where would she go? What would happen to her?

"Are they ... do they hurt you?" My throat was hoarse, thick, and scratchy with a combination of anger and pity.

"Holden." I jerked around at the whisper of my name. "Help me."

The darkness faded into a playroom I didn't recognize. "Yes?" I steadied myself, then walked around a pile of Legos. Crayons were scattered across the floor, some broken and others, the wrapper had been torn off.

"Holden," the voice said from behind me. I whirled around. The same faceless kid stood in front of me. Why the hell couldn't I see their face?

"I'm here." I held my hand out and finally realized I was young again. Most likely close to the same age.

Little fingers wrapped around mine. "Promise me they won't rip us apart." A slight lisp reached my ears.

"Why would anyone want to separate us?" I scrambled to understand what they were referring to.

"Promise me, Holden. Please."

"I promise."

Little arms circled around my torso, and I did my best to comfort them. The room flickered in and out. The little person stepped back, and their face began to take shape. Jesus, what was happening? Terror ripped through me, and I stumbled backward, staring at the person that haunted me.

"I don't understand. Stay away from me!" I crawled backward, frantically searching for a way out.

"Holden? What's wrong? Don't go. Don't leave me!"

Hot tears streamed down my cheeks, then a scream tore from my throat.

My body jerked out of the ice-cold water, and I gasped.

"Listen to my voice," Jace said. "You're here at the hotel with Chance and me. You're coming out of hypnosis, Holden. Just breathe. Inhale. Exhale."

I blinked my eyes several times and grabbed the side of the tub. "I'm fucking freezing." My teeth chattered as the guys helped me out.

Chance immediately drained the bath and turned on the shower. "Get those clothes off," Chance ordered. "Let's get you under some hot water."

My limbs were so weak and numb I couldn't shed the wet jeans and shirt. Jace and Chance continued to talk to me as they removed my wet clothes down to my boxer-briefs. I stepped under the steaming spray.

"I'm going to make it a little warmer." Chance turned the knob, and the steam began to billow into the room.

"What the fuck happened?" Jace asked. "And don't give us a line of bullshit. We know something went down. I've never heard such a terrified scream in my whole goddamned life. I almost pissed myself."

Beginning to feel my limbs again, I flexed and remained in the stream of water. How could I possibly tell them what I'd seen? I'd struggled the last time, but this ... I shook my head in an attempt to clear my mind. "I finally saw the face of the little kid that's always calling my name."

Chapter Thirty-Five

I turned off the water and Chance handed me a towel. Once I dried off, I excused myself to change in my room.

Seconds later, a soft knock grabbed my attention. "We've gotta talk about this, Holden," Jace said. "If we don't, the memories will fade. We need all of the details we can get."

I pulled on a long-sleeved shirt and a fresh pair of jeans, then I let him in. "I know."

"Chance is in the living area."

Silently, I followed behind him, still reeling from what I'd experienced. I rubbed my face with my hands and groaned. "Why do I keep reaching for the truth? This shit was buried for a reason." Exhausted, I sank into the chair. Jace collected his notebook and pen, then settled in, poised and ready. Chance rubbed his hands together, his features full of worry.

"I saw the same girl I'd seen on the leash. When I first went under, I was in a basement, I think. The smell of dirt was strong. She was in a ... cell." I closed my eyes, willing myself to verbalize the horror I'd seen. "She was naked and shivering. I think I was trying to help her, but the door required a key."

The sound of Jace's pen scratching words onto the paper filled the room.

"The cell faded when I heard the same kid call my name." My pulse throbbed wildly, and little beads of perspiration began to form on my back. Chance and Jace stared at me, waiting for me to go on. "I was young, too. I think we were the same age. Maybe four or five."

"That's the same age every time from my notes. Right around there," Jace said.

I nodded. "The kid made me promise they wouldn't rip us apart. I tried to ask who, but they hugged me instead. When ... when he stepped back, I saw his face for the first time." I cleared my throat, head dipping down.

"Do you know who he is?" Chance asked gently.

I nodded, then my attention bounced between them. "It was me." My voice cracked as goosebumps peppered my skin.

"What?" Jace asked. "Are you sure? Like was the memory fuzzy or ... "

I pursed my lips. "I'm positive. I saw my face."

Jace scribbled like a mad man in his notebook while Chance leaned back in his chair. "The scream that came out of you." He shook his head. "It was fucked up."

"Oh, the whole thing was fucked up." I ran my hand through my hair, flicking tiny droplets of water onto my jeans. "I don't feel like I'm any closer to understanding. My subconscious is obviously giving me two sides of ... of I don't even know."

"This is what we have so far: a house you don't recognize, a little boy begging you for help, adults who are abusing kids in their late teens." Jace tapped the end of his pen against the paper. "You've seen this young lady twice and the little boy calls your name every damned time."

"It's obviously someone close to you," Chance added. "You probably see yourself in him. Like you were close when you were young. What about a best friend when you were that age? Did your parents know anyone that lost a child or something difficult for your mind to understand when you were young?"

I barked out a maniacal laugh. "I have no memories from the ages of three to five, remember?"

"Fuck, I forgot." Chance steepled his fingers together, his blue eyes searching mine.

"For some reason, I keep hoping it will lead me to River. Obviously, I've lost my fucking mind."

Chance's brows knitted together. "I can see why this is important." He blew out a big breath.

"I think we need to sit on it. This was huge progress, Holden. You at least know it was a little boy calling your name. Up until now, he was faceless. I'm sure as you sleep more, the puzzle will reveal itself." Jace stood. "Why don't you try to get some rest? I have a feeling we'll all be at the hospital tomorrow. We need to be at our best for Brynn."

Jace was right, but I was terrified to fall asleep. The more I discovered about my lost memories, the more questions I had, and the more I doubted what I saw. What if it was nothing and I had a vivid imagination?

Not likely, the little voice in my head whispered.

Chapter Thirty-Six

The following day, I woke up early after a fitful night of sleep. The Portland sun streamed through the penthouse windows, casting a cheerful smile into the room. I hoped like hell I would have something to smile about as well.

Zayne, Chance, Jace, and I were quiet as we walked down the hospital hall toward Brynn's room. Chance had called before we came over to make sure there weren't any changes, and we could see her. Brynn had made some progress overnight, and they were considering bringing her out of the coma if she continued to do well.

Rounding the corner by the nurse's station, I came to an abrupt halt. "What the fuck?" I said a little too loudly.

Tim left Brynn's room and stepped into the hall. He raised his hands in surrender. "Before you lose your shit, I got your message. I wanted to see for myself that she's okay, that's all."

Chance didn't even spare him a backward glance as he darted around him and into her room. Jace was hot on his heels, and Zayne remained by my side.

My hands clenched and unclenched. "Okay. You've seen Brynn,

now you're finished. Don't you ever go near her again," I growled. Hell, he could have slipped something into her IV to finish her off for all I knew. There wasn't a single fucking thing I trusted about this monster.

"Son, I'm not trying to cause any trouble. When you said she'd died—"

I grabbed him by the lapels of his Armani suit jacket and slammed him against the wall, my face a mere inch from his. "You listen to me you pathetic motherfucker. I beat your ass once and the next time I won't stop until you're dead."

Tim stiffened, then grinned. "You don't know who you're screwing with, ya little dick."

"Let go of him, Holden," Zayne said in a calm tone. "We need to take this elsewhere."

"Listen to your little babysitter, Holden. If you don't want to hear what else I came here to tell you, then ..." He gave me a half-shrug.

I released his jacket and walked backward. "Outside. Now." I refused to play any more games with him. He'd been jerking me around for way too long.

I draped my arm over his shoulders and pulled him against me, ensuring he wouldn't take off before I was finished with him. Zayne was on high alert as he led us to the elevator. When the doors slid open, we entered, and I reached for the main floor button. Zayne's hand shot out and stopped me. He lifted a brow before he pushed the garage button. He obviously knew something about this hospital that I didn't.

Tim rubbed his stubbled jawline. "It doesn't have to be like this. It really doesn't."

My nails dug into his shoulder. "You're the one who made it this way, not me."

As soon as we arrived, Zayne stepped out first and led us behind a row of cars and into a tucked-away corner. The smell of oil and rubber assaulted my nose, and my nostrils flared.

"As long as you stay in this area, the camera won't pick up anything. It's a blind spot." Zayne nodded, then backed up far enough to give me room to do whatever I deemed necessary.

"What else do you need to tell me?" Tension slithered down my neck and between my shoulder blades.

"As I was trying to explain, I just came to see Brynn. She's been a part of our lives since she was a kid, Holden. Regardless of what you think of me, I care about her."

I chuckled. "Okay, fine. Let's say I buy into that bullshit."

"I would never hurt her." Pain flickered across his features, and I wondered if there was a soul in him after all. My hope was smashed to smithereens with his following sentence.

"I also came to tell you that I can't get River back. It's too late, Holden." Regret shadowed his face briefly. "I tried."

"Did you? Or was this payback because she put you in your place when you tried to rape her?" I asked, spittle flying out of my mouth. "Did you know what happened from the beginning?" Somewhere in the corner of my mind, I recalled that we still had his car bugged and not to blow it.

"No. I didn't know until it was already done. Logan didn't either. We were completely surprised, the same as you."

I barked out a laugh. "You make it sound like it was a fucking party instead of a kidnapping."

Tim released a weary sigh. "Best advice I can give you, son ... forget about River. She's gone. You're never going to see her again. You have a bright future ahead of you. There will always be a hot piece of ass available to you."

My fist slammed into his nose, a satisfying crunch ringing in my ears. "Why won't you tell me who has her? If you don't want to tell me, then fine. At least report it to the police."

Crimson red liquid dripped from his nose and soaked into his light blue dress shirt. He attempted to wipe the blood off with his hand but only managed to smear it across his face. "You stupid,

stupid boy. Don't you understand? The people who have her are way more powerful than I am. They'll destroy me, you, and anyone I'm associated with. So, when it came down to me protecting you or her, I chose you." He spat onto the smooth concrete floor. "I chose *you*, Holden."

Was Tim *afraid* of someone? The man who dealt with some of the most powerful and terrifying men in the world ... I didn't understand.

In a final, desperate attempt, I pleaded with him. "Who has her, Dad? If you can't outright tell me, then give me a goddamned hint."

Tim's shoulders sagged, and his eyes narrowed. "If this ever comes back to me, I'll kill you myself. I don't care if you're my fucking kid or not."

My heart pounded against my chest while I waited for him to continue.

"I can't say who, but I'll tell you where. As of this morning, she was in California. She won't be there long, though."

Zayne stepped over to me and faced Tim. "California is a big fucking state." An intimidating sneer eased across Zayne's features. "Motherfucker, I can kill you with my bare hands. I don't need a gun or any other men to help me. If you want to continue breathing, I suggest you start by giving us everything you know. Then I'll decide if you live or not."

For the first time in my life, I cheered at the idea of Tim's measly life-ending. And I was lucky enough to have a front-row seat.

I glanced around the garage since Zayne wasn't keeping a lookout. Honestly, I'd much rather see his torture skills put into practice than stand guard.

"Northern. There's a house with over twenty acres about thirty miles away from Mount Shasta. Follow Highway 97 until you see a little grocery store on the left," he sputtered, blood streaming over his lip and into his mouth.

"What's the name of it?" Zayne asked, closing the gap between them.

I was pretty sure Tim was about to piss his fucking pants. What shocked me was that Tim hadn't pulled a gun on us. I began to question his intelligence level. He either assumed I wasn't a threat, or he wasn't carrying. Both were stupid. I knew for a fact Zayne had a gun, but I didn't even think a show of his piece was necessary. Tim was singing like a little bitch.

"I don't remember," Tim squeaked. "It's the only one. You can't miss it."

"What else?" Zayne's hand twitched as if he were trying not to kill Tim before he provided us with more information.

"It's heavily guarded. The house is large and contemporary, but that's not what you're looking for. It's ..." Tim glanced at me, fear flickering in his expression. "There are hidden bunkers under the ground and cells in another area. If she's still there, she's probably in one of them."

Fuck. Cell. Basement. Jesus. Fuck no. I nearly dropped to my knees as the images of the little girl assaulted my senses. An eerie feeling of deja vu clouded my mind.

Zayne wrapped his fingers around Tim's throat and lifted him off the ground. Tim's feet kicked as his face turned beet red. He clawed at Zayne's hand, but Zayne didn't even flinch. Zayne let him go with a quick release, and Tim fell to the ground, gasping for air. Zayne stepped away from him and smoothed his black polo shirt as though what he'd just done was a part of his everyday life. It probably was.

Tim crawled forward a few paces. "They're dangerous, Holden. If you go up against them, you won't survive." He coughed between each word.

"If you were an actual human being instead of a disgusting monster, you would have told me this as soon as you found out." I closed part of the gap between Tim and me, then swung my leg back and landed a kick to his gut. He grabbed his stomach and toppled over.

Whimpers escaped him, and I glanced at Zayne. "What now?"

"Go see Brynn. Let me handle this, and I'll join you when I can."

Questions burned to be answered, but I understood that I needed to leave. The reason Zayne was my bodyguard was to protect me from Tim or any other dangers. A few minutes apart wouldn't hurt anything. I just had to stay aware in case Logan or one of Tim's colleagues showed up.

I walked casually to the elevator as if I'd simply parked my car and had every right to be here. Several people filed out before I could slip in and punch the button to Brynn's floor. I shoved my hands in my pockets, my body beginning to tremble uncontrollably. *River. Oh, God. We have to get her.* Tim's words rang in my ears,

If she's still there ...

My stomach clenched, and I ground my teeth together, scared that I was going to hurl.

A soft ding alerted me I'd arrived, and as soon as the doors whooshed open, I bolted into the hallway. I looked both ways and tried to get my bearings. After several heartbeats, I recognized where I was and hurried to Brynn's room. I poked my head in through the crack in the door and cleared my throat.

"There you are," Jace said, waving me in. His expression grew more serious as I approached them. "Dude, you look like shit."

Chance stood, smacked Jace in the arm, and hissed, "Not now, man."

Oddly enough, I was grateful for Chance's reminder. Brynn didn't need to hear any of what had just happened. My gaze landed on her. She had more color in her cheeks than yesterday, but she still looked rough.

"They're going to allow her to wake up from the coma if she's doing well by tonight," Chance explained, holding her hand.

"Well, that's some progress, at least." I sat down, my mind spinning out of control with the information Zayne had extracted from Tim. I almost wished I'd stayed with him, though. I had no idea what was happening. Was he going to finish Tim off? What if there was more information? My leg bounced, and Chance shot me a look.

"Hallway. Jace, you stay here and watch over Brynn." He stood, and I followed him.

Closing the door behind me, I ran my hands through my hair. "I'm fucking losing my mind."

"What happened with Tim?" Worry lines etched into Chance's forehead.

I began to pace, unsure of where to start. "He gave us an area to ... to look for River."

Chance grabbed my shoulders and stared a hole into me. "And you're *here*?"

"I can't do anything yet. I have to wait for Zayne to finish taking care of Tim, whatever that entails. Plus, I had to see Brynn." I rubbed my face with my hand. "Tim said the place is in Northern California, and if River is there, then we would need to search the grounds and look for bunkers. He said she'd possibly be in a hole underground." My words stuck in my throat, and I nearly gagged on the memories of my hypnosis.

Chance's eyes widened. His mouth opened and closed several times before he whispered, "Fuck."

We stupidly looked at each other. I trusted Zayne. I knew that he was giving all of the information to the FBI.

"Who took her? Did he say?" Chance pinned me with an intense gaze.

"No. He refused to give me any names." I looked away, afraid of what he was going to suggest. At the same time, I was already forming ideas and plans.

"Holden, you saw a cell with a naked girl inside of it. It was in a basement, or underground, right?"

I nodded, struggling to string the right words together. "Do you think I've been where she's at?" I could literally feel the blood drain from my face.

"Yeah, man. I think so. I'm guessing that those years of memories you've blocked out were sheer horror. And somehow you're connected to what's happening with River."

Tears burned my eyes. "I'd never intentionally put her in harm's way. I love her so goddamn much."

"I know. Hell, you saved her. Now you know what you have to do," Chance said, sympathy flashing across his features.

My heart pounded against my rib cage. "Yeah. I'd better get to it."

Chapter Thirty-Seven

Zayne was going to kick my ass when he realized I'd ditched him. Jace agreed to return to the hotel with me while Chance stayed with Brynn. I'd given Brynn a quick kiss on the forehead and told her I couldn't wait to see her gorgeous green eyes when she woke up.

Jace requested a few bags of ice for the penthouse, but instead of waiting for the staff to deliver them, we grabbed them ourselves. Now that I had additional information from Tim, maybe my subconscious would help me connect the rest of the dots, and I'd learn who took her.

"Were you close to any aunts and uncles? Your parent's best friends?" Jace asked as we rode the elevator to the top floor.

"I didn't even remember Logan until River showed me the picture. Both Mom and Dad had a huge family. Thanksgiving was at my grandma's on my dad's side for years until we simply wouldn't fit."

The doors slid open, and we hurried down the hall to our room. Jace held the keycard up, and the lock clicked, alerting us it was open.

Once inside, I bolted the door in case anyone tried to barge in. I wasn't sure how Zayne would react, but as he said, he was with Tim, so jogging a few blocks to the hotel wasn't a huge deal.

I collected the large container of salt and hurried to the bathroom.

"Dude, why do you always get in with your fucking clothes on?" Jace called out as he grabbed his notebook and pen from his bedroom.

"Because the heaviness of the clothes keeps me grounded in the present. It's one of the first things I'm aware of. The feel of cold, wet clothes clinging to my body."

"That actually makes sense. I was just hoping maybe we wouldn't have to deal with the mess after you get out of the tub."

"I know. Water goes fucking everywhere." I reached the bathroom and slipped off my tennis shoes.

Jace flipped the lever on the drain. "Are you ready? We're so fucking close."

"I know. I can feel it in my bones. I'm not going to lie, though. This time, I'm fucking scared. We've been playing around with this method a lot over the last few days. I've never had hypnosis sessions this close together. But River's been gone for three weeks, and I have to push myself."

Jace set his notebook and pen on the counter and gripped my shoulders. "You're coming back. Don't you even dare to think otherwise."

I didn't miss the hint of fear clinging to his words.

"I'm going to find River." I placed my hands on top of his, then grabbed him into a huge hug.

"We've got this, Holden. We've fucking got this," he whispered.

I backed away, then inhaled deeply as I got into the tub. I settled in, stretching my legs out in front of me and placing my arms at my sides. Jace turned on the warm water, then began to guide me. I forced myself to relax as the water started to rise. *Breathe in. Breathe out.* Jace continued to talk, his soft voice lulling me into another place and time.

"Hannah?" I asked. "What are you doing here?"

She giggled. "Don't be silly." She playfully punched me in the arm.

I glanced around, recognizing the playroom instantly.

"Where are we?" I rose from the floor and sidestepped a yellow, then purple crayon.

Hannah frowned at me. "What's wrong with you? Are you sick?" She hopped up and placed her hand against my forehead. "Holden?" She gently shook me, then she faded away.

Frowning, I waited to see the little boy again. Maybe this time, it wouldn't fuck with me so badly.

A loud cry reached me, and I ran out of the room and into a long hallway that forked to the left and right.

"Hello?" I called. The only response was the sound of my voice echoing through the hall. A flicker of something caught my eye, and I spun around, catching a fleeting glimpse of the young girl crawling on the floor into another room. I ran over, but the door had disappeared.

Another scream ripped through my heart, but I didn't see anyone. I was the only one around.

"There you are, Holden," an older woman smiled warmly at me and took my little hand in hers. "I've been looking for you. Everyone is expecting you. We have to get you cleaned up and ready for the big party."

Terror spiked inside my chest. "Party?"

She turned down the hall, and I was suddenly in a bedroom. I recognized it. I'd slept there before. "Yes, silly. The Christmas party!" She rubbed my head, messing up my dark hair. "I'll get you a bath, and your new suit is pressed." She clapped her hands together and laughed.

"Will there be presents?" I asked, giddy with excitement.

"So many. Boys and girls, teens, anyone that you desire." She picked me up and placed me on the countertop.

"Anyone? Don't you mean anything?"

The sweetness drained from her features as she narrowed her eyes at me. "I mean anyone. We've been over this."

I willed myself to scream and kick her, punch her in the boobs and run like hell, but I couldn't. I had to let it play out.

The lady began to flicker and fade, and I jumped off the counter. Hauling ass as fast as my little legs could carry me, I left the bedroom and turned left down the hall. Voices and laughter called me closer. A white door glowed in front of me. I placed my hand on the knob, then turned it.

Two women broke their kiss and smiled at each other. The brunette threw her head back and moaned. It was then that I realized a young man had his head buried between her legs. She jerked a chain in her right hand, and his face turned red as he clawed at the collar around his neck. "You're not doing it right." She scooted farther back on the table and spread her legs.

A dark-haired man in a black suit walked up and chided the guy. "If you can't do it correctly and she doesn't come, then you know what will happen." He brought his hand up. A riding crop flicked, then landed on the guy's back. A tortured scream ripped through the air.

I tore my gaze away, nausea bubbling up in my stomach. I walked to the edge of the room, witnessing a sick and depraved show.

How did I help them? How the hell did I free them from these twisted monsters?

"Holden!" I recognized the little boy's voice. But where? I ran in the direction I hoped he was calling me from.

"Don't let them take me, Holden!"

Fuck. "I'm here! I'm coming to help you!" My breathing became erratic as I searched and searched, unable to pinpoint where he was.

"Focus, Holden," Jace's soothing tone broke through my terror. "You're almost there. Can you see the person who has River?"

I closed my eyes and allowed my intuition to drive my decisions. On a whim, I ran the way I came, back into the long hall. A light flickered to life, and the smell of fresh-cut grass and sweet roses tickled my nose. I needed to look for the bunkers underground. I hustled until I reached another white door. Swinging it open, I squinted against the sunlight. I held my hand against my brows, trying to adjust to the brightness.

"Hi!" The boy waved at me, sadness and fear twisting his little features.

I didn't startle this time as I looked at my own face. "Are you okay?" I struggled to understand what was happening.

"I just wanted to tell you goodbye." He hugged me, then grinned up at me. "You promised, Holden. You said they'd never rip us apart." A sad expression settled over him. "But I understand. We're just little kids."

My heart ached as he backed away. A dark-haired figure approached us. "There you are," a voice said before swooping the boy with my face into their arms. "Say goodbye now. This will be the last time you two ever see each other."

I focused as they turned toward me, but the adult was faceless, and the clothes were blurred.

"Focus. You can do this," Jace's steady words came through again.

I closed my eyes in the other reality and took a deep, cleansing breath. My eyelids fluttered open and landed on a clear face. Disgust, rage, and desperation coursed through my veins. This couldn't be right. Jesus. It couldn't be. But there was no arguing about the person that stood in front of me.

I shot out of the water and wiped my cheeks. I glanced around the bathroom, attempting to gain my footing enough to realize where I was. My body shook as I stood and placed the palm of my hand against the shower wall. The hypnosis. The screams and agonizing cries ... My brain spun faster and faster, then screeched to an abrupt halt. Fear and disgust speared my chest.

"Where's my phone?" I gasped.

Wild-eyed, Jace looked around, then ran out of the bathroom. He returned seconds later and handed it to me.

With shaking hands, I pulled up my contacts.

"Let me help." Jace took the cell out of my hand, and I lifted one leg at a time out of the bath.

I sank to the floor, my teeth chattering. "Call Pierce."

"On it." The line began to ring, and Jace put the call on speaker.

"Holden? Are you okay?" Pierce asked, his tone heavy with worry.

I shuddered and glanced up at my friend. "Pierce, I know who fucking took River."

River's fight continues as she learns who is behind her kidnapping and the depths of the evil she faces in this stunning conclusion of the Beautifully Damaged Series.
Pre-order today on Amazon.

Turn the page for the Beautifully Shattered Sample!

Beautifully Shattered Sample

They think they'll win. They're wrong.

Waking in complete darkness, I find myself naked, scared, and alone. I thought my past was as bad as it could get, but I was wrong. My nightmares are child's play compared to the place they've stashed me.

The people who took me are planning something horrible. Thinking about it makes my skin crawl.

My only comfort is knowing that Holden is searching for me. But he's not ready to learn what he'll discover. This evil has the ability to break him.

The danger is everywhere, and my time is running out. If I want to see Holden again and expose the corruption of this hellhole, I need to escape. My only chance is to befriend the one person I've met and hope like hell my plan works.

I never knew I could love someone the way I do Holden, obsessive and all-consuming. He's the fuel that drives me and protects me from the insanity. I'll do anything to return to his arms. But loving him might cost me everything, including my life.

Join River as her strength and fight to live are tested in ways she never imagines in the stunning, heart-stopping conclusion of the Beautifully Damaged series. This billionaire, opposite worlds, dark new adult novel will leave you gasping as the answers unfold. Guaranteed HEA!

**Please be advised that this series contains dark and mature content some will find triggering.

Order today on Amazon and FREE in Kindle Unlimited.

Turn the page for the Beautifully Shattered Sample!

Beautifully Shattered Sample

Chapter 1

Acidic, bitter grains of dirt rolled over my tongue. I attempted to swallow, but my throat gave me a firm "fuck you." I wasn't sure how long I'd gone without water, but at this point, if I drank any, it would turn the grit in my mouth into mud.

My cheek pressed against the cold ground as tears burned down my face and melted into the soil. After nearly drowning, I'd woken up trapped in this hellhole. I'd frantically searched for a way out, clawed at my surroundings, and screamed for help until my voice was reduced to a scratchy whisper. I found nothing. I was alone. Underground, with no windows, dirt walls, and no light except an occasional sliver from above. My desperation and fear permeated the air around me. *What had I done to end up here?* I pushed off the hard dirt and sat up. A wave of fear crashed over me, and I rested my chin on my knees and cried.

Attempting to conserve energy, I curled my naked body into a ball, hoping for a bit of warmth. Instead, I was met with my cool, clammy skin. A shudder traveled through me. "Mind over matter," I said softly. I sniffled and wiped my nose with the back of my hand.

Crying wouldn't accomplish anything. I needed a plan of action for when the door finally opened. *If it opens at all.* I swatted the dark thought away as though it were a wasp, waiting to sting me at the right moment.

Holden's name escaped my parted lips as I imagined his arms around me—safe, sound, and warm. We were supposed to be in our new home together and making love on every surface possible. Afterward, he would have pressed gentle kisses against the side of my head. Instead, I'd ditched Zayne after I'd stared at the pregnancy test. In my state of panic, I'd left myself vulnerable, wide-open for the sharp prick of the needle to my neck, bag over my face, and the fight for my life. If I'd only known ... but there was no reason to play the *what-if* game now. Eventually, someone would come for me, and I suspected that Logan was behind my kidnapping. He'd made it clear he would take me as payment in place of the money Dan, my piece of shit guardian, owed him. My guess was that Dan wasn't just drinking and smoking pot, he was strung out on the meth Logan so readily supplied.

An unseen critter scampered across my back, and I shivered, my skin crawling. It was most likely a spider, but not for long. I laid down, wishing it a slow death for having the nerve to touch me.

Memories of the shitty trailer I'd grown up in taunted me. The place had also been cold and bug-infested. I swore I would never live that way again. And yet here I was, worse off than before.

Light seeped through the cracks above my head, and the floor creaked with footsteps. I bolted upright and waited, my pulse beating wildly against my wrists. *Open the door. Open the fucking door.* I rubbed my throat and willed it to work. I pried my lips apart, and only hoarse, quiet choking sounds came out.

Almost as quickly as the light peeked through, it disappeared, leaving me in complete darkness.

I sank to the unforgiving floor as my thoughts drifted to Holden again. He had to be out of his mind with worry. At least he suspected his father, Tim, and Logan, who had been business partners at one time. After Tim had put his disgusting paws on me and I'd dropped him to the floor, he'd been pissed at me. I couldn't blame him. I'd made him look weak and stupid in front of his family. Once Holden, Brynn, and I had learned that Tim was an illegal weapons dealer, though, I realized he was capable of anything, including kidnapping me. Hopefully, there would be enough evidence for Holden to find me. But would it be soon enough?

A sharp pang stabbed me in the chest. Closing my eyes, I said, "I love you," but there was no sound. A brutal reminder tapped me on the skull. Even if my voice had been working, there wasn't anyone around to hear me. Whoever had been walking above had left.

Waves of nausea rolled in my belly. I scrambled across the small space and attempted to puke where I wouldn't sit or lay in it later. I wished the morning sickness were an indication that it was actually morning. At least then it would help me mark time. At this point, I had no fucking idea if I'd been in this hole for an hour or a week. My guess was a few days from the number of times I'd squatted against the wall and peed. My aim sucked, and the warm liquid had streamed down my leg instead, marking me with the pungent stench of urine. I got better at it, eventually.

I'd lived in some messed up conditions, but this ... this was quickly stripping me of my dignity and replacing it with the burn of shame. I was living like an animal. If I ever had the opportunity to shower, I suspected that tears of joy would run down my cheeks.

Fear settled in and wrapped her long fingers around my heart while she whispered that I wouldn't ever see the light of day again. I would never touch Holden's beautiful face, kiss his full lips, or tell him I loved him. I sucked in a lungful of air and clawed at the dirt, the grime caking under my fingernails. I'd come too far to lose now. Logan wouldn't win. I fucking refused to let him. I'd rebuilt my life with Holden, Brynn, and the guys ... even Catherine, Holden's mom, and I had grown closer. I loved my job at the club—missed the people, the interaction, and the sense of belonging I had.

I squeezed my eyes closed and listened to the beat of my pulse thumping rhythmically in my ears. I was alive.

Images of my abduction flickered across my mind, and I shook my head. It didn't make sense. The face of the monster that had attempted to drown me was someone I knew. I'd obviously been delirious from the drug that had been administered. I must have hallucinated because what I saw couldn't have happened.

My left calf started to cramp, and I shot up off the ground. I stretched my arms in front of me and began to walk back and forth in the small space while I swore a blue streak at the obnoxious pain. I'd learned really fucking fast that I'd break a toe or my nose since I couldn't see the walls. Once I'd figured out the layout, I'd counted steps in order to be able to move around without hurting myself. I barked out a laugh. I was naked, hungry, dirty, and freezing. I wasn't sure breaking a fucking toe would be that big of a deal. But I had to try and take care of myself, take care of my baby.

I leaned into my anger and allowed it to build. It fueled my mind and provided energy, keeping me warm. Holden had taught me to love and trust. Brynn had taught me to laugh and live. But now ... now I reached into the darkest part of my soul and fanned the flames of the fury toward Tim and Dan. It broke through the fear and the self-pity. It marked me as a different woman. In a short time, I was no longer the person who had kissed Holden and watched the furniture for our new home be delivered. Whatever stupid son of a bitch had thought taking me was a good idea ... I swore that I would destroy them if it was the last thing I did. Anyone that had any sense understood not to mess with a mama and her baby. Come hell or high water, I would be with Holden again, and I would keep our child safe ... unlike my mother.

The creak of a door opening reached my ears. I turned my head toward the sound and was blinded as a flood of light cut through the darkness. A combination of fear and hope sprung to life deep inside me. I rubbed my eyes and blinked rapidly, trying to clear the grit. I wasn't sure when I'd fallen asleep since I'd been locked away in this damned hole unable to tell time.

My stomach growled as I shielded my vision and stood slowly. I was weak and probably dehydrated.

"You can come out," a deep, husky voice said. As a ladder was lowered down, I gulped and hoped I had the strength to climb it.

I gripped the side, a sharp splinter immediately slicing the palm of my hand. Shaking it off, I placed my bare foot on the first rung and grabbed the sides. One shaky step at a time, my head finally peeked through the opening in the ceiling. I gasped as I scrambled to gather my wits and clear my muddled brain. It was daylight out, which meant I'd been in darkness for no less than twenty-four hours.

I crawled the rest of the way out of the hole, then sat down quickly, pulling my knees to my chest to shield my exposed body. My attention swept across the kitchen, and I mentally took notes. Every detail would be important to my freedom. A white refrigerator hummed in the corner next to an old farm sink. The white and blue linoleum floor was worn but clean. A man I didn't recognize sat at the white table, only a few feet away from me. He took a bite of what appeared to be a roast beef and cheese sandwich, then followed it with a long drink of water. Maybe he would share with me. Not only was I starving, but the baby needed food as well.

"W-w-who are you?" I stammered, my throat raw as I spoke. I didn't recognize the burly man in front of me. His red hair was sheared close to his head, and his beard was neatly trimmed. His biceps bulged against the navy, short-sleeved shirt that was tucked into the same color slacks. My focus landed on the gun holstered to his hip.

His dark, lusty gaze raked over my dirty, naked body. His mouth parted, and his coffee-stained tongue darted out over his bottom lip. I cringed but remained still. Antagonizing him didn't seem like a good idea, at least for the moment.

"I'm Barrett. You'll see a lot of me around here."

I nodded. "Where is 'here'?" My voice trembled.

"Training camp." He bit into his food, the crunch of the fresh lettuce and the smacking sounds of his open-mouthed chewing breaking through the silence.

My forehead creased in confusion. "Training? I don't understand."

Barrett stood and wiped the crumbs from his lap. He strode to the refrigerator and opened it, revealing well-stocked shelves. Barrett reached inside, then produced a plastic bottle of water and a half of a sandwich. "I'm under orders to feed you. Then it's shower time."

Tears of relief stung my eyes—a *shower*. I gulped and stared at the drink. Surely, Barrett couldn't be all bad if he allowed me to clean up and eat.

He closed the gap between us and squatted down. "Open your mouth."

I parted my lips slightly, the chapped skin painfully tearing. My attention remained on him as I waited while he removed the cap on the bottle, filled it with water, then dumped the small amount down my throat. I swallowed, nearly groaning from the sweet taste.

"Open." Barrett poured a bit more and fed me another two capfuls. He moved to recap it, and desperation rose quickly.

"More. Please."

"You'll fucking puke everywhere. It's why I'm only giving you a little at a time."

I met his gaze and searched for any sign of compassion. None. This was all part of the control game, and it started with water and food.

He continued to give me small doses, then set the bottle next to him. "Let's try a bite to eat." He opened the sealed sandwich baggy, and I looked at the ham and cheese eagerly. He ripped off the crust from the top of the bread. I parted my mouth like an obedient little puppy, and he placed the food on my tongue.

Once I'd chewed and struggled to swallow, he allowed me to have another drink.

He stood and returned to his seat at the table. "We wait." He folded his hands across his chest and stretched his muscular legs in front of him.

Something told me he was used to waiting.

"Thank you," I whispered, unsure if he was a good guy or not. My instincts told me not to trust him, but I had no other choice in my current situation. "I'm River." If I could connect with him, maybe Barrett would tell me where I was and eventually help me leave. All I wanted was to go home and pepper Holden's face with a hundred kisses.

"I know." His brown eyes remained on me, and I wrapped my arms around my legs as I tried to cover myself the best I could.

"Do you work for Logan?"

Barrett didn't even blink at my question. His stoic expression didn't offer me a glimpse of who he worked for.

"Why are you keeping me here?"

He answered with more silence. I struggled to understand. What did Barrett mean by training camp? What was I training for?

I studied the small room and finally realized I was still sitting beside the trap door. Barrett could easily shove me back into the dark hole. I shifted my weight and tried to scoot away, which was difficult since I didn't want to expose my breasts.

"You're not going back in the hole ... for now." He rose and approached me again. Over the next several minutes, he fed me small bites and allowed me to drink more.

Fear rippled through me at the idea of returning to the pit of darkness. Dirt streaked my legs and arms, and I reeked of urine, sweat, and vomit. I had no idea how Barrett was able to sit with me and not gag from the stench.

After I'd finished the sandwich, Barrett gave me what was left of the water, and I gulped it greedily. "Thank you," I panted, wiping the droplets from my mouth with the back of my hand.

Barrett tossed the baggie into the trash, then grabbed another bottle from the fridge. He looked at me with a smirk on his face. "Stand up."

"I don't have any clothes."

With two long steps, he closed the space between us. "I said stand up." He peered down at me.

I was nearly at eye level with his bulging cock that pressed against his pants. Barrett didn't even try to hide his arousal.

"Please. I need some clothes."

He reached down, fisted a handful of my hair, and jerked me painfully to my feet. "I fucking told you to stand," he growled.

My legs wobbled as I found my balance, the pain shooting through my skull.

Barrett released me and stepped away. His gaze traveled over my breasts, down my flat stomach, and to my stubbled pussy. He palmed his erection through his pants and grinned. "Let's get you cleaned up."

Barrett motioned for me to walk in front of him. I crossed an arm over my chest, but before I could cover my center, he knocked my hands away.

With a shove, I stumbled to the front door. Barrett removed his pistol and pressed the cold, hard metal to my back. "Just so you don't get any big ideas."

Ragged breaths tore through me. I had a feeling that Barrett wouldn't think twice about pulling the trigger. I suspected the only thing that would stop him were orders from above.

My bare feet landed on the sidewalk outside of the house. I squinted against the harsh sunlight and inhaled slowly. Fresh air. While in the pit, I wondered if I would ever see the light of day, smell freshly cut grass, or enjoy the bright colors of flowers again.

I took mental notes of the layout of the land. Several small homes were spread across the property. The landscape was flat, with only a few trees planted here and there. Toward the back of the acreage, a large, beautiful white home with black trim stood out like a sore thumb. Next to it were four huge outbuildings.

Barrett guided me to one of them, then rang a buzzer. Within seconds, the door swung open, and I stepped foot into my new hell.

Order today on Amazon and FREE in Kindle Unlimited.

Also by J.A. Owenby

Bestselling Romance

The Love & Ruin Series

Love & Sins

Love & Ruin

Love & Deception

Love & Redemption

Love & Consequences, a standalone novel

Love & Corruption, a standalone novel

Love & Revelations, a novella

Love & Seduction, a standalone novel

Love & Vengeance, a standalone novel

Love & Retaliation

The Wicked Intentions Series

Dark Intentions

Fractured Intentions

The Torn Series, inspired by True Events

Fading into Her, a prequel novella

Torn

Captured

Freed

Standalone Novels

Where I'll Find You

About the Author

International bestselling author J.A. Owenby grew up in a small backwoods town in Arkansas where she learned how to swear like a sailor and spot water moccasins skimming across the lake.

She finally ditched the south and headed to Oregon. The first winter there, she was literally blown away a few times by ninety mile an hour winds and storms that rolled in off the ocean.

Eventually, she longed for quiet and headed up to snowier pastures. She now resides in Washington state with her hot nerdy husband and cat, Chloe (who frequently encourages her to drink). She spends her days coming up with ways to torture characters in a way that either makes you want to throw your book down a flight of stairs or sob hysterically into a pillow.

J.A. Owenby writes new adult and romantic thriller novels. Her books ooze with emotion, angst, and twists that will leave you breathless. Having battled her own demons, she's not afraid to tackle the secrets women are forced to hide. After all, the road to love is paved in the dark.

Her friends describe her as delightfully twisted. She loves fan mail and wine. Please send her all the wine.

You can follow the progress of her upcoming novel on Facebook at Author J.A. Owenby and on Twitter @jaowenby.

Sign up for J.A. Owenby's Newsletter:
BookHip.com/CTZMWZ

A note from the author:

This book may contain sensitive material for some readers. Gemma and Hendrix's story is considered a dark romance with language, sex, and violence.

www.ingramcontent.com/pod-product-compliance
Lightning Source LLC
Chambersburg PA
CBHW050817190726
48286CB00007B/1901